The Fractured Path to Emerald Vale

A Boy, His Dog, and a World Beyond

by

Jackie L. Smith

Copyright Page

The Fractured Path to Emerald Vale

Copyright © 2026 by Jackie L. Smith

All rights reserved.

No part of this book may be reproduced, distributed, or transmitted in any form or by any means, including photocopying, recording, or other electronic or mechanical methods, without the prior written permission of the author, except in the case of brief quotations embodied in critical reviews and certain other noncommercial uses permitted by copyright law.

This is a work of fiction. Names, characters, places, and incidents either are the product of the author's imagination or are used fictitiously. Any resemblance to actual persons, living or dead, events, or locales is entirely coincidental.

Published by Jackie L. Smith

Staffordsville, Kentucky

ISBN: 979-8-9959280-0-3 (paperback)

First Edition: 2026

Cover design by Jessica Stacey

Published and Printed in the United States of America

DEDICATION

For every kid who ever needed a way out

and the dog who found it for them.

And for Eydan.

The mothers who hold it all together

when everything is falling apart.

Courage is not staying where it is safe.

Courage is going where you are needed.

— Elysian Mosswood

Contents

Chapter One - The Boy with the Dog

The last bell at Ridgewood High rang at 2:45, and Cade Thompson was out the door before the echo died. He moved through the hallway with his head down and his backpack slung over one shoulder, weaving past clusters of freshmen who lingered at lockers and seniors who leaned against walls like they owned the place. Nobody called out to him. Nobody tried to stop him. That was fine. That was how he preferred it.

The October air hit him as he pushed through the double doors, cool enough to remind him that his hoodie had a hole in the left elbow and winter was coming whether they could afford a new jacket or not. He pulled his ear buds from his pocket, plugged them into his phone, and scrolled to a playlist he'd built over the summer—heavy on guitar, low on lyrics. Music that didn't ask him to feel anything.

The walk home took eleven minutes. He'd timed it once, back when he used to count things like that—the minutes until Don came home from work, the seconds between the front door slamming and the yelling starting, the number of steps from his bedroom to the back door in case he needed to grab Ashen and run. He didn't count anymore. Don was gone. Six months now. Walked out on a Tuesday morning and never came back.

Good riddance. That's what Cade told himself. Good riddance to the belt that hung on a nail by the kitchen door. Good riddance to the boots on the stairs at midnight. Good riddance to the man who'd taught him that love and pain were the same thing.

Except the belt was still there. Eydan hadn't taken it down. Cade walked past it every morning, and every morning he thought about pulling it off that nail and throwing it in the trash. He never did. Some things were easier to leave where they were.

He turned onto Maple Creek Drive, a street that sounded nicer than it was. The houses here were small and tired, with patchy lawns and driveways cracked down the middle. A few had American flags on their porches. One had a couch on the front lawn that had been there since July. The Thompsons' place was third from the end—a one-story ranch with faded blue siding and a screen door that didn't close all the way.

But there, in the front window, a blur of merle fur exploded against the glass.

Sammy.

Cade felt the corner of his mouth lift—an involuntary thing, the kind of reaction he couldn't have stopped if he'd tried. The Australian Collie was already spinning in circles by the time Cade reached the porch, his nails clicking against the hardwood on the other side of the door, his whine building into a full-throated bark of pure, uncontainable joy.

Cade opened the door and Sammy hit him like a furry torpedo—forty-five pounds of love and chaos, front paws on his chest, tongue everywhere.

"Alright, alright," Cade said, dropping to one knee. He scratched behind Sammy's ears with both hands and the dog went still for exactly two seconds before erupting again, spinning, barking, tail whipping hard enough to clear a coffee table. "I was only gone seven hours, you maniac."

But Sammy didn't care about the math. Sammy cared that his person was home. That was the whole equation.

Cade stood and looked around the house. The living room was dim, curtains half-drawn. The kitchen light was off. A cereal bowl sat in the sink from that morning—Ashen's, with the little pink spoon she insisted on using even though she was nine years old and Cade had told her a dozen times that it was a baby spoon. She didn't care. Some things were easier to keep than to let go of.

The house was quiet in the way it always was on weekday afternoons. Eydan was at her first job—cashier at the Walgreens on Route 9. She'd clock out at four, drive to the diner on Elm Street, tie on an apron, and work the dinner shift until close. She'd get home around ten-thirty, maybe eleven, with aching feet and a Styrofoam container of whatever the cook hadn't sold that night. She'd eat standing up in the kitchen because sitting down meant she might not get back up.

Cade knew the routine by heart. He'd memorized it the way other kids memorized football stats or video game codes. His mother's schedule was a map of survival, and he'd learned to navigate it without being told. When Eydan worked, Cade was the adult in the house. He'd been the adult in the house long before Don left, if he was honest about it. Someone had to be.

Ashen would be home in an hour. The elementary school bus dropped her at the corner at 3:50. Cade would have a snack ready—peanut butter on toast, or crackers if the bread was gone. He'd ask about her day and she'd give him three words or less, because that's how Ashen was now. Quiet. Pulled inward. Like a flower that had learned to close its petals before the frost came.

She used to be loud. She used to laugh so hard she'd fall off chairs. That was before Don's voice started filling every room in the house like smoke, before she'd learned to make herself small and invisible because small and invisible didn't get hit.

Cade dropped his backpack on the couch and walked to the kitchen. He passed the nail by the door. The belt was still there—brown leather, cracked, with a heavy brass buckle that had a tiny American eagle stamped into the metal. Don had bought it at a truck stop in Oklahoma. He'd been proud of that buckle. He'd told Cade once, while wrapping the leather around his fist, that a man's belt said something about his character.

Cade's back still said something about Don's.

He opened the fridge. Milk, half a pack of deli turkey, mustard, and three apples Eydan had brought home two days ago. He grabbed an apple and bit into it, leaning against the counter while Sammy sat at his feet, ears forward, eyes locked on the apple like it might be the most interesting object in the known universe.

"You already ate," Cade said to Sammy.

Sammy tilted his head.

"Don't give me that look," Cade told him.

Sammy tilted his head the other way.

Cade sighed and tossed him a small piece. Sammy caught it midair, and for a moment, the kitchen felt almost normal.

His phone buzzed in his pocket. Cade pulled it out and glanced at the screen. A text from Carla.

Carla wrote: Hey! How was your day? Missed you at lunch.

Cade stared at the message longer than he needed to. Carla Reeves. Brown eyes, dark hair that smelled like coconut shampoo, and a laugh that made him forget things—which was exactly why he liked her and exactly why she scared him. People who made you forget were dangerous because eventually they'd remind you of everything.

Cade typed back: Fine. Had to study in the library. Sorry I missed you.

That was a lie. He'd eaten lunch alone behind the gym, sitting on the concrete with his back against the wall and his ear buds in, watching a squirrel fight a crow over a potato chip. He hadn't been studying. He hadn't been doing anything. He'd just needed to be somewhere that no one would look at him and try to figure out what was wrong.

Three dots appeared on the screen. Carla was typing.

Carla wrote: No worries! Want to hang out this weekend? We could go to the park with Sammy.

Something warm moved through Cade's chest, and he hated it. Warm meant vulnerable. Warm meant there was something to lose.

Cade wrote back: Maybe. I'll let you know.

He shoved the phone back into his pocket and finished the apple. Carla deserved better than "maybe." She deserved someone who could say "yes" without it feeling like stepping off a cliff. But Cade had learned something from growing up in Don Thompson's house—the people you love the most are the ones who can hurt you the worst. And the only real protection was to never let anyone that close.

The only exception to that rule was currently sitting at his feet, staring at the back door.

Sammy had his ears up. Not the happy, alert ears that meant he'd heard a squirrel or the mail truck. These were different—rigid, pointed, locked onto something beyond the glass.

"What's up, boy?" Cade said to the dog.

Sammy didn't move. Didn't wag. Just stared.

Cade followed Sammy's gaze through the glass door to the backyard. "The backyard was enclosed by a rusted chain-link fence that sagged in places but still held. Beyond it, past the property line, the woods began."They weren't deep woods—at least, Cade had never thought they were. He and Sammy had walked in there plenty of times, chasing sticks and kicking through leaves. A quarter mile in, the trees thinned out and you hit the creek. That was as far as they ever went.

But Sammy wasn't looking at the near trees. He was looking beyond them, into the deep green where the light didn't reach, where the oaks grew thick and the brush piled up in tangled walls.

A low whine built in the dog's throat.

"Sammy. Hey." Cade knelt and put his hand on the dog's back. The muscles were tight, trembling slightly, like a spring wound too far. "It's just the woods, pal. You've been out there a hundred times."

Sammy whined again, louder this time, and pressed his nose against the glass hard enough to leave a smudge.

Cade watched the tree line for a long moment. Nothing moved. No deer, no raccoons, nothing. Just the October wind pushing through the branches and the slow fade of afternoon light.

"You're losing it, Sammy," Cade said quietly.

But the dog didn't stop staring.

Ashen came home at 3:52. Two minutes late, which meant the bus driver had made the extra stop on Cedar Lane again. Cade had the toast ready—peanut butter, cut diagonal, the way she liked it—and a glass of milk on the table.

She came through the front door without a word, dropped her backpack by the couch, and walked to the kitchen table like she was following a script she'd memorized. Her dark hair was pulled back in a ponytail that was coming loose on one side, and her sneakers were scuffed at the toes from dragging her feet on the playground—a habit she'd picked up when things at home got bad.

"How was school?" Cade asked his sister.

"Fine," Ashen said.

"Learn anything?" Cade asked.

"Stuff," Ashen said.

Two words. Better than yesterday's one. Cade counted the small victories.

He sat across from her and watched her eat. She was small for nine—always had been—with Eydan's dark eyes and Don's stubborn jaw. She'd lost a tooth last week and hadn't told anyone until Cade noticed the gap when she yawned. He'd put a dollar under her pillow that night from his own pocket. She hadn't mentioned it the next morning, but the dollar was gone and the tooth was sitting on her windowsill in a little cup like a trophy.

There were things Cade remembered about Ashen from before—before Don got worse, before the bad nights outnumbered the good ones. She used to do this thing where she'd climb onto Cade's back and wrap her arms around his neck. "Fly me, Cade! Fly me!" Ashen would shout. And he'd run through the house with her bouncing on his shoulders, both of them laughing until they couldn't breathe. Eydan would yell at them from the kitchen. "You two stop before someone breaks a lamp!" But their mother would be smiling when she said it.

That was a long time ago. Before Ashen learned that loud noises meant danger. Before she started sleeping with her door locked and a stuffed bear she'd had since she was three clutched against her chest like a shield.

Cade wanted to fix that. He wanted to reach into his sister and pull out the little girl who used to laugh until she fell off chairs. But he didn't know how. He was fourteen, not a therapist. He could make toast and walk her to the bus stop and make sure no one at school gave her a hard time. Beyond that, he was just guessing.

Sammy trotted over and laid his head on Ashen's lap. That, at least, got a reaction. Her hand went to the dog's ears, and something in her face softened—not a smile, not quite, but the ghost of one. Sammy had that effect. He was the one member of the Thompson family who had never raised his voice, never slammed a door, never made anyone flinch. In a house where trust had been broken so many times the pieces didn't fit together anymore, Sammy was the only thing that was whole.

Cade watched his sister pet the dog and felt the thing he always felt—the tight, burning knot below his ribs that was equal parts love and helplessness. He was fourteen years old. He shouldn't be the one holding this family together with peanut butter toast and fake smiles. He shouldn't know how to check Ashen's arms for bruises or how to lie to a teacher about where a mark on his neck came from. He shouldn't have a map in his head of every creak in the hallway floor so he'd know when Don was coming.

But Don was gone now. The hallway was just a hallway. The creaks were just old wood in a cheap house. And the belt on the nail by the kitchen door was just a belt.

Just a belt.

Cade thought about calling Eydan. He did that sometimes—picked up his phone and stared at her contact photo, a picture he'd taken last Christmas of her smiling in front of the little tree they'd put up on the end table because they couldn't afford a real one. She looked tired in the photo. She always looked tired. But the smile was real, and it was aimed at him, and sometimes just seeing it was enough.

He didn't call. She'd be ringing up customers, and hearing the worry in her voice when she answered—"Is everything okay? Is Ashen okay?"—would just make both of them feel worse. So he put the phone on the counter and let it sit there, screen dark, full of messages from Carla he'd answer later and photos of a life that looked almost normal if you didn't know where to look for the cracks.

Cade helped Ashen with her math homework at the kitchen table while Sammy lay between their chairs, his chin resting on Cade's sneaker. Long division. Ashen was good at math when she could focus, but focus was hard when your brain was always listening for footsteps that weren't coming anymore. Cade walked her through each problem with more patience than he felt, because she didn't need his frustration on top of everything else she was carrying.

"You got it," Cade said when Ashen finished the last problem.

Ashen didn't look up. But the corner of her mouth moved, just barely, and Cade filed it away with the two words from earlier. Small victories.

By five o'clock, the light outside had gone amber, and the house settled into its evening quiet. Ashen was on the couch watching cartoons with the volume low—she always kept it low, a habit from the days when too much noise brought Don out of whatever room he'd been drinking in. Cade heated up canned soup for dinner because it was easy and there wasn't much else. They ate in the living room, bowls on their laps, Sammy positioned strategically between them in case someone dropped a cracker.

Cade turned and looked through the kitchen window at the woods beyond the fence. The trees were going golden with autumn, and the late sun turned the canopy into something almost beautiful.

Sammy was at the back door again. Ears up. Tail still. That same fixed stare, pointed into the deep woods.

Cade frowned. The dog had been doing this for three days now. Every afternoon, same spot, same look. Like something out there had caught his attention and wouldn't let go.

"What do you see out there, boy?" Cade asked Sammy.

Sammy's tail gave one slow wag. Just one. Then he went still again, his blue-brown eyes locked on the tree line.

Cade put his hand on the dog's head. "Whatever it is, it can wait," Cade said.

He pulled out his phone and plugged his ear buds back in. The guitar filled his head, and for a little while, the world was just noise and rhythm and the weight of nothing at all.

Sammy stayed at the door until dark.

Chapter Two - *What He Carries*

The alarm on Cade's phone went off at 5:45. He reached out from under the blanket and silenced it before the second buzz, a reflex trained into him by years of not wanting to wake Don. The habit had outlived the reason, but habits were like that—stubborn, stupid things that hung around long after the danger passed.

He lay in the dark for a few seconds, listening. The house was quiet. Eydan had already left for Walgreens—her shift started at six, which meant she was out the door by five-fifteen. Cade had heard her moving through the hallway an hour ago, the soft pad of her slippers on the hardwood, the click of the front door latch. She always tried to be silent. She always failed, but Cade never told her that.

Sammy was curled at the foot of the bed, a warm weight against Cade's ankles. The dog lifted his head when Cade sat up, tail thumping once against the mattress.

"Yeah, I know," Cade said to him. "Another day."

He swung his legs off the bed and stood. His room was small—a twin mattress on a metal frame, a dresser with a drawer that stuck, and a desk he never used because doing homework at a desk felt like something kids in movies did. A poster of a mountain range he'd torn out of a National Geographic at the school library was taped above his bed. He didn't know where the mountains were. He just liked looking at them because they were far away from here.

He pulled on jeans and a gray T-shirt that had a small bleach stain near the collar, then went down the hall to Ashen's door. He knocked twice.

"Ashen," Cade called through the door. "Time to get up."

Nothing.

He knocked again, softer this time. "Ash. Come on. Bus comes in an hour."

He heard the lock click. The door opened a crack and one dark eye peered out at him.

"Mom already left?" Ashen asked.

"Yeah," Cade said. "But I'm here. Cereal or toast?"

"Cereal," Ashen said, and closed the door.

Cade went to the kitchen and poured two bowls of off-brand Cheerios. He set Ashen's bowl in her spot with the pink spoon beside it and poured the milk. Sammy followed him through every step, nails clicking on the linoleum, occasionally glancing at the back door with that same locked-on stare from yesterday.

"Stop it," Cade told the dog. "There's nothing out there."

Sammy looked at Cade, then back at the door, then at Cade again, as if to say, *You sure about that?*

Ashen appeared in the kitchen doorway wearing the same jeans from yesterday and a purple hoodie two sizes too big that had been Cade's before he outgrew it. Her hair was unbrushed. Cade didn't say anything about it—picking battles was another skill Don had taught him without meaning to.

They ate in silence. The kitchen clock ticked. A car passed outside. Sammy lay under the table with his chin on his paws, and for a few minutes the Thompson house was just a house where two kids ate cereal before school, and nothing was broken, and nobody was afraid.

Cade walked Ashen to the bus stop at the corner of Maple Creek and Cedar Lane. He waited with her, hands in his pockets, while she stood a few feet away, clutching the straps of her backpack like it was the only thing holding her to the ground. Two other kids from the neighborhood were there—a boy kicking a rock and a girl scrolling through her phone. Neither of them talked to Ashen. She didn't seem to mind, or maybe she'd just gotten used to it.

The yellow bus rounded the corner and wheezed to a stop. Ashen climbed on without looking back.

"Have a good day, Ash," Cade called after her.

She didn't answer. The doors closed and the bus pulled away, and Cade stood on the sidewalk watching it go until it turned the corner and disappeared.

* * *

Ridgewood High was a flat, sprawling building that looked like it had been designed by someone who'd never met a teenager and didn't particularly want to. Brown brick, narrow windows, and a front entrance flanked by two half-dead boxwoods that the custodian watered every Tuesday out of either duty or spite. The parking lot smelled like diesel from the buses, and the hallways smelled like floor wax and cheap body spray.

Cade moved through it like a ghost. He'd figured out early in freshman year that the trick to surviving high school was simple—don't be noticed. Don't raise your hand. Don't make eye contact with the wrong people. Don't sit in the front row. Don't sit in the back row either, because that's where the kids who wanted attention sat. Middle of the room, third seat from the window. Invisible.

His teachers had noticed the invisibility, which was ironic. Mrs. Delgado, his English teacher, had pulled him aside two weeks ago.

"Cade, your writing is excellent," Mrs. Delgado had told him. "Your essay on *To Kill a Mockingbird* was one of the best I've read from a freshman. But you never participate in class. You never raise your hand. Is everything okay at home?"

"Everything's fine," Cade had told her.

Mrs. Delgado had looked at him the way adults looked at you when they knew you were lying but didn't know how to say so. "Well, if you ever want to talk, my door's open," she had said.

Cade had thanked her and left. He didn't want to talk. Talking meant explaining, and explaining meant admitting that his home life was a mess, and admitting that meant people would get involved—social workers, counselors, maybe even police—and Cade had learned the hard way that when adults got involved, things didn't get better. They just got different kinds of bad.

He drifted through first and second period like a body in a current—present but not really there. Algebra. Biology. Notes he took without thinking, problems he solved without caring. He was smart enough to keep his grades in the B range without trying, which was exactly where he wanted them. A's attracted attention. D's attracted concern. B's were the grade of the invisible.

At noon, Cade headed for the cafeteria. He almost didn't go—the concrete spot behind the gym was calling to him, the quiet, the solitude. But Carla had texted him that morning.

Carla had written: Lunch today? Please? I saved you a seat.

The "please" got him. Carla Reeves didn't beg. She wasn't the type. The fact that she'd typed that word meant she'd been thinking about it, and the fact that she'd been thinking about it meant she was worried about him, and the fact that she was worried about him made something behind his ribs ache in a way he didn't have a word for.

Cade had written back: OK. See you there.

She was already at the table when he walked in, sitting with her friend Maya and a kid named Jordan who was always talking about whatever video game he'd been playing the night before. Carla spotted Cade the second he came through the doors. Her face lit up—not a big dramatic reaction, just a softening around her eyes and a smile that was meant only for him. She patted the empty seat beside her.

Cade sat down and pulled a sandwich from his backpack—turkey and mustard on white bread, made that morning while Ashen ate her cereal.

"You came," Carla said, bumping her shoulder against his.

"You asked," Cade said.

"I ask every day," Carla said. "You don't always show up."

There wasn't any accusation in her voice. That was the thing about Carla—she stated facts without turning them into weapons. Don had been the opposite. Every observation was a blade. *You're eating too much. You're too loud. You're just like your mother.* Words that left marks you couldn't see.

"So how's Sammy?" Carla asked. "Still being a maniac?"

"Always," Cade said. "He's been acting weird, though. Staring at the woods behind the house like he sees something. Been doing it for days."

"Maybe he sees a deer," Carla said. "Or a ghost." She grinned. "Maybe your yard is haunted."

"With my luck, probably," Cade said, and Carla laughed.

He almost relaxed. Almost let himself lean into the warmth of her beside him, the easy way she included him without pressure. She was talking about a movie she wanted to see that weekend and asking if he'd go with her, and he was about to say yes—actually, genuinely yes—when Maya said something that knocked the air out of him.

"My dad's being so annoying," Maya said, rolling her eyes. "He won't let me go to Kelsey's party Friday. He's like, 'You're too young.' I'm fourteen! God, dads are the worst."

The table went on talking, but Cade didn't hear any of it. The word "dads" sat in his chest like a stone. Maya's dad wouldn't let her go to a party. That was her problem. Her crisis. The worst thing her father did was say no.

Cade's father had held him down on the kitchen floor and hit him with a belt until the skin on his lower back split open. He'd been eleven. Ashen had been six, hiding in her bedroom closet with her hands over her ears. Eydan had screamed at Don to stop, and Don had shoved her into the refrigerator hard enough to crack the handle. The next morning, Don had made pancakes and whistled while he cooked, and nobody said a word about the night before because that was the rule in the Thompson house. You didn't talk about it. You just survived it.

Cade put his sandwich down. He wasn't hungry anymore.

Carla noticed. She always noticed. Her hand found his under the table and squeezed.

"Hey," Carla said quietly, leaning close so only he could hear. "You okay?"

"Yeah," Cade said. "Just tired."

Carla held his hand a moment longer, then let go. She didn't push. She never pushed. And that was either the best thing about her or the thing that would eventually make him lose her, because Cade knew that even the most patient person in the world eventually gets tired of knocking on a door that never opens.

"Every weekday, Eydan had a two-hour gap between jobs. She finished at Walgreens at four and had to be at the diner by six, which meant she was out the door again by five-thirty. Most days she spent that window on laundry, groceries, or whatever else was falling apart. But today, when she came through the door a little after four, she dropped her purse on the counter and sank into a kitchen chair like her body had decided that was far enough."

She was sitting at the kitchen table with a cup of coffee that had probably gone cold twenty minutes ago, still wearing her red Walgreens polo. A half-eaten granola bar from Walgreens sat on the table next to her coffee, and a banana peel was in the trash — the closest thing to lunch she'd had all day. Her hair was pulled back in a clip, and the skin under her eyes was the color of old bruises—not from being hit, not anymore, just from not sleeping enough for too many months in a row.

"Hey, baby," Eydan said when Cade came in. She tried to smile. It almost made it all the way.

"Hey, Mom," Cade said. He dropped his backpack and opened the fridge, more out of habit than hunger. "How was work?"

"Oh, you know," Eydan said. "Same as always. Mrs. Patterson came through with forty coupons again. I think she collects them for sport."

Cade half-smiled. His mother had a way of making the worst things sound manageable. She'd done it for years—turned bruises into "I bumped into the door" and empty bank accounts into "We're just having a tight month." She was so good at it that sometimes Cade wondered if she'd convinced herself too.

"How was school?" Eydan asked.

"Fine," Cade said.

"Just fine?" Eydan asked.

"Yep," Cade said.

Eydan looked at him. Cade looked at the fridge. The silence between them was thick and familiar, packed with all the things neither of them knew how to say. *Are you okay? Are we going to make it? Do you hate me for staying with him as long as I did?* None of it came out. It never did.

"Cade," Eydan said, and something in her voice made him turn around. She was gripping the coffee mug with both hands, and her eyes were wet. "I know things have been hard. I know I'm not around enough. I'm trying—"

"Mom," Cade said. "You don't have to—"

"Yes, I do," Eydan said. Her voice cracked, just slightly, like a window with a chip in it that hadn't shattered yet. "You shouldn't have to take care of your sister every morning. You shouldn't have to make dinner. You're fourteen, Cade. You should be—" She stopped. She pressed her lips together and looked down at her coffee.

Cade stood very still. He didn't know what to do with this—his mother breaking, even just a little, in front of him. In the old days, she'd never broken. She'd held it together through every bad night, every bruise, every lie she told the neighbors. She'd been a wall. But walls get tired too.

He walked over and sat across from her. "We're okay, Mom," Cade said.

Eydan looked up at him. "You sound like me," she said.

"Maybe that's not a bad thing," Cade said.

Eydan reached across the table and squeezed his hand. Her fingers were rough from register keys and dish soap, and her nails were cut short because long nails broke at the diner. She held on for a few seconds, and Cade let her, even though something in his throat was tightening and he didn't trust himself to speak.

Then she let go, took a breath, and became Eydan Thompson again—the woman who kept moving because stopping meant falling apart.

"I left money on the counter for pizza tonight," Eydan said, standing and rinsing her mug in the sink. "Make sure Ashen eats something besides the breadsticks this time."

"I'll try," Cade said. "No promises."

Eydan almost laughed. Not quite, but close. She grabbed her keys and her purse and paused at the door.

"I love you, Cade," Eydan said. "You know that, right?"

"Yeah, Mom," Cade said. "I know."

The screen door slapped shut behind her. A moment later, the old Honda coughed to life in the driveway and pulled away, and the house was quiet again.

Cade stood at the kitchen sink, washing the cereal bowls from that morning, when Sammy started whining.

It wasn't the feed-me whine or the let-me-out whine. It was the same sound from yesterday—high, thin, almost anxious. Cade turned off the water and looked.

Sammy was at the back door. Same position. Same rigid ears. Same stare aimed at the deep woods beyond the fence. His front paws were planted on the floor and his body leaned forward like a runner waiting for the gun.

"Sammy," Cade said firmly. "Leave it."

"Cade opened the back door and let Sammy out into the fenced yard. The dog trotted straight to the far fence line, the side closest to the woods, and stood there with his nose pressed against the chain-link. He didn't sniff around or mark anything. He just stood and stared. After a few minutes, Cade called him back in. Sammy came, but he came slow, looking over his shoulder the whole way."

The dog didn't even glance at him. That was unusual. Sammy was well-trained—not because Cade had taken him to classes, but because the two of them had an understanding built on three years of being each other's only reliable company. When Cade said "leave it," Sammy left it. Always.

Except now.

Cade dried his hands on a dish towel and walked over. He crouched beside the dog and followed his gaze out through the glass. The backyard. The fence. The tree line. Same as always. The October light was going soft and orange, and the shadows between the oaks were lengthening, but there was nothing out there that should have held a dog's attention for four days running.

"What is it, boy?" Cade asked, more to himself than to the dog. "What's got you so wound up?"

Sammy let out a bark—one sharp, insistent bark aimed directly at the woods—then went back to his rigid stare.

Cade shook his head. "You're a weird dog, Sammy," Cade said. He rubbed the dog's neck and stood up.

He picked up his phone from the counter and checked the time. Ashen's bus would be at the corner in twenty minutes. He had pizza money, half a homework assignment to finish, and a dog who'd apparently lost his mind over a bunch of trees.

A text from Carla popped up on the screen.

Carla wrote: Thanks for coming to lunch today. It meant a lot. See you tomorrow?

Cade looked at the message. He thought about what she'd said—*I ask every day. You don't always show up.* He thought about her hand under the table. He thought about the movie she wanted to see.

Cade wrote back: Yeah. Save me a seat.

It was two steps forward and one step back, but at least it was steps. And maybe that was all anyone could ask from a kid who'd been taught that every open hand was just a fist that hadn't closed yet.

He pocketed the phone and headed for the door to meet Ashen's bus.

Behind him, Sammy stayed at the back door. Watching. Waiting. Staring at something in those woods that only he could see.

Chapter Three - *Into the Woods*

Saturday morning came in gray and cool, the kind of October day that couldn't decide if it wanted to rain or just threaten. Cade woke late for the first time in weeks — no alarm, no school, no Ashen to get ready. The clock on his phone read 8:17. He had a text from Carla that must have come in late the night before.

Carla had written: *Saturday! Any chance you want to do something? I'm free all day.*

Cade stared at it. All day. That sounded like a foreign concept — a whole day with nothing to survive, nothing to manage, just time. He typed a reply.

Cade wrote back: *Maybe later. Got a history essay to finish first.*

It wasn't entirely a lie. He did have the essay. But "maybe later" was the fence he kept building between himself and Carla, one board at a time, and he knew it. He put the phone in his backpack and got out of bed.

Sammy was curled on the floor beside the bed instead of on it, which was unusual. The dog lifted his head when Cade's feet hit the hardwood, but he didn't do the usual morning routine — no spinning, no tail going crazy, no full-body wiggle of joy. He just looked at Cade with those blue-brown eyes, then looked toward the bedroom door, then back at Cade.

"You're still being weird," Cade said to him. "Come on. Let's eat."

Eydan was off from Walgreens on Saturdays but still had the diner shift at six. She was in the kitchen when Cade shuffled in, standing at the stove in sweatpants and an old T-shirt, scrambling eggs. The house smelled like butter and coffee, and for a moment it felt like someone else's home — the kind where Saturday mornings were slow and safe and nobody flinched when a pan clanged.

"Morning," Eydan said without turning around. "Eggs are almost done."

"Thanks, Mom," Cade said. He sat at the table and Sammy materialized beside him, tail giving a half-hearted wag, eyes drifting toward the back door before settling on the stove.

"Don't even think about it," Cade told the dog.

Ashen was already at the table, eating a piece of toast and drawing on the back of a grocery receipt with a stubby pencil. She didn't look up when Cade sat down, but she shifted her chair a few inches closer to his. It was the kind of thing she did without thinking — drifting toward Cade the way a plant drifts toward sunlight. He was her safe place, and they both knew it even if neither of them said it.

"What are you drawing?" Cade asked his sister.

Ashen tilted the receipt so he could see. It was a dog. Or something close to a dog — four legs, a tail, two pointy ears. It looked more like a fox that had been through a windstorm, but the effort was there.

"That's pretty good," Cade said. "That supposed to be Sammy?"

Ashen nodded without looking up. She added a tongue hanging out of the dog's mouth. Cade watched her draw and felt that familiar ache — his little sister, hunched over a grocery receipt because they didn't have sketch paper, drawing the one member of the family who had never scared her.

Eydan set plates on the table — scrambled eggs, toast, and a few slices of turkey she'd fried in the pan. She grabbed a yogurt from the fridge for herself and ate it standing at the counter with a spoon, the way she ate everything — fast, between tasks, like sitting down for a meal was a luxury she couldn't afford. Then she caught herself, looked at the two kids at the table, and pulled out a chair.

"Scoot over," Eydan said to Ashen.

Ashen scooted. Eydan sat down with a plate of eggs and for ten minutes the Thompsons ate together like a family. Nobody mentioned Don. Nobody mentioned money. Nobody mentioned the fact that this was the only meal they'd share all day because Eydan would be at the diner by six. Sammy lay under the table waiting for something to fall, and the kitchen clock ticked, and the rain that had been threatening held off, and it was enough.

"I was thinking we could go to the store later," Eydan said, looking at Ashen. "You need new sneakers. Those things are falling apart."

Ashen looked down at her scuffed shoes. "They're okay," Ashen said.

"They're not okay," Eydan said. "Your toe is practically poking through. We'll go to the outlet place on Route 4. They've got a sale."

Cade knew what "sale" meant — the clearance rack at the back of the store where last season's shoes ended up in bins sorted by size. But Ashen didn't need to know the math behind it. She just needed new shoes.

"Can Sammy come?" Ashen asked.

"To the shoe store?" Eydan asked.

"He likes car rides," Ashen said.

"He also likes eating seat belts," Cade said. "Last time he chewed through the shoulder strap on the passenger side."

"That was one time," Ashen said, and for a half second her voice had something in it that sounded almost like argument, almost like fight, almost like the little girl who used to shout "Fly me, Cade!" from across the room. It was gone as fast as it came, but Cade caught it, and across the table he saw Eydan catch it too. Their eyes met for just a moment. A tiny victory, shared in silence.

After breakfast, Eydan started a load of laundry and then sat on the couch with Ashen to watch cartoons before their shopping trip. Cade grabbed his backpack — he had a history essay due Monday that he hadn't started — and headed for the back porch. The air was cool but not cold, and the porch had a wooden bench along the wall that was good enough to sit on if you didn't mind the peeling paint.

He set the backpack beside him, pulled out his notebook and textbook, and started reading about the American Revolution. He opened the back door and let Sammy out into the fenced yard. The dog trotted straight to the far fence line, the side closest to the woods, and stood there with his nose pressed against the chain-link. He didn't sniff around or mark anything. He just stood and stared. After a few minutes, Cade called him back.

"Sammy, come," Cade said.

Sammy came, but he came slow, looking over his shoulder the whole way. He circled twice in the grass near Cade's feet and lay down, but his head stayed up, his ears stayed forward, and his eyes never left the tree line.

Cade shook his head and went back to his notes.

For about thirty minutes, it was quiet. He got through two pages on Valley Forge. A squirrel ran across the top of the fence and Sammy watched it with mild interest but didn't move. A car passed on Maple Creek Drive. A bird landed on the gutter and sang three notes before flying off. Inside, he could hear the low murmur of cartoons and Eydan's voice saying something to Ashen that made his sister respond with more than one word, though Cade couldn't make out what they said.

His phone buzzed. He pulled it from the backpack.

Carla had written: *History essay on a Saturday. You really know how to live. Want help? I already finished mine.*

Cade smiled. He couldn't help it. The idea of Carla sitting on this porch with him, both of them doing homework, Sammy at their feet — it was such a normal, simple picture that it hurt a little.

Cade wrote back: *Show off. I'm good. Maybe we can hang out tomorrow?*

He meant it this time. Actually, truly meant it. And the fact that he meant it scared him almost as much as the thought of not meaning it.

Carla wrote: *Tomorrow works! I'll bring snacks. Tell Sammy I said hi.*

Cade put the phone back in the backpack and picked up his pen. He was writing a sentence about George Washington crossing the Delaware when Sammy stood up.

Cade didn't notice at first. He was copying a quote into his notebook when the dog's shadow shifted at the edge of his vision. He glanced down. Sammy was on his feet, body rigid, ears locked forward, staring at the back fence — at the woods beyond it.

"Not this again," Cade said to him.

Sammy didn't acknowledge him. The dog took a step forward. Then another. His walk was slow and deliberate, nothing like his usual bouncing trot. He moved toward the back fence like he was being pulled by a string.

"Sammy," Cade said, louder. "Come here, boy."

The dog reached the fence and pressed his nose against the chain-link. A low whine built in his throat. His tail was down, not tucked — just still. Every muscle in his body was taut.

"Sammy!" Cade called again, setting his notebook down. "Come!"

Sammy turned and looked at Cade. And what Cade saw in the dog's eyes was something he'd never seen there before — not excitement, not fear, but something between the two. An urgency. A need. Like the dog was trying to tell him something and didn't have the words.

Then Sammy turned back to the fence, dropped his head, and pushed through a gap at the bottom where the chain-link had pulled loose from the post.

"No!" Cade shouted, jumping to his feet. "Sammy, no!"

But the dog was through. He squeezed under the sagging fence and hit the ground running — not a playful run, not chasing a squirrel. A full sprint, ears back, legs stretching, tearing across the narrow strip of grass between the fence and the tree line and disappearing into the woods like he'd been shot from a cannon.

"Sammy!" Cade yelled.

Nothing. The dog was gone. Swallowed by the trees in three seconds flat.

Cade didn't think. He didn't go inside to tell Eydan. He didn't stop to consider what he was doing. He grabbed his backpack off the bench — his phone was in it, his notebook, a pen, the half-empty water bottle from yesterday — slung it over his shoulder, and ran. He hit the fence, found the gap Sammy had squeezed through, dropped to his knees, and forced himself under the chain-link. The metal scraped his back through his T-shirt and caught on the backpack strap, but he yanked free and kept moving.

He was in the woods.

The trees closed around him fast. Within fifty yards the suburban sounds — a lawnmower somewhere on the next street, a car door slamming, the faint murmur of Ashen's cartoons through the window — faded to nothing. The ground was soft with fallen leaves, damp from the morning dew, and the canopy overhead filtered the gray sky into something dimmer and quieter.

"Sammy!" Cade shouted. His voice bounced off the trunks and died. "Sammy, come!"

He heard barking. Distant but clear, deeper into the woods than Cade had ever gone. Past the creek. Past the part he knew.

He ran toward the sound. Branches snagged his hoodie and scratched at his arms. His sneakers slipped on wet leaves and he nearly went down twice, catching himself on a trunk the second time, bark biting into his palm. He jumped the creek — a narrow thing, barely three feet across with muddy banks — and kept pushing. The trees were getting bigger here, the oaks wider, the brush thicker. This wasn't the tidy fringe of woods behind the neighborhood anymore. This was old forest, dense and tangled, the kind of place that didn't care if you were in it or not.

"Sammy!" Cade called again, breathing hard now.

A bark answered him. Closer. To the left.

Cade veered and pushed through a wall of brush, thorns raking his forearms hard enough to draw thin lines of blood. A vine caught his ankle and he stumbled, went to one knee, got back up. The barking was louder now, more insistent. Sammy was close.

He shoved through a final curtain of undergrowth and stumbled into a small clearing.

Two boulders.

They sat at the far end of the clearing like sentinels, massive and gray, each one taller than Cade and wider than a car. They were pressed close together with a narrow gap between them — maybe two feet across, just enough for a person to squeeze through if they turned sideways. Moss covered their bases and a single oak root had grown over the top of the left boulder like a gnarled arm reaching across to the other.

Cade had never seen them before. He'd been in these woods dozens of times over the three years they'd lived on Maple Creek Drive, and he'd never come this far, never found this clearing, never laid eyes on anything like these two ancient slabs of rock that looked like they'd been dropped here by something enormous a thousand years ago.

Sammy's barking was coming from the other side.

"Sammy!" Cade shouted through the gap.

The barking continued — insistent, sharp, the way Sammy sounded when he'd treed a squirrel and couldn't understand why Cade wasn't as excited as he was.

Cade stepped closer to the gap between the boulders. The air felt different here. Warmer. Not by much, but enough to notice against the October cool on the back of his sweating neck. And there was something else — a faint shimmer in the air between the rocks, like heat rising off summer asphalt. He blinked, thinking it was a trick of the gray light filtering through the canopy. But it was still there. A ripple. A distortion. The air between the two boulders looked like it was bending.

He didn't have time to think about it. Sammy was on the other side, and that was all that mattered.

Cade turned sideways, squeezed into the gap, and pushed through. The rock was cold against his chest and his backpack scraped against the stone behind him. The warm air pressed against his face and the shimmer danced at the edges of his vision — close, all around him, like walking through a curtain made of light. For a moment he was stuck — wedged between the two boulders with his backpack caught on a jut of rock. He twisted his shoulders, pulled hard, and felt the strap tear slightly as it came free.

Then he was through.

And the world was wrong.

The gray October sky was gone. Above him was a canopy of green so vivid it hurt his eyes — leaves the size of dinner plates in shades of emerald and jade, vines thick as rope hanging from branches that could have held a car. The trees stretched so high their tops vanished into a soft white mist that clung to the upper canopy like cotton. The air was warm and heavy, thick with moisture and the smell of earth and vegetation and something else, something wild and ancient that Cade had no name for.

The ground under his feet was soft — not the dry leaf cover of the woods behind his house, but dark, rich soil carpeted with moss and ferns that came up to his knees. Flowers he didn't recognize bloomed in clusters of orange and deep purple along the base of the trees. Insects hummed in the undergrowth — not the lazy buzz of backyard mosquitoes, but a layered chorus of clicks and trills and hums that sounded like the forest itself was alive and talking.

Something called out in the distance, a long, low sound that didn't belong to any bird Cade had ever heard. It rose, held, and faded into the canopy like smoke. A moment later, another call answered it from a different direction, deeper, resonant, shaking the air with a vibration Cade could feel in his chest.

Cade stood completely still. His heart was hammering so hard he could hear it in his ears. His brain was trying to make sense of what his eyes were telling him, and failing. Every tree, every leaf, every sound was too much — too big, too green, too alive. The woods behind Maple Creek Drive were a thin strip of oaks and maples between two subdivisions. This was something else entirely. This was a forest that had never been cut, never been mapped, never been touched by anything human.

This was not the woods behind his house.

This was not anywhere he had ever been or seen or imagined.

"Sammy?" Cade whispered.

A bark. Right behind him. Cade spun around.

Sammy was sitting five feet away, tail wagging, tongue out, looking at Cade with an expression of pure canine satisfaction. Like this was exactly where he'd been trying to go for the past five days, and it was about time Cade caught up.

"Where are we, boy?" Cade said to the dog. His voice came out shaky and thin, and he didn't care.

Sammy wagged harder.

Cade turned back toward the boulders. They were there — the same two massive rocks, the same narrow gap. But the shimmer was fading. The warm ripple in the air between the stones was thinning, dimming, like a candle guttering in a draft. As Cade watched, it flickered once more and went still. The air between the boulders was just air now. Cold stone and nothing else.

He reached out and touched the gap. Just rock. Just air. Whatever had been there — whatever had brought him here — was gone.

Cade's stomach dropped. He pushed his hand deeper into the gap. Nothing. He squeezed back in sideways and hit solid rock where open space had been moments ago. The passage was sealed. The way home was gone.

"No," Cade said. "No, no, no."

He slammed his palm against the boulder. The stone didn't care. He hit it again, harder, and pain shot through his hand.

Cade pressed his back against the rock and slid down until he was sitting on the mossy ground. His hands were shaking. His breath was coming fast and shallow. He thought about Eydan on the couch with Ashen, watching cartoons, not knowing her son had just disappeared. He thought about Ashen's drawing of Sammy on the grocery receipt. He thought about Carla's text — *Tomorrow works! I'll bring snacks* — and something in his chest cracked, because tomorrow wasn't going to work. Tomorrow might not exist. Not the tomorrow she meant.

Sammy trotted over and pushed his nose into Cade's chest, whining softly.

Cade grabbed the dog and held him. He held Sammy the way Ashen held her stuffed bear — tight, desperate, like the only solid thing in a world that had just turned to water under his feet.

"What did you do, Sammy?" Cade whispered into the dog's fur. "Where did you bring us?"

Something moved in the trees. Something large. The ground trembled slightly beneath Cade, a vibration he felt through the moss and the soil and the rock at his back. A sound came through the forest — a deep, resonant boom, like a drum the size of a house being struck once.

Then again.

Then again.

Footsteps. But not human footsteps. Something much, much bigger. The ferns at the edge of the clearing swayed, pushed aside by something Cade couldn't see yet but could feel in the ground, getting closer with each step.

Cade pulled Sammy against his chest and pressed his back harder against the boulder. He didn't breathe. He didn't move.

He didn't know where he was. He didn't know how to get home. And something was coming through the trees.

Cade didn't move. He sat with his back against the boulder, Sammy pressed tight against his chest, and watched the ferns at the edge of the clearing sway with each thundering footstep.

The sound was getting closer. Whatever was making it was heavy — heavier than anything Cade had ever encountered outside of a truck or a building. The ground pulsed with each impact, a rhythmic tremor that traveled up through the moss and into his spine. He could feel it in his teeth.

Sammy was rigid in his arms but not shaking. The dog's ears were pinned forward, tracking the sound, and a low growl was building in his throat. Cade clamped his hand gently around Sammy's muzzle.

"Quiet," Cade whispered to the dog. "Please be quiet."

Sammy went silent. His body vibrated with tension, but he didn't make a sound. Three years of trust between them held.

The ferns parted.

Cade saw the legs first. They were thick as tree trunks, covered in rough, gray-green skin that looked like bark or stone. Each foot had three massive toes, splayed wide, pressing deep impressions into the soft earth. The legs rose up and up, disappearing into a body so large that Cade had to tilt his head back to take it in.

It was a dinosaur.

The word formed in Cade's mind, but it didn't make sense there. It was like thinking the word "spaceship" while looking at the sky — the concept existed, but not in any reality he'd ever lived in. Dinosaurs were bones in museums. Dinosaurs were pictures in textbooks. Dinosaurs were things that had been dead for sixty-five million years.

This one was very much alive.

It was an herbivore — Cade knew that much from sixth-grade science, a lifetime ago. The head was small compared to the body, perched on a neck that curved like a crane arm, maybe thirty feet above the forest floor. The body was enormous, a living mountain of gray-green flesh that moved through the trees with a slow, deliberate grace that seemed impossible for something that size. Its tail swung behind it like a counterweight, thick at the base and tapering to a point, brushing aside ferns and saplings without effort.

It hadn't seen them. Or if it had, it didn't care. It moved through the clearing on the far side, maybe forty yards from where Cade sat frozen against the boulder, its massive head dipping to strip leaves from a branch high above. The sound of its jaws working was like someone ripping a bed sheet — slow, heavy, deliberate. Leaves and small branches disappeared into its mouth, and the tree swayed and shuddered under the assault.

Cade watched it with his mouth open. He forgot to be afraid. For about ten seconds, fear stepped aside and pure, paralyzing wonder took its place. He was looking at a living dinosaur. A real, breathing, eating dinosaur, standing in a forest that shouldn't exist, in a world he didn't understand, and it was the most incredible and terrifying thing he had ever seen.

Then the animal shifted its weight and one massive foot came down fifteen yards closer to them than the last step, and fear came back like a slap.

Cade pressed harder against the boulder. Sammy trembled in his arms. The dinosaur's foot left an impression in the soil six inches deep and wide enough to sit in. If that foot came down on them, they wouldn't even be a stain.

But the creature kept moving. Step by enormous step, it passed through the edge of the clearing and back into the deeper forest, its body pushing through the canopy like a ship through water. The trees creaked and swayed in its wake. The ground trembled for another thirty seconds, then gradually stilled. The booming footsteps faded. The insects, which had gone silent, began their chorus again, cautiously at first, then building back to full volume.

Cade let out a breath he didn't know he'd been holding. His arms were locked around Sammy so tight the dog squirmed and licked his chin.

"Sorry," Cade said to Sammy, loosening his grip. His voice was hoarse. "Sorry, boy."

He sat there for a long time. He didn't know how long — five minutes, maybe ten. His legs didn't want to work and his brain was stuck in a loop, cycling through the same three facts over and over. There was a dinosaur. It was alive. He was somewhere that dinosaurs existed.

Finally, Sammy pulled free from his arms and stood, shaking his coat out like he'd just had a bath. The dog sniffed the ground where the dinosaur had walked, tail wagging cautiously, then looked back at Cade as if to say, *You coming or what?*

"I don't know where to go, Sammy," Cade said to the dog. His voice sounded small in the vastness of the forest.

Sammy tilted his head.

Cade pulled himself to his feet. His legs were stiff and his hands were still trembling, but standing was better than sitting. Sitting was giving up, and giving up was something Don had tried to beat into him — the idea that he was too small, too weak, too worthless to fight. Cade had never believed it, even on the worst nights. He wasn't going to start believing it now.

He took stock. Backpack: still on his shoulders. Inside it: his phone, a notebook, a pen, a half-empty water bottle, and the remains of a granola bar he'd shoved in there last week. That was it. That was everything he had in a world he didn't understand.

He pulled out his phone. The screen lit up, familiar and bright and completely useless. No signal. Not one bar. The little icon in the top corner showed nothing — no cell network, no Wi-Fi, nothing. He was as disconnected as if he'd been dropped on the moon.

He tried calling Eydan anyway. He tapped her contact photo — the Christmas picture, her tired smile, the little tree on the end table — and held the phone to his ear. Nothing. Not even a ring. Just dead, empty silence.

He tried 911. Same thing. Nothing.

He tried Carla. Nothing.

Cade lowered the phone and stared at the screen. Carla's last text was still there — *Tomorrow works! I'll bring snacks. Tell Sammy I said hi.* — and looking at it now, in this impossible forest with the smell of ancient earth in his nose and the memory of a dinosaur's footstep still vibrating in his bones, it felt like a message from another planet. Another life. A life that was still happening somewhere without him in it.

He opened his photos. There was Eydan in the kitchen, stirring something on the stove, caught mid-laugh because Cade had said something stupid to make her smile. There was Ashen on the couch with Sammy, the dog's head in her lap, both of them asleep. There was Carla at school, leaning against her locker, making a face at the camera. There was the backyard on Maple Creek Drive, the chain-link fence, the tree line beyond it — the same woods he'd chased Sammy into, the same woods that had swallowed him whole and spit him out here.

Cade's thumb hovered over the photos. His throat tightened. These people — his mother, his sister, his girlfriend — they were out there somewhere, on the other side of a passage that had closed behind him, and they didn't know where he was. Eydan would notice he was gone. She'd call his name. She'd check the yard, the neighborhood, the creek. She'd call his phone and it wouldn't ring. She'd call the police. There would be searches, flyers, news stories maybe. And none of it would matter because Cade wasn't missing in any place they could look.

He turned the phone off to save battery. He didn't know why — there was nothing to save it for. No one to call, no maps to check, no signal to find. But turning it off felt like a decision, and decisions meant he was still thinking, and thinking meant he was still alive, and alive meant there was still a chance.

He slid the phone into the backpack and zipped it shut.

"Okay," Cade said out loud. He looked at Sammy. The dog was sitting patiently, watching him with those mismatched eyes, waiting. "Okay. We need water. We need shelter. We need to figure out where we are."

Sammy's tail wagged.

"Glad one of us is optimistic," Cade said to the dog.

He looked around the clearing. The boulders were behind him — sealed, useless, a locked door with no key. Ahead, the forest stretched in every direction, an ocean of green with no landmarks, no paths, no signs. The canopy above was so thick he couldn't see the sky clearly, just patches of white mist and filtered light that gave no clue about the time of day or which direction was which.

But Cade could hear water. Somewhere to his right, faint but unmistakable — the sound of running water. A stream or a river. Water meant survival. It also meant animals would come to drink there, including whatever predators lived in a world where dinosaurs roamed, but Cade pushed that thought aside. One problem at a time.

"This way," Cade said to Sammy. "Come on, boy."

They moved through the forest together. Cade kept one hand on Sammy's collar for the first hundred yards, not because the dog would run — Sammy seemed perfectly content to walk beside him — but because the contact steadied him. The dog's fur under his fingers was warm and real and familiar, the one thing in this world that made sense.

The forest was unlike anything Cade had experienced. Every tree was enormous, with trunks wide enough that three people couldn't have wrapped their arms around them. The bark was rough and dark, covered in patches of bright green moss and clusters of fungus that glowed faintly in the dim light — soft blues and pale oranges, like tiny lanterns scattered across the wood. The ferns on the forest floor rose to Cade's waist in places, and he had to push through them like wading through green water. Vines hung from the canopy in long, looping curtains, some as thick as his arm, others thin and delicate, covered in tiny white flowers that gave off a sweet, heavy scent.

And it was loud. Not the roaring, crashing loud he'd expected from a world of dinosaurs, but a constant, layered hum of life — insects clicking and buzzing, birds calling from the canopy in voices he didn't recognize, the rustle of small things moving through the undergrowth. Twice he heard the distant boom of heavy footsteps, somewhere far off, and both times he froze until the sound faded.

Sammy was calm. That was the strange part. The dog who'd been anxious and rigid for five days, staring at the woods with obsessive intensity, was now trotting through this alien forest with his tongue out and his tail swinging. He sniffed at the giant ferns. He investigated a fallen log covered in luminous fungus. He paused to watch a beetle the size of Cade's fist crawl across a root and showed no fear, only curiosity. Whatever had been calling to Sammy from across the worlds, whatever had pulled him through that gap in the fence and into the portal between the boulders, the dog had answered it. He was home in a way Cade couldn't understand.

The sound of water grew louder. The trees thinned slightly and the ground sloped downward, and then Cade pushed through a final curtain of ferns and found himself standing on the bank of a river.

It was wide — maybe fifty feet across — with clear water running over smooth stones. The current was gentle, not dangerous, and the banks were lined with flat rocks and patches of dark sand. On the far side, the forest continued, but the canopy opened above the river and for the first time since arriving, Cade could see the sky.

It was blue. Not the gray October sky of home, but a deep, clear, endless blue that stretched from horizon to horizon without a single cloud. The sun was high and warm — mid-afternoon, maybe, though Cade had no way to know if the sun here followed the same rules as the one back home.

He knelt at the river's edge. The water was cool and clear enough to see the bottom — smooth pebbles in shades of brown and gray, a few small fish darting between them. He cupped his hands and drank. It was the cleanest, coldest water he'd ever tasted, and he drank until his stomach hurt, then filled his water bottle and capped it.

Sammy was already in the river, chest-deep, lapping water with his tail going like a propeller.

"At least you're having fun," Cade said to the dog.

He sat on a flat rock beside the river and let himself breathe. The sun was warm on his face. The water rushed past, steady and constant and completely indifferent to the fact that a fourteen-year-old boy from the suburbs was sitting on its bank trying not to fall apart.

He was alone. He was in a world he couldn't explain. He had no food except a stale granola bar, no shelter, no way home, and no idea what else was out there in the forest besides plant-eating dinosaurs the size of buildings.

But he had water. He had Sammy. And he had enough of Don Thompson's hard lessons beaten into him to know one thing — you don't quit. You don't lie down. You don't give up, because giving up is what they want, and Cade had spent his whole life refusing to give anyone what they wanted when what they wanted was to see him break.

He ate the granola bar. He split the last piece with Sammy. He filled his water bottle again.

Then he stood up, shouldered his backpack, and looked downstream. The river had to go somewhere. Rivers meant life — animals, people, settlements. If there was anyone in this world, they'd be near the water.

"Come on, Sammy," Cade said. "Let's find out where we are."

The dog shook himself dry, spraying water in a wide arc that caught Cade across the legs, and fell into step beside him. Together, they followed the river into the unknown.

The sun was dropping lower in the sky by the time Cade admitted to himself that he was in trouble. He'd been walking for hours. The river had widened and then narrowed, curving through the forest in long, slow bends. He'd seen more dinosaurs — two more herbivores in the distance, different from the first one, shorter and broader with heavy ridged plates along their backs. They'd been grazing at the river's edge on the far bank, and Cade had given them wide clearance, pressing into the tree line and moving past as quietly as he could.

He hadn't seen any predators. Not yet. But the forest was changing as the light faded. The insect chorus shifted to a deeper, slower rhythm. The bird calls stopped. And from somewhere far upriver came a sound that turned Cade's blood to ice — a roar. Not the booming footstep of a plant-eater. A roar. High, cutting, hungry. The sound of something that ate meat and was announcing itself to anything within earshot.

Sammy's ears flattened. The dog pressed against Cade's leg and growled low in his throat.

"I know," Cade said to the dog quietly. "I heard it too."

He needed shelter. Now. Not a bush, not a tree — something solid, something with walls, something that would put a barrier between him and whatever had made that sound.

He found it fifty yards from the river — a rock outcropping at the base of a low ridge, with an overhang deep enough to sit under and sides narrow enough that nothing much bigger than a large dog could squeeze in. It wasn't a cave. It was barely a dent in the rock. But it was the best he was going to get before dark.

Cade crawled under the overhang, pulling Sammy in with him. The rock was cold against his back, the ground underneath covered in dry leaves and small stones. He pushed the debris into a rough pile at the opening — it wouldn't stop anything determined, but it might slow something down long enough for him to react.

React how, he didn't know. He had no weapon, no fire, no knowledge of this place. He was a fourteen-year-old kid with a backpack and a dog, sitting under a rock in a world that shouldn't exist, listening to something roar in the distance.

Night fell fast. One moment the sky through the canopy was orange and gold. The next it was deep blue, then purple, then black. Stars appeared — more stars than Cade had ever seen, more than he'd known existed, a sky so thick with light it looked like someone had spilled milk across a black table. No moon, or at least not one he could see through the canopy.

The forest came alive in the dark. The roaring didn't come again, but other sounds took its place — clicks, grunts, the snap of branches, the heavy breathing of things moving through the undergrowth. Something walked past the outcropping, close enough that Cade could hear its feet on the forest floor. It paused. Sniffed. Moved on.

Cade didn't sleep. He sat with his back against the rock, Sammy curled against his chest, and watched the darkness. His phone was in his backpack. He thought about turning it on for the flashlight, but some instinct told him that light in this darkness would attract attention he didn't want.

So he sat. And he listened. And he held his dog.

Hours passed. The sounds came and went. Something screamed once — a high, sharp sound that cut off abruptly and left a silence worse than the noise had been. Cade's hand found Sammy's fur and gripped it, and the dog pressed closer, warm and alive and the only thing in this world that knew his name.

Somewhere in the deepest part of the night, Cade whispered into the dark.

"We're going to be okay, Sammy," Cade said to the dog. "We're going to figure this out."

Sammy's tail thumped once against the ground.

Cade didn't believe himself. But saying it out loud was better than the silence, and the dog believed him, and that was enough to hold onto until morning.

Chapter Five – *Found*

Morning arrived slowly, the darkness giving way to a gray-green twilight that seeped through the canopy like water through cloth. Cade hadn't slept. His back ached from the rock, his neck was stiff, and his legs were cramped from sitting in the same position for hours. His mouth tasted like dirt and his stomach was a hollow, angry knot.

Sammy stirred against his chest, yawned wide enough to show every tooth he had, and wriggled out from under Cade's arm. The dog stretched — front legs out, back arched, tail up — then trotted to the edge of the outcropping and sniffed the morning air like it was the most interesting thing he'd ever encountered.

"Glad one of us got some rest," Cade said to him.

He crawled out from under the rock and stood. Every joint protested. The forest looked different in the morning light — less menacing, more alive. The mist that clung to the upper canopy had thickened overnight, and droplets of water hung on every leaf and vine like tiny glass beads. The air was cool and damp, and the insect chorus had shifted back to its daytime rhythm — higher, brighter, busier.

No roaring. That was the first thing Cade checked for, standing still and listening with every nerve in his body tuned to the forest. Whatever had made that sound last night was either gone or sleeping, and Cade intended to be far away before it woke up.

He went to the river and drank. He filled his water bottle. Sammy waded in and drank beside him, then shook himself dry with the kind of full-body violence that only dogs seemed capable of. Cade got soaked from the waist down.

"Thanks for that," Cade said to the dog.

His stomach growled. The granola bar was gone — he'd split the last of it with Sammy the night before. There was nothing left in the backpack but his notebook, his pen, his dead-weight phone, and the empty wrapper. He needed food. Real food. And he had no idea what was safe to eat in a world where the plants were three times the size of anything back home and the insects were the size of his hand.

He pulled out his phone and turned it on. The screen lit up — forty-one percent battery. Still no signal. He looked at the home screen for a moment. The wallpaper was a photo of Sammy sitting on the back porch with his tongue out, taken on a day last summer when the heat had been brutal and Cade had sprayed the dog with the garden hose. Sammy had loved it. Cade had laughed so hard his ribs hurt.

That felt like a hundred years ago.

He turned the phone off again. Forty-one percent. He didn't know how long that would last with no charger and no outlet in a world that hadn't invented electricity. He needed to save whatever was left.

"Okay," Cade said to Sammy. "Same plan as yesterday. Follow the river. Find something. Someone. Anything."

They walked. The forest was dense along the riverbank, and Cade had to pick his way through ferns and over roots that jutted from the soil like the knuckles of buried giants. The river curved to the right in a wide, slow arc, and as they rounded the bend, the trees thinned and the terrain opened into a broad valley. The mist burned off as the sun climbed, and for the first time Cade got a real look at the world he'd fallen into.

It was enormous.

The valley stretched out before him, miles wide, carpeted in green — grassland and scattered trees and clusters of thick vegetation. In the distance, mountains rose in a jagged line against the sky, their peaks wrapped in white cloud. The river he'd been following widened as it entered the valley, becoming a broad, lazy waterway that wound through the landscape like a silver ribbon.

And there were dinosaurs everywhere.

Not one or two. Dozens. Maybe hundreds. Herds of them, moving across the grassland in loose groups, their massive bodies casting long shadows on the green earth.

Cade could see at least three different kinds from where he stood — the tall, long-necked ones like the first he'd seen, moving slowly through stands of trees; the shorter, broader ones with ridged plates on their backs, clustered near the river; and a new type he hadn't seen before, medium-sized animals that moved on two legs, their bodies tilted forward, tails held stiff behind them for balance, traveling in a tight group of eight or ten like a flock of enormous birds.

Cade stood at the edge of the tree line and stared. His brain had given up trying to process what he was seeing and had settled into a kind of numb acceptance. Dinosaurs. A valley full of dinosaurs. He was standing in a world where dinosaurs had never gone extinct, where they roamed in herds across open grassland under a blue sky, alive and real and impossible.

Sammy sat beside him, panting happily, completely unfazed.

"You know what, Sammy?" Cade said to the dog. "I think you've been here before. In your head, at least."

The dog looked up at him and wagged.

Cade was about to step out of the tree line when Sammy's ears snapped forward. The dog's body went rigid — not the staring-at-the-woods rigid from back home, but the alert, sharp focus of an animal that had detected something close. A growl started low in his throat.

Cade froze. He scanned the tree line. Nothing. He looked left. Nothing. He looked right.

A girl was standing twenty feet away, half-hidden behind the trunk of an enormous oak, with a bow in her hands and an arrow pointed directly at his chest.

Cade's hands went up before his brain told them to. An automatic response, programmed by years of Don — when someone threatens you, you make yourself small, you show your palms, you try not to get hit.

"I'm not — I don't —" Cade stammered.

The girl didn't move. She was about his age, maybe a year younger, with dark hair pulled back in a braid that hung over one shoulder. Her skin was sun-browned and her eyes were sharp and steady, the color of dark amber. She wore clothing Cade had never seen outside of a history book — leather and woven cloth, layered and practical, with a belt at her waist that held a knife in a sheath. Her boots were laced to the knee. The bow in her hands was not a toy. It was a weapon, and she held it like she knew exactly how to use it.

She said something. The words should have been foreign — her mouth formed sounds that didn't look like English — but what reached Cade's ears was clear and sharp and perfectly understandable.

"Who are you?" the girl asked. "Where did you come from?"

Cade blinked. She was speaking to him and he could understand her. The words arrived in his head as English, clean and clear, as if someone had translated them between her mouth and his ears. He didn't have time to wonder how or why. The arrow was still pointed at his chest.

"My name is Cade," Cade said. "Cade Thompson. I was — I was chasing my dog. I came through the woods and I ended up here. I don't know where I am."

The girl studied him. Her eyes moved from his face to his clothes — the gray T-shirt, the jeans, the sneakers caked in mud — to the backpack on his shoulders. Nothing he was wearing made sense in her world. He could see her processing it, cataloging the strangeness.

Then her eyes dropped to Sammy.

The dog was sitting beside Cade, no longer growling. His tail was swaying in a slow, cautious wag, and his head was tilted to one side, studying the girl with the same intensity she was studying him. Sammy's ears were forward but relaxed. His body language said the same thing it always said when he met someone new — *I'm deciding if I like you. Give me a minute.*

The girl lowered her bow an inch. "What is that?" the girl asked, nodding toward Sammy.

"That's my dog," Cade said. "His name is Sammy. He won't hurt you."

"Dog," the girl repeated, like she was tasting the word. "I have never seen an animal like this."

"He's friendly," Cade said. "He's the reason I'm here. He ran into the woods and I followed him and I — I went through something. Between two big rocks. Boulders. And then I was here."

The girl's eyes narrowed slightly. She lowered the bow another inch. "You came from beyond the vale?" the girl asked.

"I don't know what the vale is," Cade said. "I come from a place called — well, it doesn't matter. I don't think you'd know it. I just need to figure out where I am and how to get back."

The girl was quiet for a long moment. The arrow was still nocked but the bow was nearly at her side now. She was making a decision, and Cade could see the calculation happening behind those amber eyes — trust or don't trust, help or walk away, risk or safety.

Sammy made the decision for her. The dog stood, trotted forward with his tail wagging full speed, and walked right up to the girl. He sat at her feet and looked up at her with that expression Cade knew by heart — ears soft, eyes wide, tongue slightly out. The look that said, *I have chosen you. You're welcome.*

The girl looked down at Sammy. Her hand moved slowly — carefully, the way you'd reach toward a wild animal — and touched the top of his head. Sammy leaned into her palm. His tail swept the ground. And the girl's face changed. The wariness cracked, and underneath it was something bright and warm and startled, like she'd just been handed a gift she didn't know she wanted.

She laughed. It was short, surprised, and real — the kind of laugh that escapes before you can stop it. She knelt and scratched behind Sammy's ears with both hands, and the dog melted into her, leaning his full weight against her knees, tail going so hard his whole back end was swinging.

"He is soft," the girl said, wonder in her voice. "His fur is like — I do not have a word. Nothing here feels like this."

Cade watched them. Something in his chest loosened — not all the way, but enough to let him breathe. Sammy was the best judge of character he'd ever known. The dog had growled at Don from the day they'd brought him home as a puppy, a low, steady rumble every time the man walked past. Eydan had thought it was a phase. Cade had known better. If

Sammy trusted this girl, then Cade could take a step in that direction.

"What's your name?" Cade asked her.

The girl looked up from Sammy. "Elowen," the girl said.

"Elowen," Cade repeated. "I'm Cade."

"You said that already," Elowen said. The corner of her mouth lifted. Not a full smile — she hadn't decided about him yet — but the beginning of one.

"Yeah," Cade said. "I did. Sorry. It's been a rough couple of days."

Elowen stood, keeping one hand on Sammy's head. She looked Cade over again — the muddy sneakers, the scratched forearms, the dark circles under his eyes. She saw a boy who hadn't slept, hadn't eaten, and was barely holding it together.

"You are hungry," Elowen said. It wasn't a question.

"Starving," Cade said.

Elowen reached into a pouch on her belt and pulled out something wrapped in a large leaf — a piece of dense, dark bread and a strip of dried meat. She held it out to him.

Cade hesitated. In Don's house, nothing came free. Every kindness had a cost, every gift came with strings attached, and the hand that fed you was the same hand that hit you. Taking things from people meant owing them, and owing people meant being under their control.

But he was starving. And Elowen's hand was steady, and her eyes were patient, and Sammy was sitting at her feet like he'd known her his whole life.

Cade took the food. "Thank you," Cade said.

"Eat," Elowen said. "Then I will take you to my village."

"Village?" Cade asked between bites. The bread was dense and nutty, and the dried meat was salty and tough and the best thing he had ever tasted.

"Verdant Haven," Elowen said. She pointed down the valley, toward the river. "My home. You cannot stay in the forest alone. The raptors hunt at dawn and dusk, and the great hunters come at night. You would not survive another darkness out here."

Cade swallowed. "Great hunters?" Cade asked.

Elowen looked at him with an expression that was half pity and half amusement. "You truly know nothing of this place," Elowen said.

"I told you," Cade said. "I just got here."

"Then you are lucky I found you," Elowen said. "And not someone else. Come. Stay close. And keep your dog near."

She turned and started walking along the tree line, bow over her shoulder, moving with the easy, silent confidence of someone who'd been navigating this forest her whole life. Cade fell into step behind her, Sammy trotting between them.

As they walked, the valley opened up below them. Cade could see the river more clearly now, and along its banks, in the distance, he saw something that made him stop.

Structures. Buildings. Not skyscrapers or houses — something older, rougher, made of timber and stone and what looked like enormous bones. Walls of sharpened logs surrounded a cluster of buildings, and smoke rose from several points within. Figures moved between the structures — people, actual people, going about their lives in the shadow of a world full of dinosaurs.

And beyond the walls, in the fields that surrounded the settlement, massive dinosaurs — herbivores, the broad ones with the ridged plates — were pulling wooden plows through dark soil while people walked beside them, guiding them with ropes and voice commands. Farming. They were farming with dinosaurs.

Cade stared. His mouth was open and he didn't care.

"That's your village?" Cade asked.

"Verdant Haven," Elowen said. There was pride in her voice.

"And those — those dinosaurs are —" Cade started.

"Working the fields," Elowen said. "The same as they do every morning. What did you think we did with them?"

Cade didn't have an answer. He didn't have words for any of this. He was standing on a ridge in a world where humans and dinosaurs lived side by side, looking down at a village that shouldn't exist, next to a girl with a bow and a braid who'd just saved his life with bread and dried meat.

Sammy barked once, tail wagging.

"Your dog is strange," Elowen said, looking down at Sammy with that half-smile again. "But I think I like him."

"He likes you too," Cade said. "He's a good judge of people."

Elowen glanced at Cade. "And you?" Elowen asked. "Are you a good judge of people?"

Cade thought about Don. He thought about Carla. He thought about Eydan doing her best with nothing, and Ashen drawing dogs on grocery receipts, and every person who'd ever looked the other way when his family was falling apart.

"I'm learning," Cade said.

Elowen studied him for a moment, then nodded once, as if that answer was good enough for now. She turned and started down the ridge toward the village.

"Stay close," Elowen said over her shoulder. "And do not touch the thornbacks. They bite."

Cade didn't know what a thornback was, and he wasn't about to ask. He just followed her down the hill, Sammy at his side, his empty backpack on his shoulders, walking toward a village full of strangers in a world full of dinosaurs.

His phone was dead weight in his pack. His old life was sealed behind two boulders somewhere in the forest behind him. And the only things he had left were a dog, a water bottle, and whatever was waiting for him at the bottom of that hill.

It would have to be enough.

Chapter Six - *Verdant Haven*

The village was bigger than it looked from the ridge. What Cade had taken for a small cluster of buildings turned out to be a sprawling settlement spread across both sides of the river, connected by a wide bridge built from heavy timber and lashed together with thick rope. The outer wall was a ring of sharpened logs, each one as tall as a telephone pole, driven deep into the earth and fitted so tightly together that Cade couldn't see between them. The tops were cut to points and angled outward. Whatever the wall was designed to keep out, the people of Verdant Haven took it seriously.

Elowen led Cade and Sammy along a worn path that curved down from the ridge and approached the village from the south. The closer they got, the more Cade could see — and the more his brain struggled to keep up.

The fields outside the walls were enormous, stretching out from the village in wide, neat rows of crops Cade didn't recognize. Dark green stalks taller than him grew in dense patches, heavy with fat pods that hung from the stems like lanterns. Shorter plants with broad, silver-veined leaves carpeted the ground between the rows. And working among them, guided by farmers with ropes and steady voices, were the dinosaurs.

Up close, they were even more staggering than they'd been from the ridge. The ones pulling plows were herbivores

— heavy, four-legged animals with wide, flat heads and thick ridged plates running down their spines. Their skin was a deep olive green, rough and leathery, and their legs were like tree stumps, short and powerful, built for pulling weight. Each one was the size of a delivery truck, and they moved through the fields with a slow, patient rhythm, dragging wooden plows that cut deep furrows in the black soil. The farmers walked beside them, one hand on a guide rope, talking to the animals in low, calm tones.

Cade stopped walking and stared.

"Don't stand in the path," Elowen said to Cade without looking back. "The haulers come through here."

"The what?" Cade asked.

Before Elowen could answer, the ground shook. Cade turned and saw another dinosaur coming up the path behind them — smaller than the field animals but still enormous, with a broad back fitted with a wooden frame loaded with cut timber. A man walked beside it, one hand on the creature's flank, steering it with gentle pressure. The dinosaur's eyes were small and calm, and it moved with the steady, unhurried pace of a draft horse.

Cade stepped off the path. Sammy pressed against his leg as the animal passed, close enough that Cade could have reached out and touched its rough hide. The ground vibrated with each step. The smell was thick and earthy — not unpleasant, just overwhelming. Like standing downwind from the biggest barn in the world.

The man walking beside the hauler glanced at Cade, then at Sammy, then did a double take. He stared at the dog for a long moment, clearly confused by what he was seeing, then looked at Elowen.

"Who is this?" the man asked Elowen, nodding toward Cade.

"A traveler," Elowen said. "I found him in the forest. I'm taking him to the chief."

The man frowned but didn't argue. He gave Cade one more look — suspicious but not hostile — and continued up the path with his dinosaur.

"People are going to stare at you," Elowen said to Cade. "And at your dog. We don't get outsiders here. Ever."

"I noticed," Cade said.

They reached the main gate — a double door of heavy timber set into the log wall, tall enough for a dinosaur to pass through. Two men stood on either side, each carrying a spear with a stone blade the length of Cade's forearm. They wore leather armor across their chests and shoulders, and their faces were painted with thin lines of red and black. Guards. Real guards, standing watch over their village the way soldiers guarded a fort.

The guards saw Elowen and nodded. Then they saw Cade and their expressions hardened. Then they saw Sammy and confusion replaced suspicion.

"Elowen," the taller guard said. "What have you brought us?"

"His name is Cade," Elowen said to the guard. "He came through the forest. He is no threat — look at him. He doesn't even have a weapon. I'm taking him to see Chief Fenvar."

The guard studied Cade for a long, uncomfortable moment. Cade stood still and kept his hands visible. He knew this feeling — being evaluated, measured, judged by someone with authority and a weapon. Don had taught him that too. When a man with power looks at you, you don't flinch and you don't look away. You stand still and you let them see that you're not afraid, even if you are.

"And that?" the guard asked, pointing his spear at Sammy.

"His dog," Elowen said. "It's harmless."

Sammy chose that moment to sit down and yawn, showing every tooth in his mouth. The guard took a half step back.

"Harmless," the guard repeated, not sounding convinced.

"He's friendly," Cade said to the guard. "He just yawns a lot."

The guard looked at Elowen. Elowen looked at the guard. Something passed between them — a negotiation conducted entirely in raised eyebrows and tilted heads — and the guard stepped aside.

"Fenvar will decide," the guard said. "Go."

Elowen led Cade through the gate and into Verdant Haven.

The village was alive. That was the first thing that hit Cade — not the buildings, not the people, but the sheer noise and energy of the place. It was a community in full motion. Women and men moved between buildings carrying baskets, tools, bundles of cloth. Children ran through the dirt paths, chasing each other, laughing, ducking between the legs of adults who scolded them without much conviction. Smoke rose from cooking fires and drifted across the paths, carrying smells that made Cade's empty stomach clench — roasting meat, something sweet and bready, herbs he couldn't identify.

The buildings were unlike anything Cade had seen. They were constructed from timber and stone, with roofs thatched in layers of dried fronds and sealed with some kind of dark clay. Many of them incorporated bones — massive bones, dinosaur bones — as structural supports. Rib cages formed arched doorways. Leg bones, each one taller than Cade, served as corner posts. Skulls the size of small cars were mounted above entryways, cleaned and polished, both decoration and statement. The effect was strange and beautiful and unsettling — a civilization built literally on the bones of the creatures they lived alongside.

And the people. They moved with purpose and confidence, dressed in clothing made from leather, woven cloth, and materials Cade couldn't name. Their style reminded him of something — not quite Native American, not quite anything he'd studied in school, but something old and connected to the earth. Beadwork and feathers adorned belts and necklines. Tattoos marked the arms and faces of some of the adults — intricate patterns of lines and dots that seemed to mean something specific, though Cade had no idea what. Their skin tones ranged from deep brown to olive, and their hair was universally dark, worn long or braided or gathered in knots.

Every single one of them stopped and stared as Cade walked past.

He felt their eyes on him like heat. His clothes alone would have drawn attention — the gray T-shirt, the jeans, the muddy sneakers were as alien here as a space suit would have been on Maple Creek Drive. But it was Sammy who really stopped people in their tracks. Children pointed and whispered. Adults paused their work and watched the strange animal with a mix of curiosity and caution. One small girl, maybe five years old, broke away from her mother and ran toward Sammy with her hands out.

"Careful," Elowen warned the girl.

But Sammy was already wagging. The little girl touched his fur and squealed — a high, delighted sound that cut through the noise of the village like a bell. She buried her hands in his coat and laughed, and Sammy licked her face, and suddenly there were four more children crowding around, all of them reaching for the dog, all of them talking at once in excited voices that Cade's ears translated into a blur of questions.

"What is it?"

"It's so soft!"

"Does it bite?"

"Can I keep it?"

Cade almost smiled. Almost. Even here, in a world he didn't understand, surrounded by people he didn't know, Sammy was doing what Sammy always did — making friends, breaking down walls, turning strangers into people who forgot to be afraid.

Elowen guided them through the village center toward a large building at the far end — bigger than the others, with a wide porch and a doorway framed by two massive dinosaur tusks that curved upward like ivory pillars. The chief's hall. It had to be.

"Wait here," Elowen told Cade. She disappeared inside.

Cade stood on the porch with Sammy and tried not to feel like a specimen under a microscope. People passed by, some slowing to look, others stopping outright. An old woman with white hair and a deeply lined face approached him, reached out, and touched the fabric of his T-shirt between her fingers. She rubbed it, frowned, said something under her breath, and walked away shaking her head.

Sammy sat at Cade's feet, tail sweeping the wooden porch, unbothered by everything.

"Easy for you," Cade said to the dog. "You don't have to explain where you came from."

The door opened. Elowen stepped out, followed by two people.

The first was a man — tall, broad-shouldered, with a face that looked like it had been carved from the same stone as the boulders Cade had squeezed through. His hair was black streaked with gray, pulled back and tied with a leather cord. His arms were covered in the tattooed patterns Cade had seen on other villagers, but denser, more intricate, running from his wrists to his shoulders. He wore a vest of dark leather over a woven shirt, and a necklace of polished bones and teeth hung at his chest. His eyes were dark and direct, and when they landed on Cade, they didn't waver.

This was Chief Fenvar. Cade didn't need to be told.

The second person was different. A man, older than Fenvar — maybe early forties — with a lean, angular face and eyes the color of wet slate. His hair was lighter than the others, a dark brown worn loose to his shoulders, and he was clean-shaven where many of the village men had beards or stubble. His clothing was finer than what the other villagers wore — better stitched, more detailed, with small silver clasps at the collar and cuffs. He stood slightly behind Fenvar and to the right, the position of an advisor, a counselor, a man who whispered in the ear of the man in charge.

He was smiling. It was a warm smile, practiced and polished, the kind of smile that invited trust. And something in the back of Cade's brain — something small and quiet and trained by years of living with Don Thompson — went cold.

He'd seen that smile before. Not on this man's face, but on Don's. The smile Don wore when company came over. The smile that said, *Everything is fine here. I am a good man. Nothing to worry about.* The smile that vanished the second the front door closed.

Cade pushed the feeling down. He was in no position to be suspicious of anyone. He was starving, lost, and completely at the mercy of these people. But the feeling didn't leave. It just went quiet, like Sammy's growl — low, steady, and waiting.

"This is the boy?" Fenvar asked Elowen, his voice deep and even.

"Yes, Chief," Elowen said. "I found him at the edge of the valley, near the river bend. He says he came through the forest from — somewhere else."

Fenvar looked at Cade. "Somewhere else," Fenvar repeated.

"Yes, sir," Cade said. The "sir" came out automatically — another gift from Don. You always said "sir" to the man in charge, because not saying it meant the belt. But Fenvar wasn't Don. Fenvar's eyes were hard, but there was no cruelty in them. Just authority, and the weight of responsibility.

"What is your name?" Fenvar asked.

"Cade Thompson," Cade said.

"And where is this somewhere else, Cade Thompson?" Fenvar asked.

Cade hesitated. How did you explain suburban America to a man who lived with dinosaurs? How did you describe cars and cell phones and high schools to a civilization that built its homes from bones and farmed with creatures that had been extinct in his world for millions of years?

"It's far away," Cade said. "Very far away. I came through a passage between two boulders in the forest. I was chasing my dog and I ended up here. I don't know how. I don't know how to get back."

Fenvar studied him for a long time. His expression didn't change — no surprise, no disbelief, just steady evaluation. Then he looked at the man beside him.

"Kaelthas," Fenvar said. "What do you make of this?"

The lean man stepped forward. His smile hadn't wavered. Up close, his eyes were sharp and intelligent, moving over Cade the way a buyer examines merchandise — assessing, calculating, measuring value.

"He is clearly not from the vale," Kaelthas said to Fenvar. His voice was smooth and measured, every word placed with care. "His clothing, his manner, his animal — all foreign. If he speaks the truth about a passage, it may warrant investigation. But for now, he is a boy, alone and hungry. Surely Verdant Haven can offer hospitality to a lost traveler."

The words were kind. The tone was perfect. And Cade didn't trust a single syllable.

He glanced at Sammy. The dog was sitting at his feet, but his tail had stopped wagging. His ears were forward, and his eyes were fixed on Kaelthas with an intensity Cade recognized — the same hard, unblinking focus Sammy had aimed at Don every time the man walked into a room.

Cade filed that away. Deep. Where it would keep.

"You may stay," Fenvar said to Cade. "Elowen's family will house you until we determine your situation. You will respect our laws and our people. In return, Verdant Haven will feed you, shelter you, and keep you safe." Fenvar paused. "Do you understand?"

"Yes, sir," Cade said. "Thank you."

Fenvar nodded once — a firm, final gesture that ended the conversation. He turned and went back inside. Kaelthas lingered a moment longer, his gray eyes resting on Cade with that same polished smile.

"Welcome to Verdant Haven, Cade Thompson," Kaelthas said. Then he followed the chief inside and the door closed behind them.

Elowen let out a breath. "That went well," Elowen said.

"Did it?" Cade asked.

"Fenvar didn't send you away," Elowen said. "That means he's willing to hear more. Come on. My father's farm is on the east side. You can eat and rest."

She started walking. Cade fell into step beside her, Sammy between them.

"Elowen," Cade said.

"Yes?" Elowen said.

"The man with Fenvar. Kaelthas. What does he do here?"

"He is the chief's advisor," Elowen said. "He has been at Fenvar's side for years. He helps run the village, manages trade, settles disputes. People trust him." She glanced at Cade. "Why?"

"No reason," Cade said.

But Sammy was looking over his shoulder, back toward the chief's hall, and the low growl in his throat said everything Cade didn't.

Chapter Seven - Learning to Survive

The first week was the hardest.

Elowen's father was a man named Torin — broad-shouldered, quiet, with hands scarred from decades of farm work and a face that said more with a nod than most people said in a paragraph. He didn't talk much, but what he said mattered, and when he looked at Cade on that first morning at the farm, his eyes held none of the suspicion Cade had seen at the gate.

"You eat," Torin said to Cade, setting a plate of food in front of him at the family table. "Then you work."

That was it. No interrogation, no conditions, no lectures. Eat, then work. Cade could understand that.

Torin's farm sat on the eastern edge of Verdant Haven, backed up against the outer wall with fields stretching out beyond the gate into the open valley. He grew crops — the tall dark-green stalks Cade had seen from the ridge, which Elowen called thornroot, and the shorter silver-leafed plants called moonvetch. Both were staples of the village diet. Thornroot was starchy and dense, ground into flour for bread. Moonvetch was sweeter, eaten raw or boiled into a thick porridge.

And then there were the dinosaurs.

Torin kept two of the broad, plated herbivores — the ones Cade had seen pulling plows on his first day. They were called stoneshells by the villagers, and up close they were even more intimidating than they'd been from a distance. Each one stood about six feet at the shoulder and stretched nearly twenty feet from nose to tail. Their skin was thick and rough, covered in overlapping plates of bony armor that clicked softly when they moved. Their heads were flat and wide, with small, calm eyes and blunt beaks designed for stripping vegetation.

They were, as far as Cade could tell, the dinosaur equivalent of draft horses. Slow, powerful, patient. They pulled the plows, hauled timber, and stood in their pen at night chewing whatever Torin threw in front of them with the lazy, methodical contentment of animals that had never been afraid of anything in their lives.

Cade was terrified of them.

"They will not hurt you," Elowen told Cade on his first morning in the field, watching him press himself flat against the fence as one of the stoneshells ambled past. "They are gentle. Stubborn, but gentle."

"It's the size of a truck," Cade said to Elowen.

"I do not know what a truck is," Elowen said. "But Bruna has never stepped on anyone who did not deserve it."

"Bruna?" Cade asked.

"The female," Elowen said, patting the stoneshell's armored flank as it passed. The animal didn't even slow down. "The male is Korr. He is lazier. You will like him."

Cade did not like Korr. Korr was a twenty-foot-long dinosaur with a beak that could snap a fence post in half, and the fact that he spent most of his time standing in the sun with his eyes half-closed did not make Cade feel better about sharing a field with him.

But he worked. He didn't have a choice — Torin had taken him in, and earning his keep was the only currency Cade had. So he hauled water from the river in heavy clay jugs. He pulled weeds from between the thornroot stalks until his fingers were raw. He shoveled stoneshell dung — an experience that redefined his understanding of the word "volume" — into compost piles behind the barn. He did whatever Torin pointed at and asked no questions, because that was another thing Don had taught him. When a man gives you shelter, you work for it. You don't complain and you don't ask for more.

The difference was that Torin never hit him for doing it wrong.

When Cade dropped a water jug on his second day and it shattered on the ground, spilling a morning's worth of river water into the dirt, he flinched. He actually flinched —

shoulders up, head down, bracing for the blow he'd been trained to expect. His body reacted before his brain could stop it, and for a terrible half-second he was eleven years old in the kitchen on Maple Creek Drive, waiting for the belt.

Torin looked at the broken jug. He looked at Cade. He saw the flinch — Cade knew he saw it, because something moved behind the man's eyes, something heavy and sad and understanding.

"We have more jugs," Torin said to Cade quietly. Then he turned and went to the barn to get one.

Cade stood in the wet dirt, shaking, hating himself for the flinch and hating Don for putting it there. Sammy pressed against his leg and whined.

Elowen had seen it too. She was standing by the fence with a bundle of thornroot over her shoulder, and she didn't say a word. She just looked at Cade with those amber eyes, and in them he saw something he wasn't used to seeing from people his age — not pity, not curiosity, but recognition. Like she understood that whatever had made him flinch was something she didn't need to ask about. Not yet.

She walked over and handed him a thornroot stalk. "Here," Elowen said. "These go in the barn. I will show you where."

And that was it. No questions. No awkward silence. Just the next task, the next step, the next thing to do to keep moving forward. Cade took the stalk and followed her, and something in his chest loosened just enough to let him breathe.

Days passed. Cade fell into a rhythm — up at dawn with Torin, work the fields, haul water, tend the stoneshells, eat meals at the family table. Elowen taught him things between tasks — which plants were edible, which were poisonous, how to read the weather by the behavior of the flying reptiles that circled above the valley in the mornings. She showed him how to approach a stoneshell without startling it, how to read the twitch of its tail and the angle of its head.

"If the plates on the back flatten, step away," Elowen told Cade. "It means they are annoyed."

"What if I don't step away fast enough?" Cade asked.

"Then you learn a very hard lesson about speed," Elowen said, and the grin she gave him was the kind of grin that made the whole impossible situation feel, for a moment, almost bearable.

Sammy had adapted faster than Cade. The dog had settled into village life like he'd been born to it. He followed Cade everywhere during the day, but in the evenings he'd wander the village on his own, greeting everyone he met with his usual boundless enthusiasm. The children adored him. A pack of six or seven kids followed him around every afternoon, and Sammy ate up the attention like it was his job. Even the adults had warmed to him — the village women scratched his ears when he passed their cooking fires, and one of the older men had started saving meat scraps for him.

The only person Sammy didn't warm to was Kaelthas.

Cade noticed it on the third day. They were crossing the village center when Kaelthas appeared from the chief's hall, walking with two men Cade didn't recognize. Sammy stopped in his tracks. His tail dropped. His ears went flat. And that low, steady growl — the one Cade had only ever heard aimed at Don — rolled out of the dog's throat like a warning.

Kaelthas glanced down at Sammy. His expression didn't change — the polished smile stayed in place — but his eyes went cold for just a fraction of a second before warming back up.

"Your animal does not seem fond of me," Kaelthas said to Cade pleasantly.

"He takes a while to warm up to people," Cade said to Kaelthas. It was a lie. Sammy warmed up to everyone. Everyone except the people who deserved the growl.

"Perhaps in time," Kaelthas said, and walked on.

Cade watched him go. Sammy watched him go. Neither of them believed a word the man had said.

It was on the fifth day that Elysian Mosswood appeared.

Cade was behind the barn, wrestling with a fence post that had come loose from the stoneshell pen, when he felt someone watching him. He looked up and saw an old man standing at the tree line about thirty yards away, leaning on a walking stick, perfectly still. He was tall and lean, with a weathered face the color of dark leather and white hair cut short against his scalp. His clothes were simpler than most of the villagers' — plain leather, undecorated, practical. A knife hung at his belt and a coil of thin rope was slung over one shoulder. He looked like a man who had been in the forest so long that the forest had started to grow into him.

He was watching Cade the way a hawk watches a mouse — not with hunger, but with assessment. Measuring. Deciding.

Cade stared back. The old man stared at Cade. The moment stretched.

Then the man turned and walked back into the trees without a word.

"Who was that?" Cade asked Elowen later, describing the man.

"Elysian Mosswood," Elowen said. Her eyebrows went up slightly. "He is a tracker. The best in the vale, maybe the best who ever lived. He keeps to himself mostly. Lives at the edge of the village, near the northern wall. People go to him when something needs finding — a lost animal, a trail, a predator that has wandered too close."

"He was watching me," Cade said.

"Then he is interested in you," Elowen said. "That is unusual. Elysian is not interested in many people."

The next morning, the old man was there again. Same spot, same position, same silent observation. Cade ignored him and kept working. The morning after that, same thing. On the fourth morning, Cade had had enough.

He set down his tools, walked across the field, and stopped ten feet from where Elysian Mosswood stood.

"You've been watching me for days," Cade said to the old man. "If you've got something to say, say it."

Elysian's expression didn't change. He studied Cade for a long moment, his dark eyes moving over the boy's face, his posture, his hands.

"You carry yourself like someone who has been hit," Elysian said to Cade. His voice was low and rough, like gravel rolling in a dry streambed. "Your shoulders stay high. Your weight stays on the balls of your feet. You watch doors and you flinch when men raise their hands too fast."

Cade's stomach went cold. Nobody had ever said it that plainly. Not Eydan. Not Carla. Not the teachers who'd looked at him sideways and asked if everything was okay at home. This old man had stood at the tree line for four days and read Cade's entire history in the way he stood.

"That is not an insult," Elysian said. "It is an observation. You have been hurt, and you have survived. That takes a certain kind of strength. But survival is not the same as living. You need to learn the difference."

"And you're going to teach me?" Cade asked. There was an edge in his voice — the defensive, sharp tone he used when people got too close to the truth. The voice that said *back off* without saying it.

Elysian didn't back off. "If you will let me," Elysian said.

Cade looked at the old man. His instincts were screaming two things at once — the first was *don't trust him, adults who take interest in you always want something,* and the second was *Sammy likes him.* Because Sammy had trotted up to Elysian while they were talking and was sitting at the old man's feet, tail wagging, leaning against his leg like they were old friends.

"What would you teach me?" Cade asked.

"How to move in the forest without dying," Elysian said. "How to track, how to hide, how to read the land. How to be more than a boy who flinches."

The last words landed like a punch, but a clean one — the kind that wakes you up instead of knocking you down. Cade looked at Elysian Mosswood and saw no cruelty in his face. No manipulation. No angle. Just a man who had seen something in a broken kid and decided it was worth building on.

"Okay," Cade said.

The first lesson happened that afternoon. Elysian took Cade into the forest beyond the village wall and told him to walk.

"Just walk," Elysian said. "Naturally. The way you would at home."

Cade walked. Twigs snapped. Leaves crunched. A bird startled out of a bush and flew away screaming.

Elysian winced. "You walk like a stoneshell with a limp," Elysian said to Cade.

"Thanks," Cade said.

"Your dog is worse," Elysian said, looking at Sammy, who was crashing through a fern patch with the grace of a bowling ball. The old man's mouth twitched. Then it twitched again. Then a sound came out of him that Cade didn't recognize at first because he'd heard it so rarely from grown men.

Elysian was laughing.

It wasn't a mean laugh. It wasn't the laugh Don used when he'd said something cruel and thought it was funny. It was warm and rough and genuine, the laugh of a man who found real joy in the absurdity of a suburban kid and his dog trying to sneak through an ancient forest.

Cade stared at him. Something inside his chest cracked — not painfully, but like ice breaking on a river in spring. A small, necessary fracture.

"We have much work to do," Elysian said to Cade, still smiling. "Come. I will show you where to put your feet."

They trained until the sun dropped below the canopy. Cade learned to place his feet on the outside edge and roll inward, to step on roots and stones instead of leaves, to move with the rhythm of the forest instead of against it. He was terrible at it. Elysian corrected him a hundred times, patiently, firmly, without anger.

Elowen was waiting at the village gate when they came back, arms crossed, a smirk on her face.

"How did he do?" Elowen asked Elysian.

"He has the instincts of a hatchling that has wandered from its nest and the footwork of a landslide," Elysian said to Elowen. "But he did not quit. We will try again tomorrow."

"I heard you from inside the wall," Elowen said to Cade.

"Everybody heard him," Elysian said.

Cade looked at both of them — the old tracker and the farmer's daughter, both grinning at him like he was the most entertaining thing that had happened in Verdant Haven in years. And despite everything — despite being lost in a world he didn't understand, despite the fear and the hunger and the sealed portal and the dead phone in his backpack — Cade felt something he hadn't felt in a very long time.

He felt like he belonged somewhere.

That evening, after training, Cade and Elowen sat on the low wall behind Torin's farmhouse. The sun was dropping behind the mountains and the valley was turning gold. Sammy lay between them, his chin on Elowen's boot, tail swishing lazily in the dirt.

Elowen was quiet for a while. Then she spoke.

"Cade," Elowen said. "What is your world like? You have told me pieces, but I cannot picture it."

Cade thought about it. How did you describe suburbs and highways and cell towers to someone who farmed with dinosaurs?

"Hold on," Cade said. He reached into his backpack and pulled out his phone. The screen lit up — dim, the battery icon blinking red, maybe six or seven percent left. He didn't know how much time he had, so he moved fast.

Elowen's eyes went wide the moment the screen glowed to life. She leaned back slightly, like the light itself was something dangerous.

"It will not hurt you," Cade said to her. "It's called a phone. Where I come from, everyone has one. You can talk to people, send messages, listen to music. And it holds pictures."

"Pictures," Elowen repeated, staring at the glowing rectangle.

Cade opened his photos. He turned the phone so she could see the screen and swiped to a photo of Maple Creek Drive — the street, the houses, the parked cars, the sidewalk.

Elowen's lips parted. She stared at the image, then leaned closer, then pulled back again. Her hand came up slowly and she touched the screen with one fingertip. The image swiped to the next photo and Elowen jerked her hand away like she'd been burned.

"It moved," Elowen said.

"That's okay," Cade said. "That's how it works. You slide your finger and it shows a different picture."

Elowen looked at him, then back at the screen. Cautiously, she touched it again and swiped. A photo of Ridgewood High appeared — the flat brown building, the parking lot, the flag out front.

"What is this place?" Elowen asked, staring at the image.

"That's my school," Cade said to her. "It's where young people go to learn things. Reading, writing, history."

"We have something like that here," Elowen said. "But it does not look like this."

He swiped again. A photo of Eydan in the kitchen, caught mid-laugh, stirring something on the stove. The little Christmas tree on the end table behind her.

"That is your mother," Elowen said softly. It wasn't a question. She could see it in the resemblance — the same dark eyes, the same jaw.

"Her name is Eydan," Cade said.

He swiped again. Ashen on the couch with Sammy, both of them asleep, the dog's head in the little girl's lap. Elowen smiled at that one.

"Your sister," Elowen said.

"Ashen," Cade said. "She's nine."

He swiped one more time. Carla at her locker, making a face at the camera, her dark hair falling across one eye.

"And who is this?" Elowen asked.

Cade paused. "That's Carla," Cade said. "She's my — she's a friend."

Elowen glanced at him with a look that said she understood exactly what "friend" meant, but she didn't press it.

Cade swiped back to the photo of Eydan. He stared at it. His mother's laugh, frozen in a moment he could see but couldn't reach. Elowen didn't say anything. She didn't need to. She could see it on his face — the longing, the fear, the not knowing if he'd ever see these people again.

"She looks tired," Elowen said quietly. "But kind."

"She is," Cade said. "Both of those things."

They sat in silence for a moment. The screen dimmed. The battery icon blinked.

"Thank you for showing me," Elowen said to Cade. "Now I understand. You are not just lost. You are missing."

Cade didn't trust himself to speak. He nodded once.

Elowen put her hand on his arm, just for a second. Then she stood and went inside, leaving Cade alone on the wall with Sammy and a phone that was almost dead.

Later that night, alone in the small room Torin had given him, Cade sat on the edge of his bed and pressed the power button one last time. The screen flickered — dim, struggling, the battery icon blinking red. Sammy's face appeared on the wallpaper. Then the screen went black.

He pressed the button again. Nothing. He held it down. Nothing. The phone was dead. The battery was gone, and with it the last glowing window into the life he'd left behind. No more photos. No more faces. No more proof that Maple Creek Drive and Ridgewood High and a girl with coconut shampoo existed anywhere outside his own memory.

He sat in the dark and stared at the dead screen longer than he should have. Sammy was on the bed beside him, chin on Cade's thigh, watching him with those mismatched eyes.

"It's just a phone," Cade said to the dog. His voice was thick.

Sammy's tail thumped once.

Cade slid the phone into the bottom of his backpack, underneath the notebook and the pen and the empty water

bottle. He'd carry it with him. He didn't know for how long —
weeks, months, maybe longer. A dead piece of a world he
wasn't sure he'd ever see again, weighing almost nothing and
meaning everything.

He lay back on the bed. Sammy curled against his
side. Through the window, he could hear the distant sounds
of the village settling in for the night — voices, laughter, the
low rumble of a stoneshell shifting in its pen.

Tomorrow, Elysian would teach him how to walk
without making noise. Elowen would teach him the name of
another plant. Torin would hand him a tool and point at
something that needed doing. And Cade would do it, because
that was what you did when people took you in and asked for
nothing but your effort.

"He closed his eyes. For the first time since he'd
squeezed through the gap between the boulders, Cade
Thompson slept without fear."

He lay back on the bed. Sammy curled against his
side. "Through the open window — a square cut in the timber
wall with a hide flap tied back to let in the night air — he
could hear the distant sounds of the village settling in for the
night"

Chapter Eight - The Way of the Vale

Two weeks into his time in Verdant Haven, Cade woke to the sound of drums.

Not the booming footsteps of dinosaurs — he'd gotten used to those, or at least stopped jumping every time the ground trembled. These were real drums, deep and rhythmic, coming from the village center. The sound rolled through the morning air like a heartbeat, steady and deliberate, shaking the hide flap over his window.

Sammy was already at the door, tail wagging, ears forward.

"You know something I don't?" Cade asked the dog.

Elowen appeared in the doorway of the farmhouse, dressed differently than usual. Instead of her everyday leathers and work clothes, she wore a long tunic of woven cloth dyed deep green, with beadwork along the collar and a belt of braided leather cinched at her waist. Her braid was wrapped with thin strips of red cloth, and she looked, for the first time since Cade had met her, less like a farmer's daughter and more like someone about to attend something important.

"Get up," Elowen said to Cade. "Today is the Binding. You need to see this."

"The what?" Cade asked.

"The Binding," Elowen said. "It happens once a season. The whole village comes together to honor the covenant between the people and the great ones."

"The great ones," Cade repeated.

"The dinosaurs," Elowen said, as if that were obvious. "Come. My father is already there."

Cade pulled on his clothes — still his jeans and T-shirt from home, now stained and worn, because nothing in Verdant Haven fit him right — and followed Elowen through the village. Sammy trotted beside them, drawing the usual attention from the children, who had taken to calling the dog "soft-one" in a way that had clearly become a term of affection.

The village center had been transformed. The open square in front of the chief's hall had been cleared, and a large circle of flat stones had been laid in the dirt, each one carved with symbols Cade didn't recognize. Torches burned at intervals around the circle even though it was broad daylight, their flames giving off a sweet, resinous smoke that drifted through the crowd. And there was a crowd — the entire village, it seemed, gathered in a wide ring around the stones. Families stood together, children on shoulders, elders in carved wooden chairs at the front. Everyone was dressed in their best — beadwork, feathers, dyed cloth, polished bone ornaments.

And in the center of the circle, standing motionless, were six dinosaurs.

They were not stoneshells. These were different — taller, leaner, built for speed rather than strength. They stood on two legs, their bodies tilted forward, balanced by long stiff tails. Their hides were mottled brown and green, and their heads were narrow and elegant, with large intelligent eyes that scanned the crowd with calm awareness. Each one wore a harness of leather and bone across its chest and shoulders, and on each harness was mounted a saddle.

Riders stood beside them — six men and women in leather armor, faces painted with the red and black lines Cade had seen on the gate guards. These were warriors. Scouts. The people who patrolled the borders of Verdant Haven's territory and kept the village safe from whatever roamed the deeper parts of Emerald Vale.

"Those are swiftclaws," Elowen whispered to Cade. "They are bonded to their riders from the time they hatch. A swiftclaw will carry no one but its bonded partner. The bond lasts for life."

Cade stared. The animals were beautiful in a way he hadn't expected — graceful, alert, powerful. One of them turned its head and looked directly at him with an eye the color of polished copper. It blinked once, slowly, then looked away.

"They are intelligent," Elowen said to Cade, noticing his expression. "More than any other creature in the vale. Some say they understand speech. Others say they understand more than that."

The drums intensified. Chief Fenvar emerged from the hall, dressed in ceremonial clothing — a long coat of dark leather layered over a woven shirt, with a necklace of enormous teeth hanging at his chest. His face was painted with a single line of red from forehead to chin. He walked to the center of the stone circle and raised both hands.

The crowd went silent. Even the children stopped moving.

Fenvar spoke. His voice carried across the square with a power that didn't need volume — it was the voice of a man accustomed to being heard.

"We gather as our ancestors gathered," Fenvar said. "To honor the covenant. The land provides. The great ones walk beside us. We do not own them. We do not rule them. We live with them, and in return, they allow us to survive."

He turned to face the swiftclaws and their riders. "These six have renewed their bond this season. Rider and swiftclaw, bound in trust, bound in purpose. They protect us. They patrol the borders. They stand between Verdant Haven and the darkness beyond."

Fenvar paused. His eyes swept the crowd. "The covenant is simple. We respect the land. We respect the great ones. And they, in turn, share this world with us. The day we forget that — the day we try to dominate what should be honored — is the day we lose everything."

The crowd murmured in agreement. Fenvar stepped back, and one by one the riders mounted their swiftclaws. The animals rose to their full height — each one ten or eleven feet tall — and the riders settled into their saddles with the ease of people who had done this a thousand times. The swiftclaws turned in unison, and with a sound like leather snapping, they leaped forward and were gone — six riders on six dinosaurs, moving through the village gate and into the open valley at a speed that took Cade's breath away.

The crowd erupted. Cheering, drums, voices raised in a song that Cade didn't know the words to but felt in his chest. It was joy and reverence and pride, all braided together, and for a moment Cade forgot that he was an outsider watching from the edge. For a moment, he was just a person in a crowd, witnessing something extraordinary.

"That was incredible," Cade said to Elowen.

"That is who we are," Elowen said to Cade. There was no pride in her voice this time — just certainty. A statement of fact as solid as the ground they stood on.

Cade noticed Kaelthas near the front of the crowd, standing a few paces behind Fenvar. The advisor was clapping along with everyone else, his face arranged in an expression of admiration and respect. But Cade watched his eyes. Kaelthas wasn't watching the riders. He was watching Fenvar. And the look in those gray eyes wasn't admiration.

It was calculation.

Cade looked away before Kaelthas could notice him staring. But the cold feeling in his gut tightened another notch.

After the ceremony, the village settled into a day of rest and celebration. Cooking fires burned throughout the square, and the smell of roasting meat and fresh bread filled the air. Families gathered in loose groups, eating, talking, laughing. Children chased each other between the buildings. Someone was playing a stringed instrument near the chief's hall — a low, warm sound that reminded Cade of a guitar, which made his chest ache in a way he didn't want to examine too closely.

Elowen found him standing at the edge of the celebration, Sammy at his feet, watching.

"Come with me," Elowen said. "I want to show you something."

She led him out through the east gate, past her father's fields, and up a narrow trail that wound through the trees and switchbacked up a steep hillside. Sammy bounded ahead of them, crashing through ferns with his usual lack of stealth. The trail climbed for twenty minutes until it broke out of the tree line onto a rocky ridge that overlooked the entire valley.

Cade stopped walking.

Emerald Vale spread out below them like a painting. The river wound through the center, glittering in the afternoon sun. The fields of Verdant Haven were neat green squares against the darker forest. In the distance, herds of dinosaurs moved across the grassland — massive shapes casting long shadows, their movements slow and ancient and timeless. The mountains rose beyond, snow-capped and sharp against a sky so blue it didn't look real. Birds — or things like birds, with wider wingspans and longer tails — circled on the thermals above the valley in lazy spirals.

It was the most beautiful thing Cade had ever seen.

"This is my place," Elowen said to Cade. She sat on a flat rock at the edge of the ridge and pulled her knees to her chest. "I come here when I need to think. Or when I need to not think."

Cade sat beside her. Sammy flopped down between them, panting, tongue out, perfectly content.

For a while, neither of them spoke. The wind moved across the ridge and the valley hummed with the distant sounds of life — animal calls, the rush of the river, the faint rhythm of drums still drifting up from the village below.

"Tell me about your sister," Elowen said to Cade.

Cade looked at her. "Ashen?" Cade said.

"You said her name when you showed me the pictures on your — your light box," Elowen said. "Your face changed when you looked at her. Tell me about her."

Cade was quiet for a moment. He looked out at the valley and thought about Ashen — her quiet voice, the pink spoon, the stuffed bear, the drawing of Sammy on the grocery receipt.

"She's nine," Cade said. "She's quiet. She used to be loud — used to laugh at everything, climb on my back and make me run through the house. But things got hard at home and she went inside herself. She sleeps with her door locked. She barely talks. She draws pictures of Sammy because he's the only thing in her life that never scared her."

Elowen listened without interrupting. No judgment in her eyes. Just attention.

"And your mother?" Elowen asked.

"Eydan works two jobs," Cade said. "She's gone before we wake up and she comes home after we're in bed. She's doing everything she can and it's still not enough, and I think she knows that, and I think it's killing her." He paused. "She's the strongest person I've ever met. And the most tired."

"Who hurt them?" Elowen asked quietly. "The person who made your sister go quiet. Who made your mother so tired. Who taught you to flinch."

The question sat in the air between them. Cade could feel it pressing against the walls he'd built — the walls that kept everything about Don locked inside where nobody could see it.

"My father," Cade said. Two words. The heaviest two words he'd ever spoken.

Elowen didn't flinch. She didn't gasp or look away or say she was sorry. She just nodded, slowly, like the answer confirmed something she'd already suspected.

"He is gone now?" Elowen asked.

"He left," Cade said. "Six months before I came here. Just walked out."

"Good," Elowen said. There was no softness in the word. It was hard and flat and certain, and Cade realized it was the exact right thing to say. Not "I'm sorry." Not "That must have been hard." Just "good." The man who hurt you is gone, and that is good.

They sat in silence for a long time after that. The sun moved across the sky. The shadows in the valley lengthened. Sammy dozed between them, his paws twitching in a dream.

"My mother died when I was six," Elowen said to Cade. She said it the same way she said everything — directly, without decoration. "A fever took her during the wet season. My father raised me alone after that. He taught me to farm, to hunt, to fight. He is not a man of many words, but every word he speaks is true. I have never once doubted that he loves me."

Cade thought about Torin — the quiet farmer who handed him tools without lectures, who saw the flinch and said nothing except "we have more jugs." The contrast with Don was so sharp it cut.

"He's a good man," Cade said about Torin.

"He is," Elowen said. "Not all fathers are what yours was, Cade. Some of them are what Torin is. What Elysian is. You will learn that here."

Cade didn't answer. But something shifted inside him — not a wall coming down, not yet, but a crack forming in the mortar. A thin line of light where there had only been dark.

When they walked back to the village, the celebration was winding down. Families were heading home. The cooking fires were burning low. Torin was standing at the gate of his farm, waiting for them, a plate of food in each hand.

"You missed dinner," Torin said to Elowen and Cade. He held out the plates. "Eat."

Cade took the plate. Roasted meat, bread, a handful of something sweet and purple that he'd learned was called starfruit. He sat on the bench outside the farmhouse and ate while Torin went inside and Elowen fed scraps to Sammy.

Cade was finishing the last of the bread when Kaelthas walked past on the path in front of Torin's farm. The advisor was heading back toward the chief's hall with two men Cade had seen with him before — the same ones, always the same ones. Kaelthas was talking in a low voice, his head tilted toward one of the men, his hand on the man's shoulder. The gesture looked friendly. Supportive. The kind of thing a leader did with people he trusted.

But Cade had watched Don put his hand on Eydan's shoulder a hundred times — at church, at the grocery store, in front of the neighbors. A gesture that looked like love but meant control. A hand that said, *I own you. Don't forget it.*

Kaelthas glanced sideways as he passed and caught Cade watching. The advisor's smile appeared instantly — warm, polished, effortless. He nodded once at Cade and kept walking.

Cade nodded back. He said nothing.

But he didn't forget what he saw.

Chapter Nine - Under the Surface

Three weeks in, and Cade was starting to feel like he might survive this place.

His hands were calloused from farm work. His legs were stronger from the daily hikes with Elysian. He could walk through the forest without snapping every twig in a ten-yard radius, which Elysian had grudgingly acknowledged with a nod and the words, "You no longer sound like a wounded stoneshell. Now you sound like a healthy one." From Elysian Mosswood, that was high praise.

He'd learned the rhythms of Verdant Haven — the morning horn that signaled the gates opening, the evening drums that called people in from the fields, the way the village moved like a single living thing, each person connected to the next by work and habit and trust. He ate meals at Torin's table. He trained with Elysian in the afternoons. He spent evenings with Elowen, sitting on the low wall behind the farmhouse, talking about everything and nothing while Sammy dozed at their feet.

It was, in many ways, the most stable life Cade had ever known. And that fact sat in his chest like a stone, because the most stable life he'd ever known was in a world that wasn't his, surrounded by people he hadn't known a month ago, with no way home.

But the stability had a crack in it. A thin, quiet crack that Cade couldn't stop picking at, the way you pick at a scab even though you know it's going to bleed.

Kaelthas.

It started with the meetings. Cade first noticed them during his second week, when he was hauling water from the river and took a different path back through the village. He came around the back of the storehouse — a large building near the north wall where grain and dried meat were kept — and stopped.

Kaelthas was standing in the narrow alley between the storehouse and the tanner's workshop, speaking with three men. Cade recognized two of them — they were the same men who had been walking with Kaelthas the night of the Binding ceremony. The third was new, a younger man with a scar across his jaw and the build of someone who spent more time fighting than farming.

They were speaking in low voices. Kaelthas had his back to the main path, positioned so that anyone passing by wouldn't see the group unless they came around the back of the building the way Cade had. The conversation stopped the instant Kaelthas heard Cade's footsteps.

The advisor turned. The smile appeared — instant, automatic, warm as sunlight.

"Cade," Kaelthas said pleasantly. "Hauling water? You are becoming quite useful around here."

"Trying to be," Cade said to Kaelthas.

"Admirable," Kaelthas said. "If you need help finding a quicker route to the river, ask one of the gate guards. They know all the shortcuts."

It was a dismissal wrapped in kindness. A polite way of saying *move along*. Cade recognized it because Don had done the same thing a hundred times — smooth words that steered people away from whatever he didn't want them to see.

"Thanks," Cade said. "I'll do that."

He walked away with his water jugs, and he didn't look back, but he listened. Behind him, the low conversation resumed before he'd taken ten steps.

Over the next several days, Cade saw it again. And again. Kaelthas meeting with the same small group of men — never in the village center, never in the open, always tucked behind a building or at the edge of the tree line just outside the north gate. The meetings were short, five or ten minutes, and when they ended the men scattered in different directions, as if they'd been told not to be seen together.

Cade said nothing about it. But he watched.

He was training with Elysian one afternoon, practicing the silent walk through a stretch of forest north of the village, when the old tracker stopped suddenly and crouched. Cade froze behind him. Sammy, who had been investigating a fallen log, went still.

Elysian studied the ground. His fingers touched the soil, tracing a mark Cade couldn't see.

"What is it?" Cade asked Elysian quietly.

"Tracks," Elysian said. He stood and looked into the deeper forest, his eyes narrowing. "Razormaw. A young one, but still dangerous. It passed through here sometime last night."

"Is that unusual?" Cade asked.

Elysian was quiet for a moment. "A razormaw this close to the village would have been unheard of five years ago," Elysian said to Cade. "They are deep forest predators. They hunt in the high valleys and the canyon lands, far from here. But lately they have been moving closer. Sightings at the river. Tracks near the eastern fields. Three in the last two months."

"Why?" Cade asked.

"That is what I would like to know," Elysian said. His voice was even, but Cade heard something underneath it — not fear, but concern. The quiet worry of a man who understood the forest better than anyone alive and was seeing something that didn't fit. "Predators do not change their territory without a reason. Something is pushing them this way, or pulling them."

He said nothing more about it. They resumed training, and Elysian corrected Cade's footwork for the next hour without mentioning the tracks again. But the old man's eyes kept drifting north, into the deep forest, and his jaw stayed tight.

That evening, Cade found Elowen mending a harness in front of the barn. Sammy was lying beside her, chewing on a strip of leather she'd given him to keep him occupied. Cade sat down on the bench across from her.

"Can I ask you something?" Cade said to Elowen.

"You always can," Elowen said without looking up from the harness.

"Kaelthas," Cade said. "How long has he been Fenvar's advisor?"

Elowen glanced at him. "Since before I was born," Elowen said. "He came to Verdant Haven when he was young — from one of the outer settlements, I think. He worked his way up. He is intelligent, well-spoken. Fenvar trusts him more than anyone."

"Do you trust him?" Cade asked.

Elowen stopped stitching. She looked at Cade with a slight frown. "Why would I not trust him?" Elowen asked. "He has served this village for twenty years. He manages the trade routes. He settles disputes between the farmers. When the northern wall needed rebuilding last year, Kaelthas organized the labor and the materials. People respect him."

"That's not what I asked," Cade said. "I asked if you trust him."

Elowen studied him for a long moment. "I have no reason not to," Elowen said carefully. "Why are you asking?"

Cade hesitated. He didn't have evidence. He didn't have anything except a feeling — a cold, crawling feeling in his gut that he'd learned to listen to in Don's house because ignoring it meant getting hurt. But how did you explain that to someone who had never lived with a man who smiled while he destroyed everything around him?

"I've just been watching him," Cade said. "He meets with the same group of men. Always in private. Always out of sight. And when someone walks up on them, the conversation stops."

"He is the chief's advisor," Elowen said. "Private meetings are part of his work. He manages things Fenvar does not have time for."

"Maybe," Cade said.

Elowen set the harness down. "Cade," Elowen said. "I understand that where you come from, people gave you reasons not to trust. But this is not your world. Kaelthas has done nothing wrong. You cannot judge every man by the worst one you have known."

The words landed hard. Not because they were cruel — Elowen didn't have cruelty in her — but because they were reasonable, and Cade knew that from the outside, his suspicion looked exactly like what she said it was. A damaged kid seeing threats where there weren't any. Projecting Don onto every man with a smile and a handshake.

Maybe she was right.

But Sammy had lifted his head when Cade said Kaelthas's name, and the dog's ears had gone flat, and that low growl — quiet, barely audible — had rumbled in his chest for just a moment before fading.

Dogs didn't project. Dogs didn't carry trauma from abusive fathers. Dogs just knew.

"You're probably right," Cade said to Elowen. "Forget I said anything."

Elowen picked up the harness and went back to stitching. But she glanced at Cade once more before he turned away, and in that glance was something that hadn't been there before — not doubt, not exactly, but the first faint shadow of a question she hadn't thought to ask until now.

Two days later, a farmer named Aldric came to the chief's hall in the middle of the morning, out of breath and angry. Cade was crossing the village center on his way to meet Elysian when he saw the commotion — Aldric at the door of the hall, gesturing, his voice loud enough to carry.

"Three of them," Aldric was saying to whoever was inside. "Three stoneshells, gone from the pen overnight. The fence was broken from the outside — clawed through. Something ripped it apart."

Cade stopped. Other villagers were gathering, drawn by the noise. Fenvar appeared in the doorway of the hall, his expression serious. Kaelthas was right behind him, as always.

"Predators," Kaelthas said to Fenvar calmly. "Razormaws have been sighted closer to the village lately. Elysian himself has reported tracks. It is unfortunate, but not unexpected. We should reinforce the outer pens and increase the night patrols."

Fenvar nodded slowly. "See to it," Fenvar said to Kaelthas.

"Of course," Kaelthas said. His voice was smooth, concerned, appropriately troubled. The voice of a man who had the situation under control.

Cade watched from across the square. He watched Kaelthas take charge — organizing patrols, assigning men, speaking with Aldric in calm, reassuring tones. He watched the villagers relax as Kaelthas handled things. He watched Fenvar step back and let his advisor work.

And he thought about something Elysian had said. *Predators do not change their territory without a reason. Something is pushing them this way, or pulling them.*

Pushing or pulling.

Cade looked at Kaelthas, standing in the center of the square, giving orders, surrounded by the same men he'd been meeting with in alleys and behind buildings for weeks.

Pushing. Or pulling.

That night, Cade lay in his bed in Torin's farmhouse and stared at the ceiling. Sammy was beside him, warm and steady, breathing slow. Through the hide flap over the window, he could hear the night sounds of the village — a distant conversation, the shifting of a stoneshell in its pen, the wind moving through the valley.

He couldn't sleep.

The pattern was there. He could see it the way you see a picture hidden in one of those optical illusions — once you saw it, you couldn't unsee it. The private meetings. The men who followed Kaelthas but weren't part of the regular village structure. The predators moving closer. The livestock disappearing. And Kaelthas, always Kaelthas, stepping in with the answers before anyone else had time to ask the questions.

Cade had seen this before. Not with dinosaurs and stockades and stone circles. But with a man in a house on Maple Creek Drive who controlled everything around him with charm and violence and the careful management of fear.

Don had done it too. He'd create the crisis — start a fight with Eydan, break something, terrify the kids — and then he'd fix it. He'd calm everyone down, make pancakes, tell jokes, be the hero of the mess he'd made. And everyone would think, *Thank God for Don. What would we do without him?*

Control the problem. Control the solution. Control everything.

Cade didn't have proof. He had a feeling, a pattern, and a dog who growled at the right people.

It wasn't enough. Not yet.

But he was watching. And he wasn't going to stop.

Chapter Ten - The Training Grounds

Elysian put a staff in Cade's hands on a Tuesday morning, five weeks after he'd arrived in Emerald Vale.

It was a simple weapon — a six-foot length of hardwood, stripped of bark, sanded smooth, with a slight taper at each end. It weighed almost nothing. Cade held it the way he'd hold a baseball bat, both hands together near the center.

Elysian looked at his grip and sighed.

"You are not chopping wood," Elysian said to Cade. "Spread your hands. One at the top third, one at the bottom. The staff is an extension of your body, not a club."

Cade adjusted his grip. It felt wrong — unbalanced, awkward, like trying to write with his left hand.

"Better," Elysian said. "Now hit me."

Cade stared at him. "Hit you?" Cade asked.

"I am old, not fragile," Elysian said. "Hit me."

Cade swung. It was a slow, tentative strike aimed at Elysian's midsection. The old man moved one step to the left, caught the staff with his bare hand, twisted it, and Cade was on the ground before he understood what had happened. His back hit the dirt and the air went out of his lungs and Elysian was standing over him, holding the staff he'd just taken away.

"Lesson one," Elysian said, looking down at him. "Do not announce your strikes. I knew where that was going before you did. Your shoulders dropped, your eyes went to the target, and you shifted your weight a full second before the swing. Every predator in this forest would have eaten you twice by now."

Cade lay on the ground, staring at the canopy. "Twice?" Cade asked.

"They would have come back for seconds," Elysian said. He held out his hand and pulled Cade to his feet. "Again."

They trained for three hours. Elysian taught Cade the basic strikes — thrust, sweep, overhead block, side guard. He showed him how to use the staff's length to keep distance, how to pivot on his back foot, how to redirect an attack instead of absorbing it. Every movement was precise, economical, stripped of wasted motion. Elysian moved like water around a rock — fluid, effortless, always in the right place at the right time.

Cade was none of those things. He was clumsy, stiff, and slow. Elysian put him on the ground eleven times in the first hour alone.

But something happened around the twelfth time Elysian swung at him. Cade didn't think. His body moved on its own — a sidestep, a turn of the hips, the staff coming up to catch Elysian's strike with a crack that echoed through the trees. The block held. Elysian's staff bounced off his, and for one frozen moment the old tracker looked at Cade with something that might have been surprise.

"Good," Elysian said quietly. "Do that again."

Cade did it again. And again. And each time it came faster, sharper, more instinctive. His hands found the right position without being told. His feet moved before his brain gave the order. His eyes tracked Elysian's shoulders and hips instead of his weapon, reading the attack before it happened.

Elysian stopped and leaned on his staff. He studied Cade with that measuring look — the same one from the tree line, the one that saw everything.

"You have fast reflexes," Elysian said to Cade. "Faster than most boys your age. Faster than most men. Do you know why?"

Cade knew why. He'd spent his whole life reading the body language of a dangerous man — learning to see the shift in Don's shoulders before the swing came, the tightening of his jaw before the yelling started, the way his hand moved toward the belt on the nail. Cade's reflexes hadn't been trained in a dojo or a gym. They'd been forged in a kitchen on

Maple Creek Drive, dodging fists and belt buckles and whatever else was in reach.

Don had given him this. The man who'd broken him had also, without meaning to, built something inside him that was hard to break.

"I've had practice," Cade said to Elysian.

Elysian held his gaze for a moment. He didn't ask what kind of practice. He didn't need to.

"Pain teaches," Elysian said. "But it is a cruel teacher. I will teach you the same lessons without the cruelty. Do you understand?"

"Yes, sir," Cade said.

"Do not call me sir," Elysian said. "I am not your chief and I am not your father. I am Elysian. That is enough."

Something behind Cade's ribs loosened. Just a fraction. Just enough.

"Okay, Elysian," Cade said.

The old man nodded once. "Now pick up your staff," Elysian said. "We are switching to knife work."

The knife was harder than the staff. Elysian gave Cade a short blade — stone-edged, wickedly sharp, with a leather-wrapped handle — and taught him how to hold it, carry it, and use it without cutting himself. The grip was reversed from what Cade expected — blade along the forearm, edge out, handle braced against the heel of the palm.

"This is not for stabbing," Elysian told Cade. "Stabbing is what fools do. This is for cutting, blocking, and controlling distance. You do not fight a predator with a knife — you survive long enough for help to arrive. Against a man, you use the knife to create space. Against an animal, you use it to discourage. Nothing more."

Cade practiced cuts and blocks until his forearm burned. Elysian corrected his angles, adjusted his footwork, and put him on the ground four more times when his guard dropped. By midday, Cade's arms felt like they were filled with sand, and his shirt was soaked through with sweat.

"Enough," Elysian said. "Rest. Drink water. We will continue tomorrow."

Cade collapsed against a tree and drank from his water bottle — a clay jug now, replacing the plastic one from home that had cracked during his second week. Sammy flopped down beside him, panting. The dog had spent the entire training session chasing butterflies at the edge of the clearing, completely indifferent to the violence being practiced twenty feet away.

"Your dog has no interest in combat," Elysian observed, watching Sammy roll onto his back in a patch of sun.

"He's a lover, not a fighter," Cade said to Elysian.

"Hmm," Elysian said. "Perhaps he is smarter than both of us."

Elowen arrived that afternoon.

Cade heard her before he saw her — the whisper of feet on leaves, barely audible, followed by the soft creak of a bowstring. He spun, staff up, and found Elowen standing at the edge of the clearing with her bow drawn and an arrow pointed at a target she'd nailed to a tree thirty yards away. She released. The arrow hit dead center with a thwack that made Sammy's ears perk up.

"Show-off," Cade said to Elowen.

"I heard Elysian has been teaching you to fight," Elowen said, walking to the target to retrieve her arrow. "I thought I would see how bad you are."

"Thanks for the confidence," Cade said.

"You are welcome," Elowen said. She pulled the arrow free and turned to face him, a grin spreading across her face. "Pick up your staff."

"Right now?" Cade asked.

"Unless you would rather sit and watch," Elowen said.

Cade picked up his staff. Elowen grabbed a training staff from the rack Elysian had set up at the edge of the clearing — a collection of weapons in various sizes that the old tracker maintained for exactly this purpose. She rolled the staff across her shoulders, loosening up, and stepped into the center of the clearing.

"Rules," Elowen said. "No strikes to the head. No strikes below the knee. First to land three clean hits wins."

"What do I get if I win?" Cade asked.

"You will not win," Elowen said. "But if by some miracle you do, I will teach you how to shoot the bow."

"And if you win?" Cade asked.

"Then you haul water for my father's farm for the next three days without complaining," Elowen said.

"I already do that," Cade said.

"Without complaining," Elowen repeated. "That is the key part."

They circled each other. Elowen moved differently than Elysian — lighter, quicker, with a dancer's balance and a fighter's focus. Where Elysian was a river, steady and relentless, Elowen was a whip — still one moment, striking the next.

She hit Cade three times in two minutes.

The first was a sweep to his ribs that came so fast he didn't see it until the staff was already connecting. The second was a thrust to his sternum that he partially blocked but couldn't fully stop. The third was a tap to the back of his knee — technically below the line, but by the time he thought to call foul, he was already on the ground and Elowen was standing over him with the same look Elysian had given him that morning.

"Three days," Elowen said. "No complaining."

"That knee shot was low," Cade said from the ground.

"Then you should have blocked it," Elowen said.

She reached down and pulled him up. Her hand was strong, calloused, warm. She held on for a second longer than she needed to, and the grin on her face softened into something else — something quieter, something that made Cade's chest do a thing he didn't have a name for.

"You are not terrible," Elowen said to Cade. "For someone who started three weeks ago."

"High praise," Cade said.

"The highest you will get from me," Elowen said. "Now again."

They sparred for another hour. Cade didn't win a single round, but by the end he was lasting longer — blocking more, reading her movement, anticipating the angles. Elowen pushed him hard, harder than Elysian in some ways, because she fought the way a real opponent would — fast, unpredictable, with no time to think.

And she laughed while she fought. Not mocking laughter — joyful laughter, the kind that came from doing something she loved with someone she was starting to care about. Cade found himself laughing too, which was dangerous because laughing meant dropping his guard, which meant ending up on the ground again.

Elysian watched from the edge of the clearing, leaning on his walking stick, saying nothing. But Cade caught the old man smiling once — a small, private smile, like a man watching something he'd hoped would happen.

It was late afternoon when the best moment of Cade's time in Emerald Vale happened, and it had nothing to do with fighting.

They were walking back toward the village, Cade and Elowen side by side, Elysian a few paces ahead, when Sammy suddenly broke away from the group and sprinted toward Torin's farm. Cade called after him, but the dog was gone — a blue-gray blur tearing through the ferns.

They heard the commotion before they saw it. Barking — Sammy's high, frantic bark, the one he used when he was absolutely beside himself with excitement. And underneath it, a sound Cade had never heard before — a high-pitched honking, panicked and indignant and very, very annoyed.

They came around the barn and stopped.

Sammy was herding a baby stoneshell.

The animal was about the size of a large pig, with stubby legs, a tiny ridged back, and a tail it hadn't grown into yet. It was honking and waddling as fast as its short legs would carry it, which was not very fast at all. And Sammy was behind it, crouched low, moving in the precise zigzag pattern of a herding dog doing exactly what generations of breeding had built him to do. Every time the baby stoneshell tried to veer left, Sammy cut it off. Every time it tried to stop, Sammy barked and it started waddling again. The dog was in absolute heaven.

The baby stoneshell was not.

Bruna, the mother, was watching from her pen with an expression that Cade could only describe as deeply unimpressed. Korr, the male, hadn't even bothered to open his eyes.

Elowen started laughing. Not a polite laugh — a full, helpless, doubled-over laugh that made her drop her staff and grab Cade's arm for balance. Elysian made a sound that might have been a laugh or might have been a cough, but his shoulders were shaking.

Torin came out of the barn, saw what was happening, and stopped in the doorway. He watched the dog herd the baby dinosaur in a perfect circle around the water trough. His mouth twitched. Then it twitched again. Then the quietest, most reluctant laugh Cade had ever heard came out of the man, like it had escaped against his will.

Village children appeared from nowhere — they always did when Sammy was involved — and within minutes a crowd had gathered, everyone watching the dog work the baby stoneshell with the professional intensity of an animal that had finally found its calling. The baby honked. Sammy barked. The children screamed with delight.

Cade watched Elowen laugh until her eyes watered, and he felt something click into place inside him — not a wall going up, but a door opening. This girl, this place, this ridiculous dog herding a baby dinosaur in a world that shouldn't exist. It was absurd and beautiful and the most alive Cade had felt in fourteen years.

He would remember this moment. Whatever happened next, wherever this world took him, he would remember the sound of Elowen's laugh and the sight of Sammy herding a honking baby dinosaur in circles around a water trough.

That evening, Elowen built a small fire behind the farmhouse. The nights were getting cooler, and the firelight pushed back the dark enough to make the world feel small and safe. Cade sat on one side, Elowen on the other, Sammy stretched between them like a furry bridge.

They were quiet for a while. Comfortable quiet — the kind that doesn't need to be filled.

Then Elowen spoke.

"Cade," Elowen said. Her voice was careful, measured. "When you were sparring today, your shirt rode up. On your back. I saw marks."

The air around the fire went cold. Cade's body went rigid — a full-system shutdown, every wall he'd built slamming into place at once. He didn't move. He didn't speak. He stared at the fire and felt the heat on his face and heard the blood rushing in his ears.

"They are old marks," Elowen said quietly. "Scars. Thin lines, like something thin and hard was used to —" She stopped herself. "You do not have to tell me."

Cade's jaw was clenched so tight his teeth ached. The scars on his back — three of them, running diagonal from his left shoulder blade to his lower right side — were the only physical evidence of the worst night in his life. The night Don had come home drunk and found Cade standing between him and Ashen's bedroom door. The night the belt hadn't been enough and Don had grabbed a curtain rod.

He'd been twelve. Eydan had driven him to the emergency room at two in the morning and told them he'd fallen off a fence.

"I don't talk about it," Cade said. His voice was flat. Dead. The voice he used when the walls were up and the drawbridge was raised and nothing was getting in.

"Then we will not talk about it," Elowen said.

She didn't move closer. She didn't reach for his hand. She didn't try to hug him or comfort him or say any of the things people said when they discovered something ugly about your past. She just sat on the other side of the fire, exactly where she'd been, and let the silence hold the space between them.

Sammy shifted, lifted his head, and laid it on Cade's thigh.

They sat like that for a long time. The fire crackled. The night sounds of the village drifted over the wall. Somewhere in the distance, a stoneshell rumbled in its sleep.

"Elowen," Cade said finally.

"Yes?" Elowen said.

"Thank you for not pushing," Cade said.

"That is what friends do," Elowen said.

Cade looked at her across the fire. The light played across her face — the amber eyes, the dark braid, the steady, patient expression of a girl who had lost her mother at six and been raised by a quiet farmer and had turned out strong and kind and sure of herself in ways Cade was only beginning to understand.

"Yeah," Cade said. "I guess it is."

Weeks were passing now. Two months in Emerald Vale, and Cade was becoming someone different. Stronger in his body — the farm work and the training had replaced the skinny, hunched frame of the boy who'd walked home from Ridgewood High with his head down. Stronger in his mind — Elysian's teaching had given him focus, discipline, a sense of purpose he'd never had before. And stronger in something he couldn't name — something that had to do with Elowen, and Torin, and Elysian, and the village that had taken in a stranger and asked nothing of him except that he try.

But at night, when the village was quiet and Sammy was asleep beside him, Cade stared at the ceiling and thought about Maple Creek Drive. About Eydan working herself to death. About Ashen drawing dogs on grocery receipts. About Carla saving him a seat at lunch.

He was changing. He was growing. But he still hadn't figured out how to get home.

And somewhere in the back of his mind, underneath the training and the friendship and the slow, dangerous warmth he felt every time Elowen smiled at him, the pattern he'd seen in Kaelthas was still there. Still waiting. Still watching.

Chapter Eleven - *Sammy's Trail*

Cade woke in the dark to an empty bed.

He reached for Sammy before his eyes were open —
the automatic, half-asleep gesture of a boy who'd spent three
years with a dog pressed against his side every night. His
hand found cold blanket. Nothing else.

He sat up. The room was dark. Through the hide flap
over the window, the first gray light of predawn was creeping
into the sky, but the sun wasn't up yet. The village was silent.

"Sammy?" Cade said.

"Nothing. No click of nails on the stone floor." No tail
thump. No warm weight shifting at the foot of the bed.

Cade swung his legs off the bed and stood. He checked
the room — small, nowhere to hide. He checked the hallway.
Empty. He moved through the farmhouse quietly, past
Torin's closed door, past the kitchen where last night's fire
had burned down to ash.

The back door was open. Not wide — just a few inches,
enough for a forty-five-pound dog to push through.

Cade's stomach dropped.

He stepped outside. The fenced yard behind the
farmhouse was empty. The gate in the low stone wall that led
to the fields was unlatched — Cade had closed it last night,

he was certain of it. Sammy had pushed it open and gone through.

"Sammy!" Cade called into the gray morning. His voice was louder than he intended, sharp with a fear that cut through the drowsiness like cold water. "Sammy, come!"

Silence. Then, from somewhere beyond the fields, from the direction of the northern forest, a single bark. Distant. Fading.

The fear in Cade's chest turned into something worse. The last time Sammy had bolted — the only other time — they'd ended up in another world. The dog had run, and Cade had chased, and everything had changed. Now Sammy was running again, into a forest that held things far more dangerous than the woods behind Maple Creek Drive.

But underneath the fear was something else — a feeling Cade couldn't explain, an instinct that had been growing for weeks without him noticing. Sammy mattered. Not just as his dog, not just as his best friend, but in some deeper way connected to the portal and the boulders and the reason they were here. The dog had found the way in. The dog might be the way out. And if something happened to Sammy in that forest, Cade might be trapped in Emerald Vale forever.

He grabbed his knife from the table by his bed — the stone-bladed one Elysian had given him — and his staff from where it leaned against the wall. He didn't bother with shoes. His feet had toughened over the past two months, calloused from farm work and forest training, and the leather boots Torin had made for him were by the front door and there wasn't time.

He ran.

Through the gate, across the fields, the thornroot stalks brushing against his legs in the half-light. Past the outer wall through the small north gate that the farmers used to access the forest trails. Into the trees.

The forest was different before dawn. The canopy blocked what little light the sky offered, and the undergrowth was a maze of shadow and shape. The night creatures were still active — clicks and rustles in the brush, the distant hoot of something Cade had never identified. The air was cool and damp, heavy with the smell of wet earth and rotting vegetation.

Cade stopped and listened. His training with Elysian took over — slow your breathing, open your ears, let the forest tell you what's happening. He heard the normal sounds — insects, wind, the creak of branches. And underneath them, far ahead and to the left, the faint crash of something moving through the undergrowth. Something dog-sized, moving fast, not bothering to be quiet.

Sammy.

Cade followed. He moved the way Elysian had taught him — feet on roots and stones, weight rolling from heel to toe, staff held close to avoid catching on branches. He wasn't silent — nobody was truly silent in this forest — but he was quiet enough. The sounds ahead stayed consistent, which meant Sammy wasn't pulling away from him.

He tracked the dog for nearly an hour. The forest thickened as he moved north, the trees growing denser, the undergrowth more tangled. He passed landmarks he recognized from training with Elysian — a lightning-scarred oak, a creek crossing with flat stones, a ridge where the old tracker had taught him to read tracks. Then he passed beyond them, into forest he'd never entered before.

Elysian had warned him about the deep north. "The village patrols go as far as the stone ridge," Elysian had told him once. "Beyond that, we do not go. The forest is wild there. The predators are larger, bolder. There is nothing in the deep north worth dying for."

Cade was in the deep north now. He knew it because the forest felt different — older, heavier, the trees so massive their roots formed walls and tunnels in the earth. The light was dimmer here even as the sun climbed. The insect chorus was muted. And the air had a smell Cade hadn't encountered before — sharp, musky, like the scent of a large animal's den.

He heard Sammy bark. Close now. Just ahead, over a low rise covered in ferns.

Cade crouched and moved forward carefully, pushing through the ferns on his hands and knees. He reached the top of the rise and looked down.

A canyon.

It was narrow — maybe a hundred yards across — with steep walls of dark stone on three sides. The fourth side, where Cade was crouched, sloped down gradually into the canyon floor, which was flat and cleared of vegetation. It looked like it had been cleared deliberately — stumps dotted the ground where trees had been cut, and the brush had been burned back to bare earth.

And in the canyon, in a row of heavy wooden cages built against the far wall, were dinosaurs.

Not stoneshells. Not swiftclaws. These were predators.

There were six of them, each in a separate cage built from logs as thick as Cade's waist, lashed together with rope and braced with stone. The animals were lean and muscular, built low to the ground, with powerful hind legs and short, grasping arms tipped with curved claws. Their heads were narrow and long, filled with teeth that Cade could see even from this distance — rows of serrated blades designed to tear flesh. Their hides were mottled dark brown and black, patterned for camouflage in deep forest.

Razormaws. Had to be. The same predators Elysian had been tracking. The ones that had been moving closer to the village. The ones that had torn through Aldric's fence and taken three stoneshells.

Except these razormaws weren't wild. They were caged. And they weren't alone.

Four men were in the canyon. Two of them were standing near the cages, holding long poles with loops of rope at the end — control poles, the kind you'd use to handle a dangerous animal without getting within reach of its jaws. A third man was at the far end of the canyon, doing something with a wooden crate that Cade couldn't make out. And the fourth was standing in the center of the clearing, arms crossed, watching the others work.

Cade recognized him. The man with the scar across his jaw — the one he'd seen meeting with Kaelthas behind the storehouse weeks ago.

Cade's blood went cold.

He pressed himself flat against the ground and watched. One of the men with the control poles approached a cage. Inside, the razormaw paced — three steps forward, three steps back, its eyes tracking the man with the fixed intensity of a predator measuring its prey. The man made a sharp clicking sound with his tongue — three clicks, fast, then a pause, then two more. The razormaw stopped pacing. It turned toward the man. It sat.

It sat like a dog obeying a command.

The second handler made a different sound — a low whistle, rising — and the razormaw in the next cage pressed itself against the far wall of its enclosure and went still. Obedient. Controlled.

These men were training predators.

Cade's mind raced. The missing livestock. The razormaw tracks near the village. Elysian's observation that predators were moving closer — not because something was pushing them out of their territory, but because someone was bringing them in. Caging them. Training them. Building something.

An army. Kaelthas was building an army of predators.

The scar-jawed man spoke. His voice carried in the still morning air, bouncing off the canyon walls clearly enough for Cade to hear every word.

"Two more weeks," the man said to the handlers. "Kaelthas wants them ready by the new moon. All six, responding to commands. He says when the time comes, the village won't know what hit them. By the time Fenvar understands what's happening, it'll be too late. The beasts go in through the north gate, the south gate, and the eastern fields at the same time. Panic. Chaos. People running. And Kaelthas steps in to save what's left."

One of the handlers laughed. "And Fenvar?" the handler asked.

"Fenvar will be dealt with," the scar-jawed man said. "Kaelthas has a plan for the chief. An accident during the attack. Tragic. Unavoidable. And when it's over, who does the village turn to? Who has been managing everything for twenty years? Who saved them from the disaster?"

"Kaelthas," the handler said.

"Kaelthas," the scar-jawed man confirmed. "Chief Kaelthas. Has a nice sound to it, doesn't it?"

Cade couldn't breathe. His hands were gripping the ferns so hard his knuckles were white. His heart was hammering against his ribs and he was sure — absolutely certain — that they could hear it down in the canyon, that the sound of his pulse was echoing off the stone walls like a drum.

It was all there. Everything he'd suspected, everything his gut had been screaming at him for weeks, laid out in plain words by a man with a scar on his jaw who thought no one was listening.

Kaelthas was going to attack his own village. He was going to murder his own chief. He was going to use trained predators to slaughter innocent people and then step into the wreckage as a savior.

A movement below him caught his eye. At the edge of the canyon, near the slope where Cade had come in, a familiar shape was trotting along the tree line.

Sammy.

The dog had his nose to the ground, following a scent, tail low, moving with the focused determination of an animal tracking something important. He was heading straight toward the canyon floor. Straight toward the men and the cages and the razormaws.

"No," Cade breathed. "Sammy, no."

One of the handlers saw the dog. "What is that?" the handler said, pointing.

The scar-jawed man turned. His eyes narrowed. "That's the outsider's animal," the man said. "The one from the village. Which means—"

He looked up the slope. Directly at where Cade was lying in the ferns.

Their eyes met.

Cade didn't wait. He was on his feet and moving before the man finished his sentence. He slid down the slope, grabbed Sammy by the collar, and hauled the dog backward.

"Hey!" the scar-jawed man shouted. "Stop him!"

Cade ran. He dragged Sammy up the slope, through the ferns, over the rise. Behind him he heard shouting, the crash of men moving through brush, the snarl of a razormaw reacting to the commotion.

He ran like he'd never run before. Not the panicked sprint of a kid chasing his dog through the woods behind Maple Creek Drive. This was something different — focused, controlled, every step placed with the precision Elysian had drilled into him over weeks of training. He moved through the forest like the forest had taught him, ducking branches, vaulting roots, cutting through gaps in the undergrowth that a larger man would have had to go around.

Sammy ran beside him, finally understanding the urgency, ears flat, legs stretching.

The sounds of pursuit faded behind them. Cade didn't slow down. He ran until his lungs burned and his legs shook and the forest around him started to look familiar again — the lightning-scarred oak, the creek crossing, the ridge. He was back in known territory. Back in range of the village patrols.

He stopped behind the scarred oak, pressing his back against the trunk, chest heaving. Sammy collapsed at his feet, panting. The forest was quiet. No footsteps. No shouting. They hadn't followed him this far.

Cade slid down the trunk and sat in the dirt. His hands were shaking. His whole body was shaking. Sweat ran down his face and dripped off his chin and he couldn't stop it, couldn't control anything, because his brain was replaying what he'd seen and heard and every repetition made it worse.

Kaelthas was going to destroy Verdant Haven. The man everyone trusted, the advisor who managed the trade routes and settled disputes and organized wall repairs — he was going to burn it all down and build himself a throne on the ashes.

And Cade was the only person who knew.

He looked at Sammy. The dog looked back at him, tongue out, eyes steady.

"You found it, boy," Cade said to the dog. "You found what he's been hiding."

Sammy's tail wagged once.

Cade stood. His legs were still trembling but his mind was clear. He knew what he'd seen. He knew what he'd heard. And he knew exactly who he needed to tell first.

He picked up his staff, tightened his grip on Sammy's collar, and headed for the village. Not to the chief's hall. Not to Fenvar.

To Elowen.

He found her behind the barn, feeding the stoneshells. She took one look at his face and set the feed bucket down.

"What happened?" Elowen asked.

Cade told her. All of it. The canyon. The cages. The razormaws being trained with commands. The scar-jawed man — the same one they'd both seen with Kaelthas. The plan to attack the village. The plan to kill Fenvar. Kaelthas stepping in as chief.

He told her everything, and he watched her face while he did it. He watched for doubt. For the same careful, reasonable skepticism she'd shown weeks ago when he'd first raised his concerns about Kaelthas. He braced himself for the words — *You are imagining things. You are projecting. You cannot judge every man by the worst one you have known.*

Elowen's face went hard. Not angry — something beyond anger. Something cold and certain and fierce.

"I believe you," Elowen said.

Three words. The three words Cade had needed to hear his entire life from someone other than a dog.

"We need to tell Fenvar," Elowen said. "Now."

"Will he believe us?" Cade asked.

Elowen's jaw tightened. "He has to," Elowen said. "We will make him believe us."

She grabbed her bow from where it leaned against the barn wall and slung it over her shoulder. Sammy stood between them, tail still, ears forward, watching both of them with the quiet alertness of a dog who understood that something important was happening.

"Come on," Elowen said. "We go to the chief."

Chapter Twelve - *Nobody Listens*

They crossed the village at a near run, Elowen leading, Cade behind her, Sammy between them. The morning was still early — most of the village was just waking up, smoke beginning to rise from cooking fires, the first farmers heading toward the gates. A few people looked at them as they passed — two teenagers and a dog moving through the village center with urgency written on their faces — but no one stopped them.

The chief's hall stood at the far end of the square, its tusk-framed doorway open to the morning air. Two guards flanked the entrance, spears upright. They recognized Elowen and stepped aside without question. One of them gave Cade a look — the same cautious, measuring look he got from half the village — but said nothing.

Elowen pushed through the doorway. Cade followed.

The hall was large, built from heavy timber with a high ceiling supported by dinosaur bone pillars. A fire pit sat in the center, cold now, the ashes raked flat. Along the walls, carved wooden benches lined up in rows — seats for the village council, Cade assumed. At the far end, on a raised platform, was a single chair made from dark wood and bone. Not a throne — nothing that ornate — but clearly the seat of the man in charge.

Fenvar was standing beside the chair, talking with two older men Cade didn't recognize — council members, maybe, or village elders. He looked up when Elowen and Cade entered, and his expression shifted from conversation to attention.

"Elowen," Fenvar said. "It is early."

"Chief Fenvar," Elowen said. Her voice was steady but tight, the voice of someone holding a great deal of urgency under control. "We need to speak with you. It is important."

Fenvar studied her face, then Cade's. Whatever he saw there was enough to make him dismiss the two elders with a nod. They left, glancing at Cade as they passed with expressions that ranged from curious to suspicious.

"Speak," Fenvar said.

Cade stepped forward. His heart was pounding, but he kept his voice level. Elysian had taught him that — control your breath and your voice will follow. He started from the beginning. The private meetings he'd observed between Kaelthas and the same group of men. The scar-jawed man he'd seen multiple times. Sammy running into the forest that morning. The canyon. The cages. The six razormaws being trained with commands and signals.

And then the words. The scar-jawed man's words, spoken clearly in a canyon where they thought no one was listening.

"He said Kaelthas wants them ready by the new moon," Cade said to Fenvar. "All six razormaws, responding to commands. He said they'd go in through the north gate, the south gate, and the eastern fields at the same time. He said there would be panic and chaos and people running. And he said Kaelthas would step in to save what was left."

Cade paused. This was the hardest part.

"He said Fenvar would be dealt with," Cade said. "An accident during the attack. And when it was over, Kaelthas would become chief."

The hall was silent. Fenvar's expression hadn't changed during the telling — he'd listened the way a man listens to a report from a scout, absorbing information, weighing it. But at the last words, something moved behind his eyes. Not fear. Not anger. Something heavier. Something that looked like a door being tested to see if it would hold.

"These are serious accusations," Fenvar said. His voice was measured and careful. "You are accusing my most trusted advisor of treason. Of plotting murder. On the word of a boy who has been among us for two months."

"I know what I saw," Cade said. "I know what I heard."

"You saw men in a canyon with caged predators," Fenvar said. "There could be explanations for that. Hunters trapping razormaws to thin their numbers. Trackers studying their behavior. I have authorized such operations in the past."

"They were training them," Cade said. "With commands. Clicks and whistles. The razormaws were obeying."

"That is unusual," Fenvar acknowledged. "But not proof of what you claim."

"The man with the scar said Kaelthas's name," Cade said. He could hear the frustration rising in his own voice and fought to keep it down. "He laid out the entire plan. The attack. Your death. Kaelthas taking over. I heard it, Chief. Every word."

Fenvar was quiet for a long moment. Then the door behind Cade opened, and a voice floated into the hall like silk over stone.

"I could not help but overhear," Kaelthas said.

Cade's spine went rigid. He turned. Kaelthas stood in the doorway, backlit by the morning sun, his expression one of gentle concern. He walked into the hall with the unhurried ease of a man entering his own home and stopped a few paces from Cade. His gray eyes moved over the boy's face — the sweat, the dirt, the scratches from running through the forest — and his brow creased with what looked exactly like worry.

"Cade," Kaelthas said, his voice warm and measured. "You seem distressed. What has happened?"

"He has made accusations against you," Fenvar said to Kaelthas. His tone was neutral — not accusatory, not dismissive, just stating a fact and waiting for a response.

Kaelthas turned to Fenvar. His expression shifted to surprise — convincing surprise, the kind that moved through his whole face, eyes widening slightly, mouth opening a fraction. Then concern. Then understanding.

"Accusations," Kaelthas repeated. He looked at Cade. "What kind of accusations?"

"He claims you are training razormaws in a hidden canyon north of the village," Fenvar said. "That you plan to use them to attack Verdant Haven. That you intend to have me killed and take my place."

Kaelthas was silent for exactly the right amount of time — long enough to show he was taking the accusation seriously, short enough to show he wasn't worried. Then he exhaled slowly, the way a man exhales when he has heard something sad rather than threatening.

"Cade," Kaelthas said. His voice was soft now. Careful. The voice of a man speaking to a child who was confused and needed guidance. "I understand. I truly do. You have been through something extraordinary — pulled from your world, dropped into ours, separated from your family. The strain of that would break most adults, let alone a boy of fourteen."

"This isn't about that," Cade said. His hands were clenched at his sides.

"Of course not," Kaelthas said. "Not intentionally. But the mind does things under pressure that we do not always recognize. You saw something in the forest this morning — perhaps a hunting party, perhaps a trapping operation — and your fear filled in the rest. The details, the overheard conversation, the plan — these things can seem absolutely real and vivid when the mind is under stress."

He turned to Fenvar. "I have been Fenvar's advisor for twenty years," Kaelthas said to the chief. "I have served this village with everything I have. I have no ambition beyond what I already hold. The idea that I would train predators to attack my own people —" He paused, letting the absurdity of the statement speak for itself. "It is the product of a frightened mind, nothing more."

Cade felt the ground shifting under him. Not literally — figuratively, emotionally, in the pit of his stomach where truth lived. He watched Kaelthas perform, because that's what it was — a performance, smooth and polished and perfectly calibrated — and he recognized every note of it. The concerned tone. The reasonable explanation. The gentle suggestion that the accuser was the one with the problem.

Don had done this. Standing in the living room after the neighbors heard the yelling, explaining to the concerned couple from next door that everything was fine, the kids were just rambunctious, Eydan had been stressed lately. His voice warm and steady. His hand on Eydan's shoulder. The smile that said, *Nothing to see here. I am a good man. This family is fine.*

And the neighbors had believed him. Every time.

"Chief Fenvar," Cade said. He kept his voice as steady as he could. "I am not confused. I am not imagining things. I know what I saw and I know what I heard. The man with the scar on his jaw — I have seen him with Kaelthas multiple times. In alleys. Behind buildings. Always in private. Always with the same group."

"Drennan," Kaelthas said smoothly. "You are describing Drennan. He is one of my trade coordinators. We meet privately because trade negotiations require discretion. I can hardly discuss supply agreements in the village square."

He had an answer for everything. Of course he did. Men like Kaelthas always had answers. The answers were the armor. The answers were the weapon.

Fenvar looked at Cade. Then at Kaelthas. Then back at Cade. The chief's face was a mask of careful neutrality, but Cade could see the calculation happening behind it — twenty years of trust weighed against two months of a stranger's word.

"Cade," Fenvar said. "I have heard what you have said. I do not dismiss it lightly. But I cannot act on an accusation of this magnitude without evidence. You have told me what you saw and heard. Kaelthas has offered an explanation. Without proof — without something I can hold in my hand and show to the council — I cannot move against a man who has served this village faithfully for two decades."

"Then let me take you to the canyon," Cade said. "I can find it again. I can show you the cages, the razormaws, everything."

"And if what you find is a trapping operation?" Fenvar asked. "If the men there are hunters doing work I have authorized?"

"Then I'm wrong," Cade said. "And I'll accept that. But if I'm right —"

"If you are right, then we will deal with it," Fenvar said. "But I will not send armed men into the northern forest on the word of a boy who has been among us for eight weeks. Not without more."

The finality in his voice was a wall. Cade had hit walls before — the wall of Don's denial, the wall of teachers who asked if everything was okay and then accepted "fine" as an answer, the wall of a system that didn't want to see what was happening in a house on Maple Creek Drive. This wall was different — Fenvar wasn't cruel, wasn't negligent, wasn't looking the other way. He was a chief making a decision based on the information he had and the trust he'd built over twenty years.

But the result was the same. Nobody listened. Nobody believed him. The truth sat in Cade's mouth like a stone, heavy and useless, and the man who was going to destroy everything stood five feet away with a concerned smile on his face and twenty years of credibility as his shield.

"Thank you for hearing me, Chief," Cade said. His voice was hollow. He turned and walked out of the hall.

Elowen was waiting outside. She had stayed by the door — close enough to hear, far enough to let Cade speak for himself. One look at his face told her everything.

"He did not believe you," Elowen said.

"Kaelthas was there," Cade said. "He explained everything away. Trade meetings. Trapping operations. I'm just a scared kid seeing things."

Elowen's eyes flashed. The amber in them went dark, the way a fire goes dark before it burns hotter.

"You are not a scared kid seeing things," Elowen said. "You are the bravest person I have met, and I believe every word you said."

Cade looked at her. The hollow feeling in his chest cracked — not enough to let much in, but enough to keep him from drowning in it.

"Fenvar needs proof," Elowen said. "Then we will get him proof. We go back to the canyon. We find something — a tool, a harness, something with Kaelthas's mark on it. We bring it back and we put it in Fenvar's hand and we make him see."

"If Kaelthas knows I found the canyon, he'll move the operation," Cade said. "He'll have the cages torn down and the razormaws released before we can get back there."

"Then we move fast," Elowen said. "Tonight. We go tonight."

Cade looked at her — this girl with a bow and a braid who had found him starving in the forest and fed him bread and dried meat. This girl who had taught him which plants would kill him and which ones wouldn't. This girl who had beaten him in every sparring match and laughed while doing it and never once asked him to be anything other than exactly what he was.

She believed him. When nobody else did, when the chief of the village sided with the man who was going to destroy it, Elowen believed him.

"Okay," Cade said. "Tonight."

Sammy sat between them, looking from one to the other, tail still, ears forward. The dog who had started all of this by staring at the woods behind a house on Maple Creek Drive. The dog who had found the portal. The dog who had found the canyon. The dog who, in his own quiet, stubborn way, had been right about everything from the very beginning.

"We are going to need help," Elowen said. "Someone Fenvar trusts. Someone who will listen."

Cade knew who she meant before she said it.

"Elysian," Cade said.

Elowen nodded. "Elysian," Elowen said.

Chapter Thirteen - The Whisper Campaign

They spent the rest of the day waiting, and it was the longest day of Cade's life. Elowen told him to act normal — go to the fields, haul water, do the things he always did — because if Kaelthas was watching, and he was certainly watching, any change in routine would tell the advisor that Cade wasn't backing down. So Cade hauled water. He pulled weeds. He ate lunch at Torin's table and tasted nothing. He moved through the hours like a man walking through mud, every minute dragging, his mind locked on the canyon and the cages and the smooth voice in Fenvar's hall that had turned his truth into nothing.

When the last light drained from the sky, they found Elysian at his home near the northern wall.

The old tracker's dwelling was nothing like Torin's farmhouse. It was small and spare — a single room built from timber and stone, tucked against the village wall where the forest pressed close on the other side. No decorations. No bone carvings above the door. A sleeping mat, a fire pit, a rack of tools and weapons along one wall, and a chair that looked like it had been carved from a single piece of wood. The home of a man who needed nothing he couldn't carry.

"Elysian was sitting in the chair, working the edge of a knife with a piece of antler bone, pressing small flakes from the stone blade to restore its edge, when Cade and Elowen appeared in his doorway. Sammy trotted in ahead of them and lay down at the old man's feet like he owned the place.

Elysian looked at Cade's face. Then at Elowen's. He set the knife down.

"Sit," Elysian said. "Tell me."

Cade told him everything. The canyon. The cages. The six razormaws trained with commands. The scar-jawed man — Drennan, Kaelthas had called him — laying out the plan in plain words. The attack on three gates at once. Fenvar's murder disguised as an accident. Kaelthas stepping into the wreckage as chief.

And then the meeting with Fenvar. Kaelthas appearing at exactly the right moment. The smooth explanations. The gentle suggestion that Cade was confused, homesick, imagining things. Fenvar siding with the man he'd known for twenty years.

Elysian listened without interrupting. His dark eyes stayed on Cade's face the entire time, reading him the way he read tracks in the forest — not just the words, but the truth underneath them.

When Cade finished, the old man was quiet for a long time. The fire crackled. Sammy's tail swept the stone floor once, twice.

"You went into the deep north alone," Elysian said finally. "Without telling anyone. Without weapons beyond a knife and a staff."

"Sammy ran," Cade said. "I didn't have time to —"

"You could have died," Elysian said. His voice wasn't angry. It was flat and factual, the way he stated everything. "A razormaw in the open forest would have killed you before you knew it was there. You are fast and you are learning, but you are not ready for the deep north."

"I know," Cade said. "But I found what I found."

Elysian leaned back in his chair. He picked up the knife and turned it slowly in his hands, not sharpening it, just holding it. Thinking.

"Kaelthas," Elysian said. The name sat in the air between them.

"You have doubts about him," Cade said. It wasn't a question. He'd seen it in the old man's eyes during training — the way Elysian went quiet when Kaelthas's name came up, the way his jaw tightened when the advisor passed through the village giving orders.

Elysian was silent for another long moment. Then he spoke, slowly, choosing each word like a man placing stones across a river.

"I have noticed things," Elysian said. "Small things. Men I do not recognize leaving through the north gate before dawn and returning after dark. Supplies missing from the storehouse — rope, chain, cured meat — in quantities that do not match the village records. Drennan disappearing for days at a time with no explanation. I have asked questions. The answers I received were reasonable. They were always reasonable."

He looked at Cade. "Reasonable answers from a reasonable man. That is what makes it difficult."

"Do you believe me?" Cade asked.

Elysian held his gaze. "I believe you saw what you say you saw," Elysian said. "I believe you heard what you say you heard. Whether it means what you think it means — that I cannot confirm tonight. But I will not dismiss you. I have spent my life reading the forest, and the forest has been wrong for months. The predators moving south. The tracks where there should be no tracks. Something is pulling them, and I have not been able to find what." He paused. "Perhaps you have."

It wasn't a full commitment. It wasn't "I believe you" the way Elowen had said it — clean and total and without reservation. But it was a crack in the wall. A crack wide enough to build on.

"We need to go back to the canyon," Elowen said to Elysian. "We need proof. Something Fenvar cannot explain away."

"Not tonight," Elysian said. "If Kaelthas knows Cade found the compound — and he does, his men saw the dog — he will have guards posted. Going back now is walking into a trap."

"Then when?" Elowen asked.

"Give it time," Elysian said. "Let me watch. Let me listen. Kaelthas does not know I am paying attention. That is an advantage we cannot afford to lose."

"Time is what we do not have," Cade said. "Drennan said two weeks. New moon. That's when the attack happens."

Elysian's eyes narrowed. "The new moon," Elysian repeated. He was quiet, calculating. "That is twelve days from now."

"Twelve days," Cade said.

Elysian stood. He walked to the door of his dwelling and looked out into the darkening village. His silhouette was sharp against the fading sky — an old man carrying the weight of something he didn't want to believe but couldn't ignore.

"Go home," Elysian said to them. "Both of you. Sleep. Say nothing to anyone. Let me think. I will come to you tomorrow."

Cade and Elowen left. They walked back through the village in silence, Sammy between them. At the gate to Torin's farm, Elowen stopped.

"He believes you," Elowen said to Cade.

"He's not sure yet," Cade said.

"He is sure enough to listen," Elowen said. "For Elysian, that is everything."

She went inside. Cade stood in the dark with Sammy for a moment, looking up at the stars — that impossible sky, thick with light, no moon visible yet — and then he went to bed.

He didn't sleep well. He dreamed of razormaws and canyon walls and a man with gray eyes who smiled while the world burned.

The change started the next morning.

Cade was crossing the village center on his way to meet Elysian when he passed two women sitting outside the weaver's workshop, sorting fibers into baskets. He nodded at them the way he'd been doing for weeks — a small gesture, nothing more. The older woman had always nodded back.

Sometimes she smiled. Once she'd waved him over and given him a piece of sweet bread wrapped in a leaf.

Today she looked away. Not quickly, not rudely — just a slow turning of the head, as if something on the other side of the path had caught her attention at exactly the right moment. The younger woman beside her didn't look up at all.

Cade kept walking. It could have been nothing. People had bad days. People got distracted.

But it happened again an hour later, at the well near the south gate. A man named Hadrik — one of the farmers who worked the fields near Torin's land — was drawing water when Cade approached to fill his jug. Hadrik had been friendly since Cade's second week. He'd shown Cade how to sharpen a stone blade and had once spent twenty minutes explaining the difference between the two types of thornroot.

Today Hadrik pulled his water jug off the stone ledge and left without a word. He didn't look at Cade. He didn't nod. He walked away as if Cade weren't there.

And again that afternoon. The children who usually swarmed Sammy when he trotted through the village — the pack of six or seven who followed him everywhere, calling him "soft-one" and burying their hands in his fur — weren't there. Sammy wandered through the paths with his tail wagging, looking for his fan club, and found empty ground. The children were inside. Their mothers had called them in.

Cade stood in the middle of the path and felt it settle over him like a cold blanket. He knew this feeling. He knew it the way he knew the taste of blood in his mouth after biting his tongue to keep from crying out.

Isolation. Someone was cutting him off from the people around him, one thread at a time, so quietly that by the time you noticed the web was gone, you were already alone.

Don had done this to Eydan. Not with fists — not at first. First he'd separated her from her friends. A comment here, a suggestion there. *Your sister doesn't really like me, does she? Maybe we shouldn't have her over so much. Your friend Karen seems like she's always judging us.* One by one, the connections dropped away, and Eydan didn't notice until she woke up one morning and realized the only person left in her world was the man who was destroying her.

Kaelthas was running the same play. Cade couldn't prove it — not yet — but he could feel it in the turned heads and the empty paths and the children who weren't there anymore.

He found Elowen at the barn that evening. She was mending a harness, Sammy at her feet.

"People are avoiding me," Cade said to Elowen.

"I know," Elowen said. "Kaelthas does not need to shout. He talks to one person, who talks to another, who talks to three more. By sundown, the whole village has heard whatever he wanted them to hear."

"What is he saying?" Cade asked.

"That the troubles started when you arrived," Elowen said. "The razormaw sightings. The missing livestock. All of it began after the outsider came through the forest. He is not saying you caused it — he is too clever for that. He is asking questions. Isn't it strange? Isn't the timing curious?"

"And people are buying it," Cade said.

"People are afraid," Elowen said. "Afraid people look for explanations. Kaelthas is giving them one."

"Your father?" Cade asked.

"Hadrik came to him this morning," Elowen said. "And Aldric. And two of the elders' wives. They said it was not proper for a farmer's daughter to spend so much time with the outsider."

"What did Torin say?" Cade asked.

"My father said thank you for your concern and closed the door," Elowen said. The corner of her mouth lifted slightly. "He is a man of few words, but the words he chooses are effective."

The next morning was worse. Cade was heading to the well when a girl about Elowen's age stepped into his path. Maren — one of the village girls who sometimes trained with the bow alongside Elowen.

Maren wasn't looking at Cade. She was looking past him, at Elowen.

"Elowen," Maren said. Her voice was tight. "Why are you defending this stranger over your own people? He has been here two months. We have known you your entire life. And you choose him?"

"I am not choosing anyone over anyone," Elowen said. "I am choosing the truth over a lie."

"What truth?" Maren asked. "The truth of a boy who appeared from nowhere and accuses the man who has held this village together for twenty years?"

"Maren," Elowen said. "When you lost your brother's hunting knife in the forest last year, who helped you find it? Who tracked it for two days?"

"You did," Maren said.

"And when your mother was sick during the wet season, who brought food to your family every night for a week?" Elowen asked.

"You did," Maren said, quieter now.

"Then trust me now," Elowen said. "Something is wrong in this village, Maren. And when it arrives, you will wish you had listened."

Maren stared at Elowen for a long moment. Then she turned and walked away without another word.

Elowen watched her go. Her hands were clenched at her sides.

"She is my friend," Elowen said quietly. "Since we were children."

"I know," Cade said. "I'm sorry."

"Do not be sorry," Elowen said. "Be ready."

That afternoon, Elysian found Cade behind the barn. The old man appeared at the edge of the tree line the way he always did — silently, suddenly, like the forest had produced him.

"Walk with me," Elysian said.

They walked along the inside of the northern wall, away from the village center, Sammy trotting beside them. Elysian was quiet for a long time. When he spoke, his voice was low.

"I went to the storehouse this morning," Elysian said to Cade. "I checked the records against the inventory. Rope is missing. Forty lengths of braided hide cord — the heavy kind we use to restrain stoneshells. Cured meat enough to feed a dozen men for weeks."

The records say the supplies were allocated to the northern patrol. I spoke with the northern patrol captain. He received nothing."

Cade's heart beat harder. "Kaelthas manages the storehouse records," Cade said.

"Yes," Elysian said. "He does."

They walked in silence for a few more paces. Then Elysian stopped and turned to face Cade. The old man's expression was different than before — the careful neutrality was gone, replaced by something harder. Something decided.

"I have watched this village for forty years," Elysian said. "I have tracked every predator that has come within a day's walk of these walls. The razormaws moving south — it has bothered me for months. Predators do not change their territory without a reason. I could not find the reason. Now I believe you have."

"You believe me," Cade said.

"I believe you," Elysian said. The words were simple and final, the way Elysian said everything that mattered. "And I believe we have eleven days to stop what is coming."

Cade felt something shift inside him — not relief, not yet, but the feeling of a wall giving way. Two people believed him now. Two people, and a dog who had been right from the beginning.

"What do we do?" Cade asked.

"We get proof," Elysian said. "And we get it fast. Come to my dwelling tonight. Both of you. We will make a plan."

The old tracker turned and walked back toward the tree line. Before he disappeared into the shadows, he looked over his shoulder.

"Cade," Elysian said.

"Yeah?" Cade said.

"Your dog knew before any of us," Elysian said. "Remember that."

Then he was gone, and Cade was standing alone by the northern wall with Sammy beside him and eleven days between Verdant Haven and disaster.

Chapter Fourteen - The Staged Attack

The attack came that same night, while the three of them were still huddled over Elysian's map.

Cade and Elowen had been at Elysian's dwelling for less than an hour. The old tracker had spread a rough map of the northern forest across the stone floor — charcoal lines on scraped hide, marking the trails, the ridges, the creek crossings between the village and the canyon. Sammy lay beside the fire, chin on his paws, watching them with sleepy eyes.

"We approach from the east," Elysian said, tracing a line with his finger. "The canyon wall is lowest there, and the tree cover on the ridge will hide us from below. We move before dawn, when the guards are —"

The screaming started.

It tore through the night like a blade — a raw, animal sound that was neither human nor dinosaur but something worse, the sound of both happening at the same time. A second scream followed, then a third, then the deep guttural snarl of something large and predatory, and underneath it all the high-pitched bleating of stoneshells panicking in their pens.

Elysian was on his feet before the second scream faded, staff in hand, moving toward the door. Elowen had her bow off her shoulder and an arrow nocked in the time it took Cade to grab his knife from the floor. Sammy pressed against Cade's leg, hackles raised, growling low.

"Eastern edge," Elysian said, his head tilted, listening. "Near the outer wall."

They ran. Out of Elysian's dwelling, through the narrow paths along the northern wall, cutting across the village toward the sound. Other villagers were pouring out of their homes — men with spears and torches, women pulling children back into doorways. The village horn sounded from the guard tower near the main gate — three short bellows, the alarm call Cade had learned during his first week.

Torin was already outside his farmhouse as they passed, a heavy staff in his hands, his face grim. He fell in beside them without a word.

They reached the eastern edge of the village in minutes. What Cade saw there stopped him cold.

A farm — Aldric's farm, the same farmer who'd reported missing stoneshells weeks ago — was in ruins. The fence around the livestock pen had been torn apart, not broken but shredded, the heavy logs splintered like kindling. Two stoneshells lay dead in the wreckage, their armored bodies ripped open with a violence that made Cade's stomach lurch. A third was on its side, still alive, bellowing in pain, a gash across its flank deep enough to see the pale tissue underneath.

Blood was everywhere. It was black in the torchlight, pooled in the churned mud, splattered across the remains of the fence. The smell hit Cade like a wall — copper and meat and the hot, musky stench of a predator.

Aldric was standing in front of his farmhouse, shaking, a spear in his hands. His wife was behind him in the doorway, clutching their two young children. His face was white.

"It came from the north," Aldric said to whoever would listen. His voice was trembling. "Over the wall. It came over the wall. I heard the stoneshells screaming and by the time I got outside it was already in the pen. I could not — it was too fast. It was too —"

He couldn't finish. His wife pulled the children tighter against her.

The village guards arrived — six of them, armed with spears and torches, spreading out around the ruined pen. One of them found the tracks and crouched to examine them.

Cade moved closer, the torchlight flickering across the churned ground. The prints were deep in the mud, three-toed and spaced wide apart. Razormaw.

But Cade saw something the guards didn't. He saw the direction of the tracks — in from the north wall, through the pen, and back out through the north wall. A straight line. In and out. A razormaw hunting for food didn't move in straight lines. A wild predator would have circled, tested, approached from downwind. This animal had come in fast, done maximum damage in minimum time, and left.

It had been sent.

Cade looked at Elysian. The old tracker was crouched beside the tracks, studying them. He ran his fingers along the edge of one print, then stood and followed the trail toward the north wall. When he came back, his face was unreadable — but his eyes found Cade's across the torchlight, and in them Cade saw confirmation. Elysian had seen it too. The straight line. The precision. The pattern of an animal following instructions, not instinct.

Neither of them said a word. Not here. Not now. Not with half the village watching.

Fenvar arrived within minutes, Kaelthas at his side. The chief took in the scene — the dead stoneshells, the destroyed pen, the terrified family — and his face hardened into something Cade hadn't seen before. Anger. Real anger, the kind that a leader feels when his people have been hurt and he couldn't stop it.

"Double the guard," Fenvar ordered. "Torches on every wall section. No one leaves the village until daylight. I want trackers on those prints at first light."

"Of course, Chief," Kaelthas said. He was already moving, organizing, giving commands to the guards with the calm efficiency of a man who had been managing crises for twenty years. The perfect advisor. The indispensable man. Stepping into the chaos with steady hands and a clear voice while everyone else was shaking.

Cade watched him work and felt sick. This was the play. Create the crisis, then solve it. Make the people afraid, then be the one they turn to. Don had done it in a house. Kaelthas was doing it in a village. The scale was different. The technique was identical.

The emergency council met at dawn in the chief's hall. Cade wasn't invited, but the hall doors were open and half the village had crowded into the square outside, so he stood at the edge of the crowd with Elowen and listened. Elysian was inside — as the village's best tracker, his presence was expected. Sammy sat at Cade's feet, quiet for once, as if even the dog understood that this was not the time for wagging.

The elders spoke first. Fear dominated every voice — fear of the predators, fear of more attacks, fear that the walls weren't strong enough, that the guards weren't enough, that something fundamental had changed and Verdant Haven was no longer safe.

Then Kaelthas spoke. His voice carried through the open doors, measured and careful, every word placed with the precision of a man laying stones.

"We must consider all possibilities," Kaelthas said. "This is the third incident in recent months. Razormaw sightings where there have never been sightings. Livestock taken. And now a direct attack inside our walls. The question we must ask is — why now? What has changed?"

He paused. The pause was calculated — Cade could feel it, the way the silence drew every ear in the hall toward whatever came next.

"I do not wish to cast blame," Kaelthas said. "But we cannot ignore the truth. These incidents began shortly after the outsider arrived through the forest. We do not know what passage he came through, or what he may have brought with him. Is it possible — and I ask this with genuine concern, not accusation — that whatever doorway brought Cade to our vale also opened a path for predators that would otherwise have stayed in the deep north?"

Murmurs rippled through the crowd. Cade felt the eyes turning toward him — dozens of them, suspicious, frightened, looking for someone to blame.

A voice from the council — one of the older men, a farmer named Brennick whose fields bordered the north wall — spoke up.

"The boy should leave," Brennick said. "Send him into the forest. Let him find whatever passage brought him here and go back through it. We cannot risk our families for the sake of one outsider."

More murmurs. Agreement this time. Heads nodding. The tide of the room was turning, pushed by fear and aimed at the easiest target.

"He is a boy," another voice said. Torin. Quiet, steady Torin, who barely spoke at village gatherings, standing up in the chief's hall and saying more words in public than Cade had heard him say in two months. "He is a child, alone, far from his home. Sending him into the wild would be a death sentence. That is not who we are."

"Torin speaks with the bias of a man who houses the boy," Brennick said.

"Torin speaks with the conscience of a man who remembers the covenant," Torin said. His voice was still quiet, but it cut through the room like a blade. "We do not abandon those who need shelter. That is the first law of Verdant Haven. It was the first law before Brennick sat on this council, and it will be the first law after he is gone."

Silence. Brennick's face reddened, but he didn't respond.

Fenvar raised his hand. The hall went quiet.

"No one is being sent into the forest," Fenvar said. His voice was heavy with the weight of a man caught between competing pressures. "But I will speak with Cade Thompson directly. If there is any connection between his arrival and these attacks, we will determine it. Until then, the outsider remains under my protection — but also under my watch."

He paused, and when he spoke again, his words were clearly meant to carry through the open doors to where Cade was standing.

"If there is further trouble connected to the outsider," Fenvar said, "I will reconsider."

The council ended. The crowd dispersed. Cade stood in the square as villagers streamed past him, some avoiding his eyes, others staring openly with hostility they no longer bothered to hide.

Elowen gripped his arm. "He is framing you," Elowen said, her voice low and hard. "He released one of those razormaws to create panic, and now he is using that panic to push you out. If you are gone, there is no one left who knows what he is planning."

"I know," Cade said.

Elysian found them an hour later, behind Torin's barn, away from the paths and the eyes. The old tracker looked tired — he'd been up all night, first at the attack site, then at the council — but his eyes were sharp.

"The tracks confirm what you saw in the canyon," Elysian said to Cade. "That razormaw did not hunt its way into the village. It was brought to the north wall and released. The tracks outside the wall come from a single direction — north, in a straight line. No circling, no foraging, no deviation. An animal following a command."

"Can you tell Fenvar that?" Elowen asked.

"I told the council the tracks were unusual," Elysian said. "Kaelthas suggested the razormaw may have been desperate — starving, driven south by competition in the deep forest. His explanation was reasonable." The old man's mouth twisted slightly. "It is always reasonable."

"We go tonight," Cade said.

"We go tonight," Elysian agreed. "But the plan changes. Kaelthas struck first. He is moving faster than we expected. That means the compound will be active — more men, more patrols, more risk. We cannot afford mistakes."

He looked at Cade, then at Elowen.

"The dog cannot come," Elysian said. "He cannot move quietly in the forest. He will give us away."

Cade's hand went to Sammy's head. The reflex was instant — protective, instinctive. Sammy had been with him every day since they'd come through the portal. Every night. Every moment. The dog was his anchor, his compass, the one constant in a world that kept shifting under his feet.

"I know," Cade said. His throat was tight.

"He stays with my father," Elowen said. "Torin will keep him safe."

Cade looked down at Sammy. The dog looked back at him with those blue-brown eyes — calm, trusting, unaware that tonight his boy would walk into the dark without him for the first time since they'd come to this world.

"Okay," Cade said. "He stays."

Sammy's tail thumped once against the ground.

Elysian laid out the new approach. They would leave through the north gate two hours before dawn, when the guards changed shifts and attention was thinnest. They'd follow the creek bed north to mask their tracks, then cut east to approach the canyon from the high ground. They needed to be in position on the eastern ridge before daylight, observe the compound, and find physical evidence — a map, a planning document, anything with Kaelthas's mark on it that Fenvar could not explain away.

"We need something he cannot deny," Elysian said. "Something I can put in Fenvar's hand and say, this came from the compound where your advisor is training predators to kill your people. Words can be dismissed. Evidence cannot."

"And if they catch us?" Elowen asked.

Elysian looked at her with the honest, unflinching gaze of a man who did not soften the truth. "Then Kaelthas wins," Elysian said. "And Verdant Haven falls."

The three of them sat in silence for a moment. The weight of what they were about to do pressed down on them like the sky pressing down on the valley.

"Rest this afternoon," Elysian said. "Eat. Sleep if you can. We move at the fourth watch."

Cade and Elowen walked back toward the farmhouse without speaking. There was nothing left to say. The plan was made. The clock was running. And somewhere in the deep north, in a canyon full of caged predators, a man with a scar on his jaw was preparing to tear this village apart.

That evening, Cade sat on the floor of his room with Sammy. He held the dog's face in both hands and looked into those mismatched eyes — one blue, one brown, both steady, both trusting.

"I have to go somewhere tonight, boy," Cade said to the dog. "And you can't come. I know that doesn't make sense to you. It barely makes sense to me. But I need you to stay here and be good for Torin. Can you do that?"

Sammy licked his face.

"I'll take that as a yes," Cade said.

He held the dog for a long time. Longer than he needed to. Longer than he should have, with the clock ticking and the darkness coming and everything balanced on what happened in the next twelve hours.

Then he lay down, Sammy against his chest, and closed his eyes. He didn't think he'd sleep, but his body overruled his mind, and within minutes the exhaustion of the past two days dragged him under.

He dreamed of Maple Creek Drive. Of Eydan at the stove. Of Ashen's grocery receipt drawings. Of Carla's text — Tomorrow works! I'll bring snacks — glowing on a screen that would never light up again.

And then someone was shaking his shoulder, and Elowen's voice was in his ear, quiet and firm.

"Cade," Elowen whispered. "It is time."

Chapter Fifteen - *Into the Dark*

They left through the north gate at the fourth watch, when the sky was still black and the torches along the wall had burned down to orange stubs.

Elysian went first. He moved through the gate like a shadow, exchanging a word with the night guard — something about checking tracks from the attack, following up before dawn. The guard nodded without question. Elysian Mosswood checking tracks in the dark was not unusual. Elysian Mosswood did what Elysian Mosswood wanted, and nobody in Verdant Haven had ever thought to stop him.

Cade and Elowen followed thirty seconds later, slipping through the gate while the guard's back was turned. They wore dark clothing borrowed from Torin's stores — leather and woven cloth, nothing that would catch light or make noise. Elowen had her bow and a quiver of arrows. Cade had his staff and his knife. Elysian carried nothing but his walking stick and the coil of braided hide cord slung over his shoulder.

Leaving Sammy had been the hardest thing Cade had done since arriving in Emerald Vale. He'd knelt on the floor of his room and held the dog's face and told him to stay with Torin, and Sammy had looked at him with those mismatched eyes and thumped his tail once and lain down on the bed as if he understood. Torin had appeared in the doorway and nodded — a silent promise, as binding as any oath. The dog would be safe.

But walking into the forest without Sammy felt like walking without a limb. Cade's hand kept reaching for the dog's collar and finding empty air.

They followed the creek bed north, wading ankle-deep through cold water that masked their scent and left no tracks on the bank. The forest closed around them, dense and dark, the canopy blocking even the faint starlight. Elysian navigated by memory and instinct, his feet finding the creek stones without hesitation, his body weaving through the undergrowth as if the forest were opening a path for him.

Nobody spoke. They had agreed on silence before leaving — hand signals only, taught to Cade and Elowen during the brief planning session before the attack had interrupted them. A closed fist meant stop. An open palm meant danger. A pointed finger meant direction. A flat hand waved downward meant get low.

For two hours they moved north. The creek narrowed and steepened as the terrain rose, the water running faster over rougher stones. The forest changed around them — the trees growing larger, the undergrowth thicker, the air heavier with the smell of deep earth and old growth. They were entering the deep north, the territory Elysian had warned Cade about weeks ago.

Twice they heard sounds that froze Cade's blood. The first was a low, grunting call from somewhere to the west — a predator, awake and hunting in the dark. Elysian held up a closed fist and they pressed against the trunk of a massive tree, motionless, barely breathing, until the sound faded. The second was worse — a scream, high and sharp, cut off abruptly. Something had caught something else in the dark. The forest was feeding, and they were walking through its kitchen.

After two hours, Elysian led them out of the creek bed and onto a ridge that ran east. The ground was rockier here, covered in low scrub instead of ferns, and they could move faster without fighting the undergrowth. The sky was still dark, but the eastern horizon had shifted from black to deep blue. Dawn was coming. They needed to be in position before the light arrived.

Elysian stopped at the edge of the ridge and crouched. Cade and Elowen dropped beside him. Below them, barely visible in the predawn gray, was the canyon.

It looked different from this angle. From the south, where Cade had first found it, the canyon had seemed small — a narrow cut in the rock with a handful of cages and four men. From the eastern ridge, looking down at the full layout, it was larger than he remembered.

The cages were still there — six of them along the far wall, each holding a razormaw. But there were more structures now, or maybe there had always been more and Cade simply hadn't seen them from his previous vantage point. A lean-to built against the south wall, large enough for several men to sleep under. A fire pit, cold now, with logs arranged around it for seating. A wooden rack near the cages holding the long control poles the handlers used. And at the north end of the canyon, partially hidden by an overhang of rock, a table.

Cade couldn't make out what was on the table from this distance. But it was a work surface — flat, covered in something, positioned where a man could stand and plan.

"There," Cade whispered, pointing at the table. It was the first word any of them had spoken in two hours.

Elysian nodded. His eyes were moving across the canyon floor, counting, assessing. He held up fingers. Two. Then pointed. Cade followed his gaze and saw them — two men, sitting near the fire pit, wrapped in blankets against the predawn chill. Guards. Night watch. One of them was awake, staring at nothing, a spear across his knees. The other was asleep, his head tilted back against a log.

Two guards. Six razormaws. And somewhere in the canyon or the surrounding forest, more of Kaelthas's men.

Elysian leaned close to Cade's ear. "The table," Elysian breathed. "Under the overhang. That is where we need to go. If there are maps or plans, they will be there."

"The guards," Cade whispered back.

"They are watching the south approach," Elysian said. "The slope where you came in before. They expect trouble from that direction. The eastern wall has a crack — a narrow gap in the rock, twenty feet down from where we are. It leads to the canyon floor behind the overhang. If we go through there, we come up behind the table. The guards will not see us unless they turn around."

"How do you know about the crack?" Elowen whispered.

Elysian gave her a look. "I have tracked animals through every canyon in the deep north for forty years," Elysian said. "I know this land better than Kaelthas's men ever will."

They waited. The sky brightened slowly — gray replacing black, the canyon floor emerging from shadow in stages. The awake guard shifted, stretched, and kicked the sleeping one. The sleeper grunted and sat up. They exchanged a few words Cade couldn't hear, and the first guard stood and walked toward the cages. Feeding time. The razormaws were stirring in their enclosures, pacing, snarling softly, smelling the morning.

"Now," Elysian breathed. "While they are at the cages. Move."

They moved along the ridge, crouching low, until Elysian found the crack — a vertical split in the canyon wall, narrow enough that they had to turn sideways to enter. The rock was cold and damp against Cade's chest and back, and for a terrible moment he was back between the boulders on Maple Creek Drive, squeezing through the gap that had brought him to this world. His breath caught. His hands shook.

Elowen's fingers found his wrist in the dark. She squeezed once. Steady. I'm here.

The crack opened onto the canyon floor behind the rock overhang, exactly where Elysian had said it would. They emerged into a pocket of shadow, hidden from the guards by the overhang itself and a stack of cut timber leaning against the wall.

The table was five feet away.

Cade moved first. He crouched and crossed the gap between the crack and the table in three quick steps, pressing himself flat against the rock wall beside it. Elowen followed. Elysian came last, moving with the silent grace of a man who had spent his entire life being invisible in the forest.

The table was a rough plank of wood set on stone supports. And on it, held down by small rocks to keep the wind from taking them, were exactly what they needed.

Maps. Three of them, drawn in charcoal on scraped hide — the same material Elysian used for his own maps. The first showed Verdant Haven from above, the village walls clearly marked, with arrows drawn in red clay pointing inward from three directions — north, south, and east. The three gates. The three points of attack. Beside each arrow, marks that Cade couldn't read but Elysian could — numbers, maybe, or unit designations.

The second map showed the canyon compound itself — the cages, the lean-to, the approaches, the guard positions. Notes were scrawled along the margins in a hand that was precise and practiced.

The third was not a map. It was a list. Names, written in a column, with marks beside each one. Some marks were simple dashes. Others were circles. And at the top of the list, underlined twice, was a single name.

Fenvar.

Beside it, a circle with a line through it. Even Cade, who couldn't read the written language of the vale, understood what that meant. The circle meant target. The line meant eliminate.

Elysian's face had gone white. Not with fear — with fury. A cold, controlled fury that tightened every muscle in his jaw and turned his dark eyes into something Cade had never seen there before. The old man who laughed at Sammy chasing butterflies, who teased Cade about his footwork, who smiled when Elowen beat him in sparring — that man was gone. In his place was someone harder. Someone dangerous.

"Take them," Elysian whispered. "All three."

Elowen carefully lifted the rocks and rolled the maps together. She slid them into the quiver on her back, nestled against the arrows where they wouldn't shift or rustle.

They were turning to leave when a voice came from the other side of the overhang. Close. Ten feet away, maybe less. A voice Cade recognized.

Kaelthas.

"— moved the timeline forward," Kaelthas was saying to someone. His voice was low but clear in the still morning air. "The boy found this place. He told Fenvar, and Fenvar dismissed it, but the old tracker was at the council. Mosswood is no fool. If he starts looking, he will find what the boy found. We cannot wait for the new moon."

"When, then?" another voice asked. Drennan. The scar-jawed man.

"Three days," Kaelthas said. "The village is afraid. The council is fractured. Fenvar is weakened. We move in three days. Release all six through the gates at dawn. My men inside the village will open the south gate. The north gate we breach with the largest razormaw — she can break timber that thick. The eastern fields are undefended."

"And Fenvar?" Drennan asked.

"I will handle Fenvar personally," Kaelthas said. His voice didn't change — the same smooth, measured tone he used for everything. The voice of a man discussing trade routes, not murder. "During the chaos, no one will notice. By the time the village understands what has happened, I will already be giving orders. I will already be in control."

Cade pressed his back against the rock wall and didn't breathe. Elowen was beside him, her hand on her bow, her face rigid. Elysian was motionless, his eyes closed, listening with the focus of a man memorizing every word.

"The outsider?" Drennan asked.

"The boy will be dealt with in the attack," Kaelthas said. "Make sure of it. Him and whoever is harboring him. Torin's farm is on the eastern edge. The razormaws will pass through there first."

Elowen's hand tightened on her bow. Cade saw her knuckles go white. Her father's farm. Kaelthas was planning to run trained predators through her father's farm.

Cade put his hand on her arm. Not now. Not here. She looked at him, and for a moment the fury in her eyes was so bright it almost burned. Then she swallowed it. Pushed it down. Held it where it couldn't get them killed.

Footsteps moved away from the overhang. Kaelthas and Drennan were walking toward the cages, their voices fading.

Elysian opened his eyes. He pointed at the crack in the wall. *Go. Now.*

They went. Single file, through the crack, up the canyon wall, onto the ridge. They moved fast — faster than they'd come in, caution sacrificed for speed, because what they'd heard changed everything. Not the new moon. Not ten days. Three days. They had three days.

They didn't stop until they reached the creek crossing, a full hour south of the canyon. Elysian finally halted behind the lightning-scarred oak — the same tree Cade had collapsed against weeks ago after his first panicked flight from the compound.

Cade was breathing hard. Elowen was breathing hard. Elysian looked like he'd been out for a morning walk.

"Three days," Cade said.

"Three days," Elysian confirmed.

Elowen pulled the maps from her quiver and unrolled them on the ground. In the growing daylight, the details were clear — the attack routes, the compound layout, the list of names with Fenvar's at the top. It was all there. Everything Kaelthas had built, laid out in charcoal and red clay on scraped hide.

"This is enough," Elysian said, looking at the maps. "This is more than enough. Fenvar will not be able to deny this. No reasonable explanation covers attack routes drawn on maps of his own village with his name circled for death."

"We heard Kaelthas himself," Elowen said. "All three of us. His voice. His words. His plan."

"Three witnesses and physical evidence," Elysian said. "Even twenty years of trust cannot stand against that."

The old man rolled the maps carefully and held them against his chest. His hands were steady. His eyes were hard.

"We go to Fenvar," Elysian said. "Now. Before Kaelthas returns to the village. Before he has time to prepare another lie."

They moved south through the forest, toward Verdant Haven, toward the chief who needed to hear the truth before it was too late. The sun was rising through the canopy, painting the forest floor in gold and green. Birds were calling. The insects were humming. The world was waking up, beautiful and ancient and completely indifferent to the fact that three people were carrying the evidence that would save or destroy a village.

Cade thought about Sammy, waiting at Torin's farm. He thought about Torin, who had stood up in the chief's hall and defended a stranger because it was the right thing to do. He thought about Aldric's children, clutching their mother in the doorway while their father shook with a spear in his hands. He thought about every person in Verdant Haven who had no idea what was coming for them in three days.

And he thought about Don. About the years of silence. The years of looking the other way. The years of nobody listening, nobody believing, nobody stepping in to stop what was happening in a house on Maple Creek Drive.

Not this time.

This time, someone was going to listen. And if they didn't, Cade would make them.

Chapter Sixteen - *The Evidence*

They reached the village gate as the sun cleared the canopy.

The morning guard saw Elysian first and straightened. Then he saw Cade and Elowen behind him — dirt on their clothes, sweat on their faces, the look of people who had been somewhere they shouldn't have been — and his hand moved to his spear.

"Stand down," Elysian said to the guard without breaking stride. "We need to see the chief. Now."

The guard hesitated. His eyes moved from Elysian to Cade, and Cade saw the suspicion there — the outsider, the troublemaker, the boy half the village wanted gone. But Elysian Mosswood was not a man you argued with at the gate, and the guard stepped aside.

They crossed the village at a pace just short of running. People were beginning their morning routines — fires being lit, water being drawn, the first farmers heading toward the eastern fields. A few turned to watch the three of them pass. Cade kept his eyes forward and his mouth shut.

Elysian stopped at the door of the chief's hall and turned to Cade and Elowen.

"Let me speak first," Elysian said. "Fenvar trusts me. If I present this, he will listen. If the boy who accused his advisor two days ago walks in leading the charge, his walls go up before a word is spoken."

"I understand," Cade said.

"You will have your moment," Elysian said. "But let me open the door."

He turned to the guards at the entrance. "I need a private audience with Chief Fenvar," Elysian said. "Immediately. No one else present."

The taller guard frowned. "Kaelthas is usually —"

"No one else present," Elysian repeated. His voice didn't rise, but something in it shifted — a weight, an authority that had nothing to do with rank and everything to do with forty years of being the man this village turned to when things went wrong. "Tell the chief it is urgent. Tell him Elysian Mosswood is calling in a debt."

The guard disappeared inside. Two minutes later, he returned and held the door open.

The hall was empty except for Fenvar. The chief was standing beside the cold fire pit, dressed in a plain shirt and leather trousers, his hair untied — he'd been roused from his private quarters. His face carried the heavy fatigue of a man who had not slept well since the attack on Aldric's farm. When he saw Elysian, his expression shifted to attention.

When he saw Cade and Elowen behind him, it shifted to something harder.

"Elysian," Fenvar said. "You said urgent. And you bring the boy."

"I bring the boy because the boy was right," Elysian said. "And I was too slow to see it. Sit down, Fenvar. What I am about to show you will test every bond you have built in twenty years."

Fenvar didn't sit. He stood with his arms at his sides, watching Elysian with the steady, unblinking focus of a man bracing for a blow.

Elysian unrolled the maps on the floor of the hall, one beside the other, smoothing them flat with his palms. The charcoal lines and red clay arrows were stark against the pale hide. He said nothing for a moment, letting the maps speak for themselves.

Fenvar looked down. His eyes moved across the first map — the overhead view of Verdant Haven, the village walls, the three red arrows pointing inward from the north, south, and east gates. His jaw tightened. He crouched and touched one of the arrows with his fingertip, tracing it from the gate to the village center.

"Where did you get these?" Fenvar asked. His voice was quiet, controlled, but there was something underneath it that hadn't been there before — a tremor, faint, like the ground shaking before an earthquake.

"From a compound in the deep north," Elysian said. "A hidden canyon, four hours beyond the stone ridge. Six razormaws held in cages, trained with commands by handlers using control poles. A planning table under a rock overhang where these maps were held down with stones. The three of us were there before dawn this morning. We took these from that table."

Fenvar's eyes moved to the second map — the compound layout. Then to the third. The list of names. His own name at the top, underlined twice, with a circle and a line through it.

The chief stared at his own name for a long time. The hall was silent. Cade could hear his own heartbeat.

"This is Kaelthas's hand," Fenvar said finally, his finger on the writing along the margins of the compound map. It was not a question.

"Yes," Elysian said. "I have seen his writing a thousand times. On trade agreements. On supply requests. On the very documents he brings to your table every week. That is his hand."

Fenvar stood. He turned away from the maps and walked three steps toward the wall. He put his hand flat against the timber and stood there, his back to them, his head bowed. The muscles in his shoulders were tight as rope.

Cade understood what was happening. He'd seen it before — not in a chief's hall, but in a living room on Maple Creek Drive. The moment when the truth breaks through and everything you believed about someone collapses. The moment Eydan had finally stopped making excuses for Don and looked at her children and saw what he'd done to them. The moment the wall between what you know and what you've been refusing to know comes down, and the wreckage on the other side is worse than you imagined.

Twenty years. Fenvar had trusted Kaelthas for twenty years. Had leaned on him, confided in him, built a village with him. And the man had been building a knife to put in his back the entire time.

"There is more," Elysian said. His voice was gentle now — not soft, Elysian was never soft, but careful, the way you speak to a man who has just been gutted. "We heard Kaelthas at the compound. His voice. His words. All three of us."

Elysian laid it out. The accelerated timeline. Three days instead of the new moon. All six razormaws released at dawn through three gates simultaneously. Men inside the village to open the south gate. The largest razormaw to breach the north. The eastern fields left undefended. Fenvar handled personally during the chaos. Kaelthas stepping in to take control.

Fenvar didn't move from the wall. His hand pressed harder against the timber. When Elysian finished, the silence in the hall was absolute.

Then Fenvar spoke. "Three days," Fenvar said.

"Three days," Elysian confirmed. "That is what he said. We heard it clearly."

Fenvar turned around. His face had changed. The fatigue was gone. The careful neutrality was gone. What was left was something raw and hard and dangerous — the face of a man who had been betrayed and was deciding what to do about it.

His eyes found Cade.

"You tried to tell me," Fenvar said to Cade. "Weeks ago. You stood in this hall and told me what Kaelthas was doing, and I chose his word over yours."

"You did what made sense," Cade said. "He'd been at your side for twenty years. I'd been here two months. I would have made the same choice."

It was the truth, and Fenvar heard it. Something in the chief's expression shifted — not gratitude, not yet, but recognition. The recognition of a man looking at someone who understood what it meant to be fooled by a person you trusted.

"How did you know?" Fenvar asked Cade. "Before the canyon. Before the maps. How did you know what he was?"

Cade was quiet for a moment. The question sat in the air between them, and he felt the weight of it — not just Fenvar's question, but the answer that lived underneath it. The answer that went back to a house on Maple Creek Drive and a man who smiled in public and destroyed in private.

"Because I have seen it before," Cade said. "In my world. A man who smiles to your face and tears everything apart when no one is looking. A man who makes everyone believe he is good while he is doing terrible things to the people closest to him. I know what that looks like. I know how it sounds. I know how it feels to be the only person who sees it and have nobody believe you."

His voice didn't waver. It didn't break. It was steady and clear and it carried the weight of every night he'd spent on Maple Creek Drive listening to his mother cry through the wall and knowing that nobody would help.

"I lived with a man like Kaelthas," Cade said. "For fourteen years. He was my father."And by the time he finally walked out, he had already broken everything that mattered."The hall was silent. Elowen was looking at Cade with those amber eyes, and there were tears in them — not pity, not sadness, but something fiercer. Pride, maybe. Or love. Cade didn't look at her because if he did, the walls would come down completely, and he needed them up for a little while longer.

Elysian stood beside him, one hand on his walking stick, his face unreadable. But his free hand moved — slowly, deliberately — and came to rest on Cade's shoulder. The weight of it was warm and steady and said everything the old man's mouth didn't.

Fenvar looked at Cade for a long time. Then he nodded. Once. A firm, final gesture.

"I believe you," Fenvar said. "And I am sorry I did not believe you sooner."

He turned to Elysian. The chief's voice hardened, shifting from the man who had been wounded to the leader who needed to act.

"Kaelthas does not know we have these maps," Fenvar said.

"Not yet," Elysian said. "But he will notice they are missing. Today, tomorrow at most. Once he does, he may accelerate again. We cannot assume we have three full days."

"Then we do not wait," Fenvar said. "I will send scouts to confirm the compound. My own men — warriors I trust with my life, men Kaelthas has never touched. If they find what you describe, we move against him before he can strike."

"The scouts should go immediately," Elysian said. "I can guide them to the canyon by nightfall."

"Do it," Fenvar said. He looked at the maps on the floor one more time. His own name, circled for death by the hand of a man he'd called brother. Then he looked up, and the man standing in the chief's hall was not the cautious, measured leader who had dismissed Cade's accusations weeks ago. This was a chief who had been given the truth and was prepared to act on it.

"Kaelthas built this in my shadow," Fenvar said. "In the trust I gave him. He used that trust as a weapon. That ends now."

He turned to Cade. "You have done this village a service I can never fully repay, Cade Thompson. Whatever you need, whatever you ask, Verdant Haven owes you a debt."

Cade shook his head. "I don't want a debt," Cade said. "I want the people in this village to be safe. That's enough."

Fenvar studied him. Something moved behind the chief's eyes — respect, maybe, or wonder, or the simple recognition of a boy who had been through more than any fourteen-year-old should have endured and had come out the other side with his spine intact.

"Your father," Fenvar said quietly. "The man you spoke of. He did not deserve a son like you."

Cade didn't answer. He couldn't. The walls he'd been holding up were cracking, and if he opened his mouth, what came out wouldn't be words.

Elysian's hand tightened on his shoulder. Elowen moved to his side and stood there, close enough that her arm touched his. Sammy wasn't here, but the warmth Cade felt in that moment was the same warmth the dog had always given him — the warmth of being known, being seen, being believed.

"Go," Fenvar said to Elysian. "Take the scouts. Confirm the compound. Report back to me by morning. And Elysian — if you encounter Kaelthas's men in the forest, do what you must."

Elysian nodded. He squeezed Cade's shoulder once more, then released it and walked toward the door. At the threshold, he turned.

"Cade," Elysian said.

"Yeah?" Cade said.

"Go see your dog," Elysian said. "He has been waiting all night."

Then the old tracker was gone, moving through the village with the quiet purpose of a man who had work to do and no intention of wasting a single moment.

Cade and Elowen walked back to Torin's farm. The village was fully awake now, people moving through their morning routines, unaware that the ground beneath them was about to shift. They passed Maren on the path near the well. The girl looked at Elowen, then at Cade, then looked away. Something in her expression was different from the hostility of the past few days — not friendliness, not yet, but uncertainty. A crack.

Torin was at the gate of his farm, feeding the stoneshells. Sammy was beside him, sitting patiently, tail wagging the moment he saw Cade coming up the path. The dog broke from Torin's side and sprinted toward Cade with the full-body, ear-flapping, tail-whipping joy of a dog who had been waiting for his person and was not going to wait one second longer.

Cade dropped to his knees and caught Sammy in his arms. The dog licked his face, his neck, his ears, whining and wiggling and pressing against him with every ounce of his forty-five pounds. Cade held him and buried his face in the dog's fur and breathed, and for a moment the canyon and the maps and the three-day countdown and the weight of everything he'd just said in the chief's hall fell away, and it was just a boy and his dog on a warm morning in a world that didn't make sense but somehow, right now, in this moment, felt like home.

"I told you I'd come back," Cade said to the dog.

Sammy's tail answered for him.

Chapter Seventeen - *The Calm Before*

Elysian returned the next morning with two of Fenvar's most trusted warriors. The three of them came through the north gate at first light, covered in mud and forest grime, their faces drawn tight with what they had seen.

Cade was at the gate waiting. He hadn't slept. He'd sat on the bench outside Torin's farmhouse all night with Sammy in his lap, watching the northern sky, counting the hours.

Elysian saw him and nodded once. That was all Cade needed. The scouts had found the compound. The cages. The razormaws. Everything.

The meeting with Fenvar happened behind closed doors. Only Elysian, the two warriors, and the chief were present. Cade and Elowen waited outside the hall in the morning cold, Sammy between them, watching the door and saying nothing.

When the door opened, one of the warriors came out first. He was a broad man named Gareth, with arms like tree limbs and a face built for silence. He looked at Cade as he passed. Then he did something Cade didn't expect — he put his fist against his chest, knuckles over his heart, and dipped his head. A salute. The gesture of one warrior acknowledging another.

Cade didn't know how to respond. He nodded, and Gareth moved on.

Elysian came out next. He looked exhausted — the first time Cade had ever seen the old man show fatigue. But his eyes were sharp and his voice was steady.

"Fenvar has seen enough," Elysian said to Cade and Elowen. "His scouts confirmed everything. The compound, the cages, the razormaws, the handlers. They even watched a training session from the ridge — commands, whistles, the animals responding. There is no room left for doubt."

"What happens now?" Elowen asked.

"Fenvar is preparing," Elysian said. "Quietly. He is pulling his most trusted warriors aside, one at a time, briefing them in private. By tonight, he will have thirty men ready to move. Kaelthas has maybe a dozen, plus the razormaws. The numbers favor us, but the predators change the calculation."

"Does Kaelthas know?" Cade asked.

"Not yet," Elysian said. "But he will. A man like Kaelthas has eyes everywhere. We have a day, maybe two, before he realizes the ground has shifted under him. When he does, he will either run or strike. I do not think he is the kind of man who runs."

Cade didn't think so either. Kaelthas had spent years building this — the network, the compound, the plan. A man who invested that much didn't walk away. He doubled down. He accelerated. He burned the house down rather than let someone else live in it.

Don had done the same thing. On the last night, the night before he'd finally walked out, Don had broken every dish in the kitchen. Not because he was angry at the dishes. Because if he couldn't have control, then nobody would have anything at all.

Fenvar emerged from the hall. The chief looked like he'd aged five years overnight, but there was iron in his posture and fire in his eyes. He stopped in front of Cade.

"The village will learn the truth today," Fenvar said to Cade. "I will address the council this afternoon. Kaelthas will not be present — I will make sure of that. By sundown, Verdant Haven will know what its advisor has been building in the dark."

"What about Kaelthas?" Cade asked.

"I will deal with Kaelthas," Fenvar said. The words were flat and heavy, like stones being laid on a grave. "He has been summoned to a meeting with the trade delegation at the south settlement. A false errand. It will keep him outside the village until midday. By the time he returns, the council will know, and he will walk into a village that no longer trusts him.”

“And if he doesn’t come back?” Elowen asked. “If he goes to the compound instead?”

“Then he has made his choice,” Fenvar said. “And we will be ready.”

The chief turned and went back inside. The door closed behind him, and the weight of what was coming settled over the village like a storm cloud that hadn’t broken yet.

The rest of the morning passed in a strange, suspended quiet. The village went about its business — farmers in the fields, children in the paths, cooking fires burning — but underneath the routine, something was different. Cade could feel it. A tension in the air, like the forest before a predator’s roar. People moved a little faster. Conversations were a little shorter. The guards on the wall stood a little straighter.

Fenvar’s warriors were invisible in their preparation. Cade saw none of the organizing, none of the briefings, none of the weapons being checked and sharpened in quiet rooms behind closed doors. Fenvar was doing exactly what a good leader did — preparing for war without letting the enemy know it was coming.

Cade spent the morning at the farm, helping Torin with the stoneshells. The big animals were restless — Bruna paced her pen instead of grazing, and Korr, who normally stood in the sun with his eyes closed, was alert, his heavy head turning at every sound. Animals knew. They always knew before people did.

Torin worked beside Cade in silence. The farmer hadn't asked questions when Cade and Elowen had returned from the canyon, hadn't asked questions when Elysian took them to the chief's hall, hadn't asked questions about any of it. He just kept working. Kept feeding. Kept doing what needed to be done. And when Cade looked at the man — quiet, steady, reliable Torin, with his scarred hands and his closed mouth and his open door — he felt something he'd been feeling more and more since coming to Verdant Haven, something he'd never felt on Maple Creek Drive.

Safe. He felt safe around a grown man.

That afternoon, while Fenvar addressed the council behind closed doors, Elowen found Cade behind the barn.

"Come with me," Elowen said.

She led him up the narrow trail to the ridge — her ridge, the spot overlooking the valley where she'd taken him weeks ago. Sammy bounded ahead of them, crashing through the ferns with his usual graceless enthusiasm. The sun was warm, the sky clear, and the valley stretched out below them in every shade of green the world had to offer.

They sat on the flat rock at the edge. The same rock they'd sat on when Cade had told her about Ashen and Eydan. The same rock where she'd said "good" about Don's leaving and it had been the exact right thing to say.

For a long time, neither of them spoke. The valley hummed. The wind moved through the grass. A herd of the long-necked herbivores drifted across the distant plains like ships on a green sea.

"Are you afraid?" Elowen asked Cade.

Cade thought about it. Not the quick, reflexive answer — the real one.

"Yes," Cade said. "But not the way I used to be afraid. When I lived with my father, I was afraid all the time, but it was a small fear — waiting for the next hit, the next explosion, the next bad night. It made me smaller. It made me curl up inside myself and disappear."

He looked out at the valley. "This is different. I'm afraid of what's coming, but the fear doesn't make me want to hide. It makes me want to fight. I didn't know fear could do that."

"That is because you are not the same boy who came through the forest two months ago," Elowen said to him.

"No," Cade said. "I'm not."

He meant it. The boy who had walked home from Ridgewood High with his head down, who had kept Carla at arm's length because getting close to people meant getting hurt, who had flinched when a man raised his hand too fast — that boy was still inside him. He always would be. But something had grown around him, like bark growing over a wound in a tree. Not hiding the wound. Protecting it. Making it part of something stronger.

Elysian had given him that. Torin had given him that. Elowen had given him that. And Sammy — Sammy had started it all, by staring at a tree line behind a house on Maple Creek Drive and refusing to look away.

Elowen reached over and took his hand. Her fingers were calloused and strong and warm, and they fit against his like they'd been designed to. Cade didn't pull away. He didn't flinch. He didn't build a wall. He just held her hand and looked at the valley and let himself feel something he'd been running from his entire life.

Connection. Trust. The terrifying, beautiful risk of letting someone in.

"Whatever happens tomorrow," Elowen said, "you are not alone in it. You know that."

"I know," Cade said. And for the first time, he believed it.

They sat on the ridge until the sun dropped behind the mountains and the valley turned gold, then orange, then deep blue. Then they walked back to the village together, hand in hand, Sammy trotting ahead of them with his tail high.

Elysian was waiting at the gate of Torin's farm. The old tracker was leaning against the fence, his arms crossed, watching them approach with an expression that held a dozen things at once — warmth, worry, pride, and something that looked like a man watching two young people walk toward a future he couldn't guarantee.

"Walk with me," Elysian said to Cade.

They walked along the inside of the village wall, away from the paths, away from the ears. Sammy padded between them, nose to the ground.

"Fenvar told the council," Elysian said. "The reaction was what you would expect. Shock. Anger. Denial from some, fury from others. Brennick — the one who wanted you expelled — wept. He has known Kaelthas for fifteen years."

"And Kaelthas?" Cade asked.

"He has not returned from the south settlement," Elysian said. "Fenvar's men are watching the roads. If he comes back, they will see him. If he goes to the compound, we will know."

They walked in silence for a few paces. Then Elysian stopped. He reached into the leather pouch at his belt and pulled out something wrapped in a piece of soft hide. He held it out to Cade.

Cade unwrapped it. Inside was a knife. Not the training blade Elysian had given him weeks ago — this was different. The handle was dark wood, carved to fit a hand, wrapped in thin leather cord. The blade was stone, but not rough — it had been shaped with extraordinary care, the edge worked to a razor line that caught the fading light like glass. Along the spine of the blade, three small marks had been etched into the stone — symbols Cade didn't recognize.

"I made this," Elysian said. "Years ago. I have carried it, but I have never given it to anyone. The marks on the spine are my name in the old script. When you carry this blade, you carry my name with you."

Cade looked at the knife. Then at Elysian. The old man's face was steady, his dark eyes holding something Cade had never seen directed at him from a grown man — not authority, not expectation, not the threat of consequences. Just quiet, unconditional pride.

"You have earned this," Elysian said to Cade.

Cade's hand closed around the handle. The wood was smooth and warm, like it had been waiting for him. His throat was tight and his eyes burned and he didn't trust his voice, so he just nodded.

Elysian put his hand on Cade's shoulder. The same gesture. The same weight. The weight of a father who chose to be one, not because of blood, but because of something stronger.

"When this is over," Elysian said, "you and I are going to sit by a fire and I am going to tell you things about this forest that no one else knows. And you are going to listen, because you are my student, and my students do not waste my time."

Cade almost smiled. Almost. "Yes, Elysian," Cade said.

"Good," Elysian said. "Now go to bed. Tomorrow will be a hard day."

Cade went to bed. He lay in the dark with Sammy beside him, the new knife under his pillow, the weight of it solid and real against his hand. Through the hide flap over the window, he could hear the village settling into what might be its last quiet night.

Somewhere beyond the walls, Kaelthas was making his decision. Stay or strike. Run or fight. And Cade knew, with the certainty of a boy who had lived with a man just like him, that Kaelthas would not run. Men like Kaelthas never ran. They burned.

Tomorrow, the fire would come. And Cade would be standing in it.

He closed his eyes. Sammy's heartbeat was steady against his ribs. The knife was warm under his pillow. And somewhere in the deep north, in a canyon full of caged predators, a man with gray eyes was lighting the match.

Chapter Eighteen - *Kaelthas Strikes*

Kaelthas never went to the south settlement.

Fenvar's watchers on the south road reported that the advisor and his escort had turned off the trail less than an hour out, circling east through the forest. By midmorning, they had disappeared into the deep north. By noon, Fenvar's men lost the trail entirely.

The report came to the chief's hall just as the council session ended. Cade was outside with Elowen when Elysian appeared in the doorway, his face tight.

"He knows," Elysian said. "He found the maps missing from the table. He never went south. He went straight to the compound."

"How long do we have?" Cade asked.

Elysian looked at the sky. The sun was past its peak, the afternoon light slanting through the canopy. "The compound is four hours from the village on foot. If Kaelthas reached it by midmorning, and if he decides to move immediately —"

"Tonight," Elowen said. "He comes tonight."

"Or dawn tomorrow," Elysian said. "Predators hunt best in low light. Dawn or dusk. If I were Kaelthas, I would move the razormaws through the forest tonight and attack at first light."

The village shifted into a different gear. Fenvar gave the order within the hour — quiet, controlled, delivered through his trusted warriors to every corner of Verdant Haven. Women and children to the stone storehouse at the village center, the most defensible building inside the walls. Warriors to their positions on the walls, at the gates, at every vulnerable point Kaelthas's maps had identified. Farmers brought their stoneshells inside the inner ring. The cooking fires were doused. The village horn was readied.

Cade helped where he could. He hauled water to the wall positions. He carried bundles of spears to the guard stations. He helped Torin move the stoneshells from the outer pens to the inner yard, the big animals bellowing their displeasure at being crowded together. Bruna nearly knocked him flat with a swing of her armored tail, and Torin caught his arm and pulled him clear without a word.

As the sun dropped, the village took on the tense, held-breath quality of a place waiting for something terrible. People moved quickly and spoke in low voices. Children clung to their mothers. The warriors on the walls stood with their spears ready and their eyes on the tree line.

Elowen found Cade at the eastern wall as the last light faded. She had her bow, her quiver full, and a short blade on her hip that Cade hadn't seen before.

"My mother's," Elowen said, touching the blade. "My father kept it. He gave it to me an hour ago and told me to come home alive."

"That's a good plan," Cade said.

"I thought so," Elowen said.

They stood on the wall together and watched the forest darken. Sammy was at Cade's feet, pressed against his leg. Cade had tried to leave the dog with Torin in the storehouse, but Sammy had refused — had planted his feet and pulled against the rope and barked until Torin had shaken his head and untied him.

"The dog has decided," Torin had said. "I am not going to argue with him."

So Sammy was here, on the wall, where he shouldn't be and where he absolutely needed to be. Cade's hand rested on the dog's head, and the warmth of it steadied him in ways nothing else could.

The night came. Full dark. No moon — the clouds had rolled in at sunset, thick and heavy, blotting out the stars. The torches on the wall created pools of flickering light that didn't reach far enough. Beyond them, the forest was a wall of black.

The hours crawled. Midnight passed. The cold deepened. Warriors shifted on their feet, rubbed their hands, whispered to each other. The tension was a living thing, coiled in every muscle, pressing on every chest. Cade's hand found the hilt of Elysian's knife under his shirt — the blade with the old man's name on the spine — and gripped it.

Elysian was somewhere on the north wall. Fenvar was at the main gate with his best warriors. Torin was in the storehouse with the families, standing guard with his heavy staff. Everyone was where they needed to be.

The attack came at dawn.

Not the slow gray dawn of a normal morning. This dawn was still dark, the sky barely shifting from black to charcoal, the first faint suggestion of light touching the eastern clouds. The moment when the night creatures were returning to their dens and the day creatures hadn't yet emerged. The moment when the forest was quietest and the eyes were weakest.

Sammy heard it first. The dog's head came up from Cade's feet, ears forward, body rigid. A low growl built in his chest — not the warning growl he'd given Kaelthas in the village square weeks ago, but something deeper. Something primal. The sound of an animal recognizing a predator.

Then Cade heard it. A sound from the north wall — a deep, resonant boom, like a battering ram hitting a wooden gate. Then another. Then a third, harder, and with it the shriek of splintering timber.

The village horn sounded. Three long bellows that split the predawn silence and sent birds screaming from the canopy.

And then the razormaws came.

The north gate broke first. The largest razormaw — the one Kaelthas had kept for breaching — "hit the timber like a charging stoneshell" Cade didn't see it from the eastern wall, but he heard it — the crack of logs shattering, the roar of the animal, and underneath it the screams of the warriors who had been standing behind the gate when it came apart.

The south gate opened from inside. Kaelthas's men within the village — the ones who had been hiding among the population, waiting for this moment — threw the bar and swung the gate wide. Two razormaws poured through, moving fast, their dark hides blending with the predawn shadows.

And through the eastern fields, where no gate existed and the wall was lowest, came three more. They leaped the wall like it was nothing — powerful hind legs launching them over the timber in single bounds, landing in the village with the focused precision of animals that had been trained to do exactly this.

Six razormaws inside the walls. And behind them, through the broken north gate and the opened south gate, came Kaelthas's men. A dozen of them, armed with spears and clubs, faces covered in dark paint, moving with the discipline of soldiers.

Verdant Haven erupted into chaos.

The razormaws did what they'd been trained to do. "They spread through the village in pairs, each taking a different section, tearing through fences and pens, destroying everything in their path as they drove toward the village center.

The sound was indescribable — roaring, screaming, the crash of structures being torn apart, the bellowing of terrified stoneshells. Torchlight flickered and jumped as warriors ran to meet the threat, their spears leveled, their faces white.

Cade was moving before he fully understood what was happening. He dropped off the eastern wall and hit the ground running, Sammy beside him. An explosion of noise came from the path ahead — a razormaw, tearing through a fence, its jaws snapping at a warrior who was backpedaling desperately, thrusting his spear to keep the animal at distance.

Cade didn't think. His body moved the way Elysian had trained it to move — fast, low, controlled. He came at the razormaw from the side, driving his staff into the animal's flank with every ounce of force he had. The blow landed hard. The razormaw whipped its head around, snarling, and for one terrible second Cade was looking directly into the eyes of a predator that weighed three times what he did and was built to kill things exactly his size.

The warrior recovered. His spear found the razormaw's shoulder, and the animal screamed and twisted away, retreating down the path. Not dead. Not stopped. Just redirected. Angry and redirected.

The warrior looked at Cade. It was one of Fenvar's men — a young man, barely older than Cade, with blood running from a gash on his forearm.

"Thank you," the warrior said.

"Move," Cade said. "More coming."

They separated. The warrior ran toward the north gate. Cade ran toward the farm.

Toward Torin's farm. On the eastern edge. Where Kaelthas had said the razormaws would pass through first.

He heard Elowen before he saw her. The sharp snap of a bowstring, then another, then a third — fast, rhythmic, the sound of someone firing with precision under pressure. He came around the corner of the barn and found her.

Elowen was standing on the roof of the stoneshell pen, firing down at a razormaw that was circling the base. The animal was smaller than the one at the gate — younger, faster, but less armored. Two of Elowen's arrows were buried in its hide, one in the shoulder and one in the haunch. The razormaw was limping but not stopping, its eyes fixed on the girl above it, its jaws snapping at the air.

Elowen drew again. The arrow took the razormaw through the neck. The animal staggered, coughed, and went down on its side. Its legs kicked twice. Then it was still.

Elowen looked at Cade from the roof. Her braid had come half undone and her face was streaked with dust and her eyes were blazing.

"There are two more near the storehouse," Elowen said. "Fenvar's men are holding them off, but they need help."

"Where is your father?" Cade asked.

"Inside the storehouse," Elowen said. "With the families. He is safe."

A sound from behind the barn froze both of them. A low, guttural growl — close, too close, coming from the narrow gap between the barn and the outer wall. Sammy's hackles went up. The dog backed toward Cade, growling, his body low.

A razormaw stepped out of the shadows.

This one was different from the others. Bigger. Heavier. Its hide was scarred and mottled, the patterns broken by old wounds that had healed into ridges of pale tissue. Its eyes were fixed on Sammy with the cold focus of a predator that had identified the weakest target.

The razormaw lunged at the dog.

Cade didn't think. He didn't plan. He didn't calculate distance or angle or risk. He threw himself between the razormaw and Sammy, driving Elysian's knife forward with both hands. The blade caught the animal below the jaw, sinking into the soft tissue of the throat. The razormaw's momentum carried it forward, slamming into Cade's chest and driving him backward into the dirt.

The weight was crushing. The animal's jaws snapped inches from his face — rows of serrated teeth, hot breath, the copper smell of blood. Cade held the knife handle with everything he had, twisting, pushing deeper. The razormaw thrashed above him, claws raking the ground on either side of his body, its roar turning into a wet, choking gurgle.

An arrow appeared in the razormaw's eye. Then another in its neck. The animal shuddered, spasmed, and collapsed. Its full weight landed on Cade and drove the air from his lungs.

He couldn't breathe. He couldn't move. The world went gray around the edges, compressed to the smell of blood and the weight of dead muscle pressing down on him.

Then the weight shifted. Elowen was there, pulling the carcass off him, her hands gripping the razormaw's hide and dragging it sideways. Cade gasped, sucked air, rolled onto his side. Sammy was there instantly, licking his face, whining, pressing against him.

"Cade," Elowen said. Her voice was sharp with fear. "Are you hurt? Cade, look at me."

He looked at her. The world stabilized. The gray receded. He was alive. He was breathing. And Sammy was alive, because Cade had done the one thing he had always wished someone would do for him — he had stepped between the danger and the one he loved without hesitating.

"I'm okay," Cade said.

He wasn't sure that was true. His chest ached where the razormaw had hit him, and his hands were shaking, and there was blood on his shirt that might have been the animal's or might have been his. But he was standing. He was breathing. And the razormaw was dead.

Elowen pulled him to his feet. Her hand found his and squeezed hard, just for a second, and then she let go and nocked another arrow.

"The storehouse," Elowen said. "We need to move."

They ran. Through the farm, past the dead razormaw, past the splintered fence and the bellowing stoneshells.

Sammy ran beside Cade, limping slightly — had the razormaw clipped him? Cade couldn't tell and couldn't stop to check.

The village center was a war zone. "Two razormaws were circling the storehouse, testing for a way in. Fenvar's warriors had formed a line in front of the building, spears out, shields locked, keeping the predators from reaching the doors. Behind them, through the cracks in the storehouse walls, Cade could hear children crying.

Fenvar was at the center of the line. The chief held a spear in one hand and a bone-handled axe in the other, and the man standing in the torchlight was not the cautious, measured leader Cade had met in the hall weeks ago. This was a warrior. A chief who had been betrayed by the man he trusted most, and who was channeling twenty years of broken trust into the kind of fury that could hold a line against trained predators.

"Hold!" Fenvar roared. "Hold the line! They do not get through!"

The warriors held. The razormaws lunged and snapped and retreated, circling, looking for a gap that didn't exist. Elowen took position on a rooftop across the square and began firing — measured shots, placed with deadly accuracy, each one finding the weak spots in the razormaws' hides. One of the animals screamed and broke off its attack, three arrows buried in its flank. The other pressed harder, slamming into the shield line, and a warrior went down.

Cade charged in. He didn't join the shield line — he was too small, too light, he'd be crushed. Instead he flanked the razormaw, coming from the side the way Elysian had taught him, striking at the tendons of the animal's hind leg with his staff. The blow connected. The razormaw stumbled, its leg buckling. Fenvar's warriors surged forward, spears driving deep, and the animal went down thrashing and screaming.

The second razormaw, the one Elowen had wounded, turned and ran. It crashed through a fence and disappeared into the eastern fields, trailing blood. It wouldn't get far.

The square went quiet. Not silent — there were still sounds from other parts of the village, shouts and roars and the clash of weapons — but here, in front of the storehouse, the immediate threat was gone.

Fenvar looked at Cade. Blood on his face, fire in his eyes, and something that cut through the chaos like a blade.

"Kaelthas," Fenvar said. "He came through the north gate with his men. He is heading for the hall. He thinks he can take the seat while I am here defending the families."

The chief's jaw tightened. He turned to his warriors.

"Five men stay here," Fenvar ordered. "Protect the storehouse. Everyone else — with me. We end this now."

Fenvar moved toward the chief's hall at a dead run, his warriors behind him. Cade looked at Elowen on the rooftop. She looked back at him. No words. No hesitation.

She dropped from the roof, landed beside him, and they ran together — Cade, Elowen, and Sammy — toward the center of the village, toward Kaelthas, toward the end of everything that had been building since a boy and his dog had followed a trail into a canyon full of caged predators.

Chapter Nineteen-The Battle for Verdant Haven

The chief's hall was burning.

Not fully — not yet. Smoke poured from the open doorway, thick and dark, curling into the predawn sky. Someone had set fire to the tusk-framed entrance, and the flames were climbing the carved wood with a crackling hunger that lit the village square in shifting orange.

Kaelthas stood in the center of the square with eight of his men. They had formed a tight circle, spears out, facing the approaches on all sides. Three of Fenvar's warriors lay on the ground nearby — wounded or dead, Cade couldn't tell. The advisor himself stood at the center of his men, a long blade in his hand, his face stripped of every mask he'd ever worn. No warmth. No concern. No gentle smile. What was left was lean and sharp and utterly cold — the face of a man who had stopped pretending.

Fenvar arrived at the square from the west path, his warriors spreading out behind him. The chief didn't slow down. He walked straight toward Kaelthas's circle with the steady, unhurried pace of a man who had spent twenty years trusting the wrong person and intended to correct the mistake personally.

Cade and Elowen came from the east. They stopped at the edge of the square, behind a water trough, and took in the scene. Sammy pressed against Cade's leg, panting, his eyes locked on the men in the center.

Elysian appeared from the north. The old tracker emerged from the smoke near the burning hall, his staff in one hand, blood on his shirt that didn't appear to be his own. Behind him came four more warriors — the men who had been holding the north gate after the largest razormaw had broken through. They looked battered but standing.

Kaelthas was surrounded. His eight men against Fenvar's growing force. The math was simple. The outcome should have been inevitable.

But Kaelthas didn't look like a man who had lost.

"Fenvar," Kaelthas said. His voice carried across the square, smooth and clear, cutting through the crackle of the burning hall. "You should have stayed at the storehouse. You were safer there."

"Surrender," Fenvar said. The word was flat and final. "Your predators are dead or scattered. Your men inside the village have been taken. You are outnumbered and surrounded. Put down your weapon and face the council."

"The council," Kaelthas said. He almost smiled — a thin, bitter thing that held no warmth. "The council that has done nothing for twenty years while I built everything that keeps this village alive. The trade routes. The supply chains.

The alliances with the outer settlements. All mine, Fenvar. Every bit of prosperity this village enjoys came from my mind and my work. And what did you do? You sat in your chair and took the credit."

"I trusted you," Fenvar said. His voice cracked on the word. Not with weakness — with grief. The grief of a man standing across from someone he had loved like a brother and seeing a stranger. "I gave you everything. My trust. My authority. My friendship. And you used it to build a weapon aimed at my heart."

"Your trust was the weapon," Kaelthas said. "You gave it too freely. That was always your weakness, Fenvar. You believe in people. You believe they are good. You believe that if you treat them fairly, they will return the favor." He shook his head slowly. "They don't. They take. They use. And the ones smart enough to see that — the ones willing to do what must be done — those are the ones who should lead."

"You would have murdered me," Fenvar said. "You would have killed the people you ate with, worked beside, shared fires with for twenty years."

"I would have saved them," Kaelthas said. And for one terrible moment, Cade heard something in the advisor's voice that wasn't calculation or ambition. It was belief. Kaelthas believed his own words. He had built a story in his head where he was the hero, where the destruction was necessary, where the deaths were a price worth paying for the better world he intended to build on the ashes.

Don had believed it too. Standing in the kitchen after breaking every dish, he had looked at Eydan and said, "You made me do this." And he had meant it. He had genuinely believed that the woman he'd married was responsible for his violence, that the children he'd terrorized had brought it on themselves, that the destruction he caused was everyone's fault but his own.

The most dangerous men in any world were the ones who believed they were justified.

Fenvar raised his axe. "Last chance," Fenvar said. "Surrender. Or we take you down."

Kaelthas looked at Fenvar. Then at the warriors surrounding him. Then, for just a moment, his gray eyes found Cade at the edge of the square. Something flickered in them — recognition, hatred, the cold fury of a man whose plan had been undone by a fourteen-year-old boy and his dog.

"Drennan," Kaelthas said quietly.

The scar-jawed man broke from the circle and came straight at Cade.

He was fast. Faster than Cade expected. Drennan crossed the distance between the circle and the water trough in three long strides, his spear leveled, his scarred face twisted into something savage. He was twice Cade's size, hardened by years of rough living, and he was not coming to capture.

Cade barely got his staff up in time. The spear point glanced off the wood and drove past his ear, close enough to feel the wind. Cade pivoted, the way Elysian had taught him — don't block power with power, redirect it, let the bigger man's momentum carry him past you. Drennan stumbled forward half a step. Cade cracked the staff across the man's ribs.

Drennan grunted but didn't go down. He whipped the spear back around in a wide arc that would have taken Cade's head off if he hadn't ducked. The shaft whistled over him. Cade came up inside the arc, too close for the spear to be useful, and drove the butt of his staff into Drennan's stomach.

The man doubled over. Cade swung the staff high and brought it down on the back of Drennan's neck. The man dropped to his knees, then to his face, and didn't get up.

It had taken eight seconds. Eight seconds of everything Elysian had poured into him over two months of training — footwork, timing, leverage, the understanding that a smaller fighter wins by being faster and smarter, not stronger.

Cade stood over Drennan, breathing hard, the staff trembling in his hands. The scar-jawed man groaned into the dirt but didn't move.

Elowen was beside him. She hadn't fired — the fight had been too close, too fast, too tangled for an arrow. But her bow was drawn and aimed at Drennan's back, ready.

"Nice," Elowen said to Cade.

In the square, the rest of Kaelthas's men were breaking. Two of them threw down their spears and dropped to their knees. Three more were overwhelmed by Fenvar's warriors, pinned to the ground, disarmed. The circle collapsed.

Kaelthas ran.

"He broke from the square and sprinted north, toward the shattered remains of the north gate. Toward the forest. Toward the compound where he still had men and supplies and whatever was left of the operation he had built. If he reached the deep north, they might never find him." "Stop him!" Fenvar shouted.

Elysian moved. The old tracker cut across the square with a speed that shouldn't have been possible for a man his age, angling to intercept Kaelthas before he reached the broken gate. He didn't run like a young man — he ran like water, flowing through the gaps between buildings, taking the shortest path with the instinct of someone who had spent a lifetime reading terrain.

Kaelthas reached the gate. Elysian reached it at the same time.

They faced each other in the wreckage of the north gate, the shattered timbers around them, the first true light of dawn breaking through the clouds. Kaelthas had his blade. Elysian had his staff.

"Step aside, old man," Kaelthas said. He was breathing hard, his composure finally cracking. The smooth voice was ragged. The gray eyes were wild. The mask was gone and what was underneath was not the calculating strategist or the patient manipulator but something smaller and uglier — a man who was losing and couldn't accept it.

"I watched you for twenty years," Elysian said. His voice was quiet and steady, the voice of a man standing exactly where he intended to stand. "I watched you smile at Fenvar and sharpen your knife behind his back. I told myself I was imagining things. I told myself a man who served this village so well could not be what I feared he was."

He shifted his grip on the staff.

"A boy had to come from another world to show me the truth," Elysian said. "A fourteen-year-old boy with a dog.

And he saw in weeks what I refused to see in decades. That is my shame, Kaelthas. But yours is worse."

Kaelthas lunged. The blade came fast — a killing thrust aimed at Elysian's chest. The old man turned it aside with his staff, the wood deflecting the stone blade with a sharp crack. Kaelthas struck again, slashing. Elysian blocked, sidestepped, and drove the end of his staff into Kaelthas's knee.

The advisor buckled. He went down on one leg, his blade hand swinging wild. Elysian stepped back, out of range, and waited.

"Surrender," Elysian said. "It is over."

Kaelthas looked up at him. The wildness in his eyes had shifted to something else — the cold, cornered fury of a man with nothing left to lose. He gripped his blade and rose to his feet.

He didn't get the chance to swing it.

From the left, a blur of fur and teeth hit Kaelthas in the side. Sammy — forty-five pounds of Border Collie mix with three years of loyalty and two months of growling at this man every time he passed — slammed into Kaelthas's hip and knocked him sideways. The blade flew from his hand and clattered across the broken timber.

Kaelthas hit the ground. Sammy stood over him, snarling, teeth bared, every hair on his body standing straight up. The dog who had herded baby stoneshells around a water trough, who had chased butterflies through the village paths, who had licked every child's face and wagged at every stranger — that dog was gone. In his place was something older and fiercer, an animal protecting his pack from the threat he had identified on the very first day.

Fenvar's warriors arrived seconds later. Four of them, surrounding Kaelthas on the ground, spears pointed at his chest. The advisor looked up at them, then at Sammy, then at Elysian. The fight drained out of him. Not gracefully — not with the dignity he'd always worn like a second skin. It drained out of him the way it drained out of every man who had built his world on lies and watched it collapse. Slowly. Ugly. Complete.

Fenvar walked through the broken gate. He looked down at Kaelthas.

"Twenty years," Fenvar said. "I gave you twenty years of my trust. My friendship. My home."

Kaelthas said nothing. His gray eyes stared at the sky, empty.

"Take him to the storehouse," Fenvar said to his warriors. "Bind him. Guard him. He faces the council when the village is secure." The warriors hauled Kaelthas to his feet. The advisor went without resistance, his head down, his hands bound behind his back with braided hide cord. As they led him past Cade, Kaelthas's eyes flickered toward the boy. No words. No smooth explanation. No gentle concern. Just the blank, hollow stare of a man who had lost everything and knew exactly who had taken it from him.

Cade met his gaze and held it. He didn't flinch. He didn't look away. He stood with his staff in one hand and Elysian's knife in the other and looked the man in the eye until Kaelthas was past him and gone.

The village square was quiet now. The fire in the chief's hall had been contained — villagers with water buckets had beaten it back before it spread beyond the entrance. The smoke was thinning. The first real light of morning was breaking through the clouds, painting the square in pale gold.

Around them, the sounds of battle faded into the sounds of aftermath. Warriors calling out to each other. The moaning of the wounded. The crying of children being released from the storehouse. The bellowing of stoneshells who didn't understand what had happened but knew they didn't like it.

Cade stood in the middle of it and felt the adrenaline drain out of his body like water out of a cracked jug. His hands were shaking. His chest ached where the razormaw had hit him. There was blood on his shirt and dirt on his face and his staff had a crack running through the middle where Drennan's spear had struck it.

Elowen appeared beside him. She looked as battered as he felt — her braid was completely undone now, her hair wild around her face, a shallow cut on her forearm bleeding through a torn sleeve. But her eyes were clear and her back was straight and when she looked at Cade, something in her expression made the shaking in his hands slow down.

"It is over," Elowen said.

"Yeah," Cade said. "It is."

Sammy trotted up between them, tongue out, tail wagging, looking enormously pleased with himself. The dog who had knocked Kaelthas to the ground. The dog who had growled at the advisor from the very first moment and never stopped. The dog who had been right about everything.

Cade knelt and put his arms around Sammy's neck. The dog leaned into him, warm and solid and real.

"Good boy," Cade whispered. "The best boy."

Elysian walked over to them. The old tracker had a bruise forming on his jaw and a tear in his shirt, but he moved with the same unhurried steadiness he always had, as if the morning's battle had been nothing more strenuous than a long walk in the forest.

He looked at Cade. Then at Elowen. Then at Sammy. The corner of his mouth twitched — not quite a smile, but close.

"You fought well," Elysian said to Cade. "Both of you. Drennan is twice your size, and you put him down in the time it takes to draw a breath."

"You taught me," Cade said.

"I taught you the movements," Elysian said. "The courage was yours."

He put his hand on Cade's shoulder. The weight of it was familiar now — warm, steady, the hand of a man who had chosen to be something he didn't have to be. The hand of a father.

Fenvar's voice rang across the square. The chief was standing on the steps of his damaged hall, soot on his face, blood on his hands, addressing the village as people streamed out of the storehouse and into the morning light.

"Verdant Haven stands!" Fenvar called out. "We have been tested, and we have not broken. We have been betrayed by one we trusted, and we have survived. And we owe that survival to three people who saw the truth when the rest of us were blind."

He pointed across the square. At Elysian. At Elowen. At Cade.

"Elysian Mosswood," Fenvar said. "Who has protected this village for forty years and proved it again today. Elowen, daughter of Torin, who fought with the skill of a warrior twice her age. And Cade Thompson — the outsider. The boy from another world who came to us with nothing but a dog and a broken heart, and who saved us all."

The square was quiet. Then, from somewhere in the crowd, a single pair of hands began to clap. Then another. Then more, spreading like fire through dry grass, until the entire village was applauding — warriors and farmers and mothers and children, the same people who had turned their backs on Cade days ago, the same people who had whispered and looked away and called him outsider. They were clapping for him now. Looking at him with something that wasn't suspicion or fear but gratitude and shame and the raw, honest acknowledgment that they had been wrong.

Cade stood in the morning light with Sammy at his feet and Elowen beside him and Elysian's hand on his shoulder, and he didn't know what to do with what he was feeling. It was too big. Too new. Too much. A boy who had spent fourteen years being invisible, being small, being the kid who kept his head down and his mouth shut and hoped that nobody noticed him — that boy was standing in a village square in another world while an entire community thanked him for saving their lives.

He didn't cry. He wanted to. The pressure behind his eyes was enormous, a dam holding back fourteen years of never being enough, never being believed, never being seen. But he held it. He held it because Elysian was watching and Elowen was beside him and Fenvar was looking at him from the steps of the hall with the respect of a chief who had learned the hardest lesson of his life.

Sammy's tail wagged against his leg. Steady. Constant. The heartbeat of everything that mattered.

Verdant Haven stood. Battered, burned, bleeding — but standing. And for the first time since he'd stumbled through a gap between two boulders and fallen into a world that shouldn't exist, Cade Thompson felt like he belonged somewhere.

Chapter Twenty - *After the Storm*

They buried the dead on the third day.

Four warriors had fallen in the battle. Two at the north gate when the largest razormaw came through. One in the eastern fields. One in the square, struck down by Kaelthas's men before Fenvar's force could reach him. Their names were spoken aloud by Fenvar at the burial site on the hill east of the village, where the morning sun touched the ground first and the valley spread out below like a green sea.

Cade stood with the village and listened to the names. He hadn't known the men well — warriors who had nodded at him in passing, faces he recognized from the wall and the gate. But they had died defending the people inside the storehouse, the children and the mothers and the farmers who had huddled in the dark while the razormaws tore through the village. They had died because Kaelthas had valued power more than their lives.

Sammy sat beside Cade during the ceremony, quiet and still, as if he understood.

The weeks after the battle blurred together in a rhythm of work and healing. The north gate was rebuilt first — heavier timber this time, braced with stone, strong enough that no single animal could break through. The chief's hall was repaired, the fire damage stripped away, the tusk-framed entrance rebuilt with new carvings. Fences were mended. Pens were reconstructed. The stoneshells were coaxed back to their fields, and the village slowly, carefully, began to resemble itself again.

Cade worked every day. He hauled timber with the construction crews, learning the methods of the village builders — how they joined logs without nails, using notches and pegs and braided cord pulled tight. He helped Torin repair the damage to the farm, where the razormaw Elowen had killed had torn through the outer fence and crushed part of the stoneshell pen. Bruna had survived without a scratch. Korr had a gash on his shoulder that healed slowly, leaving a pale scar across his armored plate.

The village's attitude toward Cade had shifted completely. The whisper campaign was dead, replaced by something Cade hadn't expected and didn't quite know how to handle — warmth. People nodded at him now. They called him by name. Hadrik, the farmer who had walked away from the well without a word, stopped Cade one morning and pressed a leather pouch into his hands. Inside was a set of stone tools — a small hammer, a scoring blade, and a smoothing stone — the kind a craftsman used for fine work.

"For you," Hadrik said. His eyes were wet. "I am sorry, Cade. I was wrong."

Cade didn't know what to say. He'd spent his life being invisible, being the kid nobody noticed, and now an entire village was seeing him and he had no practice at being seen.

"Thank you," Cade said. It was all he could manage, but Hadrik seemed to understand.

The children came back to Sammy. The pack of six or seven who had followed him everywhere before the whisper campaign returned in full force, calling him "soft-one" and burying their hands in his fur. Sammy accepted their return with the uncomplicated forgiveness that only dogs possess — no grudge, no memory of the days when they'd been called inside and told to stay away. He rolled on his back in the village paths and let them scratch his belly and was happy.

Maren came to Elowen on the fourth day after the battle. Cade watched from across the path as the two girls spoke — quietly, heads close together, Maren's face tight with something that might have been shame. Elowen listened. She didn't smile. She didn't make it easy. But when Maren finished speaking, Elowen reached out and took her hand, and the two of them stood there for a moment in the kind of silence that means more than words.

Elowen told Cade about it that evening. "She apologized," Elowen said. "She said she should have trusted me. She said she was afraid and it was easier to blame the stranger than to question the man everyone trusted."

"What did you say?" Cade asked.

"I said fear makes fools of all of us," Elowen said. "And that I would rather have a friend who admits she was wrong than one who pretends she was always right."

Kaelthas was judged by the council on the seventh day. Cade was not present — Fenvar had told him the council would handle it, and that Cade had done enough. Elysian attended as a witness. When it was over, the old tracker came to Torin's farm and sat with Cade on the bench outside.

"Exile," Elysian said. "Permanent. He is to be taken to the far edge of the vale, beyond the eastern mountains, and left. If he returns, the penalty is death."

"Not execution?" Cade asked.

Elysian shook his head. "Fenvar argued against it. He said killing Kaelthas would make them no better than what Kaelthas had planned for them. The council agreed — not unanimously, but enough. Brennick wanted death. Several others did too. But Fenvar held the room."

Cade thought about that. A man who had plotted to murder the chief, destroy the village, and seize power — and the chief's response was exile instead of death. It was a mercy Cade wasn't sure Kaelthas deserved. But it was the kind of mercy that said something about the man giving it, and about the village that followed him.

"Drennan and the others?" Cade asked.

"Exile as well," Elysian said. "All twelve. Stripped of their names and their standing. They leave tomorrow at dawn."

They left. Cade watched from the wall as Kaelthas and his men were led through the south gate by an armed escort of Fenvar's warriors. The advisor walked with his head up, his back straight, still carrying himself with the posture of a man who believed he was better than everyone around him. He didn't look back.

Drennan walked behind him, the scar on his jaw livid in the morning light. The others followed in a silent line, carrying nothing, heading into the wilderness with nothing but the clothes on their backs and whatever they could find to eat.

Cade watched them until they disappeared into the trees. Then he went back to work.

The weeks turned into months. Spring deepened into summer, and the valley blazed with color — flowers Cade had no names for, birds with plumage that didn't exist in any book he'd ever read, insects that hummed in frequencies that seemed to vibrate in his chest. The long-necked herbivores migrated through the valley in vast herds, their footsteps shaking the ground like slow thunder. A pair of swiftclaws nested near the village, and their hatchlings became a village attraction — tiny, wobbly things that chased each other in circles and fell over their own feet.

Sammy tried to herd the hatchlings. The village gathered to watch. Even Fenvar laughed.

Cade trained with Elysian every morning. The lessons had changed since the battle. Less combat, more knowledge. Elysian taught him how to read weather from the movement of the canopy. How to find water by the behavior of insects. How to identify every edible plant in the forest, and every poisonous one, and the dozen that could be either depending on how you prepared them. He taught him the history of the vale — the old stories, passed down through generations, about the first people who had come to Emerald Vale and the covenant they had made with the land and its creatures.

"The covenant is simple," Elysian said one morning as they sat on the ridge watching the sunrise. "We take what we need. We give back what we can. We do not destroy what we cannot rebuild. Every generation has honored it. Kaelthas forgot that. Or maybe he never believed it."

"Do you think he'll survive out there?" Cade asked.

"Kaelthas is clever and resourceful," Elysian said. "He will survive. Whether he will learn anything from it — that I doubt. Men who believe they are always right rarely change their minds. They simply find new people to blame."

Cade thought of Don. Wherever Don was — if he was still alive, still out there somewhere — he was probably telling anyone who would listen that Eydan had driven him away, that his kids were ungrateful, that everything was someone else's fault. Men like Don didn't change. They just found new victims.

The thought of Don brought the other thoughts — the ones that came at night, when the village was quiet and Sammy was asleep and the stars were so thick overhead that the sky looked solid with light.

Eydan. Working herself to the bone, trying to hold a family together on her own, exhausted and stretched thin and doing it all without help. Ashen, seven years old, going quiet the way children go quiet when the world teaches them that speaking up gets you hurt. Carla, who had texted about snacks and didn't know her best friend had fallen through a crack in the universe.

His family. His real family. The people who needed him and didn't know where he was.

One evening, weeks after the battle, Cade sat on the floor of his room and pulled his backpack from the corner where it had sat untouched for months. He opened it and spread the contents on the bed. A crumpled algebra worksheet. Two dried-out pens. A granola bar wrapper. His house key on a lanyard from Ridgewood High.

And his phone. Dead. Black screen. Cold in his hand like a stone pulled from a river.

He held it and tried to remember the photos. Eydan smiling in the kitchen on a good day. Ashen holding up a drawing of a cat. Carla making a face at the camera during lunch. His house — the house on Maple Creek Drive with the blue door and the cracked driveway and the bedroom where he'd spent a thousand nights lying in the dark listening to sounds no child should hear.

The photos were there, locked behind a dead screen, and he couldn't reach them. Just like his family was there, on the other side of whatever door had brought him here, and he couldn't reach them either.

He put the phone back in the backpack and closed his eyes.

I have to go home, he thought. *I have a life here. I have people who care about me. I have a place. But my mother is working herself to death and my sister is hurting and they don't even know if I'm alive.*

Sammy was lying on the bed, watching him. The dog's head was tilted, his mismatched eyes steady, as if he were waiting for Cade to figure out what Sammy had already known.

Because Sammy had been pulling. Not physically —
not bolting into the forest the way he had the night he found
the canyon. But in small ways. Standing at the edge of the
village and staring south, toward the forest, toward the
direction they'd come from. Lifting his nose at certain times
of day and sniffing the air with the focused intensity of a dog
catching a scent that nobody else could detect. Pacing at
night, restless, turning circles on the bed before settling.

Sammy had found the way in. Sammy would find the
way out. Cade was certain of it now — the portal was tied to
the dog, to whatever strange connection existed between
Sammy and the space between two boulders in a forest that
existed in two worlds at once.

But going home meant leaving. It meant leaving
Elowen, whose hand in his had become the steady point
around which everything else turned. It meant leaving
Elysian, who had given him the father he'd never had. It
meant leaving Torin's farm and the ridge overlooking the
valley and the children who called Sammy "soft-one" and the
stoneshells who had learned to eat from his hand.

It meant leaving the first place he had ever truly
belonged.

The hardest decision of his life was forming in his
mind, and he couldn't stop it, and he couldn't rush it. It sat
there, growing heavier each day, while the summer deepened

around him and the valley bloomed and the life he had built in Emerald Vale became more real and more precious and more impossible to walk away from.

But Eydan was out there. Ashen was out there. And Cade was here, in a world that shouldn't exist, living a life that felt like a gift and a betrayal at the same time.

He lay on the bed with Sammy beside him and stared at the ceiling and listened to the village settling into sleep. Outside, the forest hummed. The stars burned. The world turned, oblivious and beautiful.

And somewhere beyond the boulders, beyond the shimmer, beyond the crack between two worlds, a woman was coming home from work, opening the door to a quiet house, and wondering where her son had gone.

Chapter Twenty-One - *The Decision*

Cade went to Elysian first because the old man would make it easier.

Not easy. Nothing about this was easy. But Elysian dealt in truth the way other men dealt in pleasantries, and Cade needed someone who would hear what he had to say without trying to talk him out of it.

He found Elysian at his dwelling near the northern wall, sitting in his chair, working the edge of a blade with a piece of antler bone. Sammy trotted in ahead of Cade and lay down at the old man's feet. Elysian looked up; studied Cade's face for three seconds, and set the blade down.

"You are leaving," Elysian said.

Not a question. A statement. The old tracker had been watching Cade stare toward the southern forest for weeks. He'd seen the restlessness, the long silences, the way Cade held his dead phone at night like a man holding a letter he couldn't read. Elysian missed nothing. He never had.

"I have to," Cade said. He sat on the floor across from Elysian, his back against the wall, his hands on his knees. "My mother is alone. She's working herself into the ground trying to keep my sister fed and a roof over their heads. Ashen is nine. She needs her brother. They don't even know if I'm alive."

Elysian was quiet for a long time. The fire crackled between them. Sammy's tail swept the stone floor once.

"How?" Elysian asked.

"Sammy," Cade said. "He found the way in. He's been pulling south for weeks — standing at the edge of the village, sniffing the air, pacing at night. I think he can feel it. The portal, the doorway, whatever it is. It's tied to him. He found it once. He'll find it again."

"And if he doesn't?" Elysian asked.

"Then I stay," Cade said. "And I find another way. But I have to try."

Elysian leaned back in his chair and looked at the ceiling. The firelight moved across his face, deepening the lines around his eyes, turning his expression into something ancient and tired and full of a sadness he rarely showed.

"I am not going to talk you out of this," Elysian said.

"I know," Cade said.

"Not because I don't want to," Elysian said. He looked at Cade, and in his dark eyes was something Cade had never seen there before — not the teacher's pride, not the tracker's focus, but the raw, unguarded ache of a man facing a loss he couldn't prevent. "I want to tell you to stay. I want to tell you that this is your home now and that we need you here and that the people who love you in this world are enough. I want to say those things because they are true.”

He paused. His jaw worked. Then he spoke again, and his voice was steady.

“But courage is not staying where it is safe,” Elysian said. “Courage is going where you are needed. Your mother needs you. Your sister needs you. And a man who turns his back on his family because leaving is hard — that is not the man I trained.”

Cade’s throat closed. He stared at the floor because if he looked at Elysian, the dam would break and he wasn’t ready for that yet.

“You have the knife,” Elysian said. “My name is on the spine. When you hold it, you hold forty years of everything I know. That goes with you. Wherever you go, whatever world you stand in, you carry my name.”

“Elysian —” Cade started.

“I am not finished,” Elysian said. His voice was gruff, the way it always got when he was feeling more than he wanted to show. “When I found you in the forest, you were a scared boy who flinched at loud voices and didn’t know how to hold a staff. You are not that boy anymore. You are something better. You are something I am proud of. And I need you to hear that, because I suspect no man has ever said it to you."

No man ever had. Cade's father had never said he was proud of him. His father had never said anything to him that didn't come with a fist behind it or a silence that was worse than shouting. In fourteen years under Don's roof, Cade had never once heard the words that Elysian had just given him in a stone dwelling by a fire in a world that shouldn't exist.

The dam broke. Cade put his face in his hands and cried.

Not the silent tears he'd learned to hide on Maple Creek Drive, muffled into a pillow so Don wouldn't hear. These were real tears — loud, shaking, ugly, the kind that come from a place so deep you didn't know it was there until it cracked open. He cried for the father he'd never had and the one he'd found too late. He cried for the boy who'd walked through a gap between two boulders and stumbled into a world that had put him back together. He cried because leaving was going to break something inside him that would never fully heal.

Elysian let him cry. The old man didn't speak. He didn't move. He sat in his chair and waited with the patience of a man who understood that some storms had to run their course before the sky could clear.

When Cade finally lifted his head, his face wet, his eyes swollen, Elysian was looking at him with an expression that held no pity and no embarrassment. Just love. The quiet, steady, unshakeable love of a man who had chosen a son.

"When do you leave?" Elysian asked.

"Soon," Cade said. His voice was rough. "Sammy is pulling harder every day. I think the portal is opening, or getting ready to open. I don't know how it works, but he knows. He's always known."

"Then you tell Elowen today," Elysian said. "Do not wait. Do not let her hear it from someone else. She deserves to hear it from you."

"I know," Cade said. "That's the part I'm afraid of."

"You should be," Elysian said. And for the first time that morning, the corner of his mouth lifted. Not quite a smile. But close. "She is going to hit you."

"Probably," Cade said.

"Definitely," Elysian said.

Cade stood. He looked at Elysian. There were things he wanted to say — a hundred things, a thousand things, words that would take years to find and a lifetime to say properly. Thank you for teaching me. Thank you for believing me. Thank you for being what my father never was.

He couldn't say any of them. They were too big. So he said the only thing he could.

"I will never forget you," Cade said.

Elysian nodded once. "Go," Elysian said. "Find Elowen. And Cade —"

"Yeah?" Cade said.

"Do not let her hit you in the face," Elysian said. "She has a very strong right hand."

Cade almost laughed. Almost. He walked out of the dwelling with Sammy at his heels and went to find the girl who was going to be the hardest goodbye of his life.

He found Elowen on the ridge. Their ridge. She was sitting on the flat rock with her legs drawn up, her arms around her knees, looking out over the valley. The sun was high and the light was warm and the long-necked herbivores were drifting across the distant plains like slow clouds.

She knew before he spoke. He could see it in the way her shoulders tightened, the way her hands gripped her knees, the way she didn't turn around when he sat beside her. She had been watching Sammy pull south too. She had seen the restlessness, the silences, the dead phone in his hands at night. She was smarter than anyone Cade had ever met, and she had put the pieces together weeks ago and been waiting for him to say it.

"You are going home," Elowen said. She was looking at the valley, not at him. Her voice was steady. Her jaw was tight.

"I have to," Cade said. "My mother —"

"I know," Elowen said. "You do not have to explain. I know why."

They sat in silence. The valley hummed. The wind moved through the grass. A bird Cade couldn't name sang a four-note melody from a branch above them, over and over, as if the world were providing a soundtrack for the hardest conversation he'd ever had.

"I am not going to ask you to stay," Elowen said. Her voice cracked on the last word. She caught it, forced it back, held it. "I am not going to ask because I know about your mother. I know about Ashen. I know what it costs you every night to be here while they are there, and I will not add my weight to that."

She turned to face him. Her amber eyes were full, bright, holding everything she was refusing to let fall.

"But I need you to know something," Elowen said to Cade. "What happened between us was real. Every moment of it. Every conversation on this ridge. Every time you held my hand. Every time I believed you when no one else would. It was real, Cade. And I will carry it for the rest of my life."

Cade couldn't breathe. The pressure in his chest was enormous — not pain, not grief, but something bigger than both. The feeling of standing on the edge of a cliff and knowing you have to jump and knowing the fall will change you forever.

"It was real," Cade said. "You are the first person who ever believed me. Before Elysian. Before Fenvar. Before anyone. You looked at me in a forest when I couldn't even speak your language and you decided I was worth helping. You changed everything, Elowen. You changed me."

A tear broke free. Just one, sliding down her cheek, catching the sunlight. She didn't wipe it away.

She reached up and untied something from around her neck — a cord of braided leather holding a small stone, smooth and green, polished by years of contact with skin. She held it out to Cade.

"This was my mother's," Elowen said. "She wore it every day of her life. My father gave it to me when she died. I have worn it every day since."

"Elowen, I can't —" Cade started.

"You can," Elowen said. "And you will. Because when you are back in your world, in your house, with your family — when all of this feels like a dream you had once and you start to wonder if any of it was real — you will hold this stone and you will know. It was real. I was real. What we had was real."

She pressed the stone into his hand. It was warm from her skin. Smooth. Green as the valley below them.

Cade closed his fingers around it and held it against his chest. He looked at Elowen — this girl with the amber eyes and the braid and the bow, who had fed him bread in a forest and believed him when nobody else would and beaten him in every sparring match and laughed while doing it and taken his hand on a ridge overlooking the most beautiful valley in any world.

"Sammy's still here," Cade said. "The dog found the way in. He can find it again. The door isn't closed forever, Elowen."

He didn't know if that was true. He didn't know how the portal worked or whether it would ever open again or whether Sammy could find it twice. But he said it because she needed to hear it, and because he needed to believe it, and because the alternative — that this was the last time he would ever sit on this rock with this girl — was something he could not accept.

"The door isn't closed forever," Elowen repeated. She held his gaze. "I will hold you to that, Cade Thompson."

She leaned forward and kissed him. Soft. Brief. Her lips warm against his, her hand on the side of his face, her fingers touching the line of his jaw. The first kiss either of them had ever had, given on a ridge overlooking a valley in a world between worlds, with Sammy lying beside them and the sun pouring down and the whole impossible, beautiful, heartbreaking truth of what they were to each other contained in three seconds of contact.

Then she pulled back. She looked at him with those amber eyes, wet and fierce and absolutely unbroken.

"Go save your family," Elowen said. "The way you saved mine."

Sammy's tail thumped against the rock. Once. Twice. As if the dog approved.

They sat on the ridge together until the sun began to drop, holding hands, saying nothing, watching the valley turn gold. There was nothing left to say that their hands weren't already saying. The decision was made. The goodbye was coming. And between now and then, there was just this — two people on a rock, holding on to each other, while the world turned beneath them and the light changed and everything that had been became everything that was about to end.

Chapter Twenty-Two - *A Chief's Gratitude*

Fenvar summoned Cade to the chief's hall at midmorning on the day before he planned to leave.

The hall had been repaired since the fire — new timber framing the entrance, the tusk archway rebuilt, the carvings along the doorway freshly cut by the village's best craftsman. It looked stronger than before. The whole village looked stronger than before, the way a bone heals thicker at the break.

Cade walked through the entrance with Sammy at his side and found the hall full. Not just the council. Everyone. The benches along the walls were packed with villagers, and more stood in the aisles and along the back wall. Farmers, warriors, mothers with children on their hips, elders in their carved chairs. Torin was there, standing near the front, his face composed in the careful stillness of a man who was about to lose the boy he'd taken in and was determined not to show it. Elowen stood beside her father, her bow over her shoulder, her amber eyes fixed on Cade with an expression that was fierce and tender and refusing to break.

Elysian was near the back, leaning against the wall with his arms crossed. He caught Cade's eye and gave him the smallest nod. That was all. That was enough.

Fenvar stood at the center of the hall, dressed in his ceremonial clothing — the long leather coat, the necklace of teeth, the single red line painted from forehead to chin. He looked every inch the chief he was — a man who had been betrayed, tested, and hardened, and who had come through it standing.

"Cade Thompson," Fenvar said. His voice filled the hall without effort. "Step forward."

Cade walked to the center of the hall. Sammy walked with him, tail swaying, completely unaware of the formality of the moment. A few people in the crowd smiled at the dog. Even Fenvar's mouth twitched.

"You came to us from beyond the vale," Fenvar said. "You arrived with nothing but a dog and a bag of objects we did not understand. You were a stranger. You could not speak our language. You did not know our customs. You did not know our land."

Fenvar paused and looked across the crowd.

"And yet this stranger saw what we could not," Fenvar continued. "He saw the danger growing in our midst when our own eyes were blind. He spoke the truth when no one would listen. He risked his life to bring us proof. And when the attack came, he stood on our walls and fought for a village that was not his own."

The hall was silent. Cade could hear Sammy's tail brushing the stone floor.

"Verdant Haven owes Cade Thompson a debt that cannot be repaid with words," Fenvar said. "But words are where we begin."

The chief turned to Cade and placed his hand on the boy's shoulder. The weight of it was different from Elysian's — heavier, more formal, carrying the authority of a man who spoke for an entire people.

"You are not an outsider," Fenvar said to Cade. "You have not been an outsider since the day you first told me the truth in this hall, even though I was too stubborn to hear it. From this day forward, Cade Thompson is a son of Verdant Haven. His name will be spoken in the histories of this village alongside those who built it and those who defended it. He came to us a stranger. He leaves us as family."

The crowd erupted. Not the polite applause of a formal ceremony — the full-throated, stamping, shouting approval of a village that meant every word. Warriors beat their spears against the floor. Children cheered. Mothers called out Cade's name. Sammy barked, because everyone else was making noise and he wasn't about to be left out.

Cade stood in the center of it and felt the sound wash over him like a wave. The boy who had been invisible. The boy who had kept his head down and his mouth shut and hoped nobody noticed him. He was standing in a hall full of people who were shouting his name, and every single one of them meant it.

When the noise subsided, Fenvar raised his hand.

"We know you must return to your world," Fenvar said to Cade. "To your mother. To your sister. We cannot keep you, though many of us wish we could."

He gestured to two warriors standing near the side of the hall. They stepped forward, carrying between them a large hide sack, heavy enough that both men strained under its weight. They set it on the floor at Cade's feet.

Fenvar crouched and untied the sack. He pulled the hide open, and the contents caught the torchlight and threw it back in a hundred directions.

Gold. Coins the size of silver dollars, thick and heavy, stamped with symbols Cade didn't recognize. Dozens of them — maybe a hundred, layered on top of each other, gleaming in the firelight. Mixed among the coins were polished stones — deep green and blood red and ocean blue, cut into smooth shapes, each one catching the light with an internal fire that made them look alive. And beneath the coins and stones, pressed against the bottom of the sack, were pieces of jewelry — bracelets of hammered gold, pendants set with colored stones, rings etched with the same symbols that decorated the chief's hall.

"These are the treasures of Verdant Haven," Fenvar said. "Collected over generations. Some were found in the deep caves beneath the eastern mountains. Some were traded from settlements beyond the vale. Some are older than anyone can remember — relics of the first people who made this land their home."

He stood and looked at Cade.

"They are yours," Fenvar said. "All of them. Take them to your world. Use them to care for your family. Your mother should not have to work herself to the bone when her son has earned the gratitude of an entire people."

Cade stared at the treasure. His mind went blank for a moment — the sheer volume of gold and jewels on the floor at his feet was beyond anything he could process. He thought of Eydan's cracked hands. He thought of Ashen's shoes with the toe poking through. He thought of the clearance rack at the outlet store on Route 4 and the grocery receipts Ashen drew on because they couldn't afford sketch paper.

"I don't know what to say," Cade said. His voice was thick.

"Say you will take care of your family," Fenvar said. "That is all the thanks I need."

"I will," Cade said. "I promise."

He knelt and began transferring the treasure into his backpack. The coins were heavy — each one solid and dense, real gold that would be worth a fortune in any world that valued the metal. The stones went in next, wrapped in the soft hide to keep them from scratching. The jewelry last, layered carefully on top. By the time he was done, the backpack was full and heavier than anything he'd ever carried. He lifted it onto his shoulders and the straps dug into his skin and his knees nearly buckled.

But he wasn't leaving a single piece behind.

The ceremony ended, but the day didn't. What followed was something Cade hadn't expected — a farewell that lasted from midmorning until sunset, as every person in Verdant Haven came to say goodbye.

Hadrik brought him a second leather pouch, this one filled with dried meat and travel bread. "For the journey," Hadrik said. "Wherever it takes you."

Gareth — the warrior who had saluted Cade outside the chief's hall the morning after the canyon — clasped his arm in the warrior's grip and held it. "You fought well," Gareth said. "I would stand beside you again."

Brennick found him near the well. The farmer who had wanted Cade expelled stood in front of him with red-rimmed eyes and a jaw that worked for ten seconds before any words came out.

"I was wrong," Brennick said. "I was afraid and I was wrong and I am sorry."

"You weren't the only one," Cade said. "Fear does that to people."

Brennick nodded, wiped his eyes with the back of his hand, and walked away.

The children came last. The pack of six or seven who had followed Sammy everywhere, who had called him soft-one and buried their hands in his fur, who had been pulled away during the whisper campaign and had come running back the moment it ended. They gathered around Sammy in the village path and hugged him and cried and fed him scraps and told him he was the best animal in the entire vale, and Sammy accepted every bit of it with the patient, bottomless love of a dog who had never once in his life turned away from a hand that reached for him.

The smallest girl — a child of maybe four, with dark curls and enormous eyes — put her face against Sammy's neck and said something so quiet Cade almost missed it.

"Will the soft-one come back?" the girl asked.

Cade knelt beside her. "I hope so," Cade said. It was the most honest answer he could give.

The girl looked at him with those enormous eyes. Then she kissed Sammy on the nose and ran to her mother.

As the sun dropped toward the mountains, Cade stood at the edge of the village and looked at Verdant Haven one last time. The timber walls, repaired and reinforced. The smoke rising from cooking fires. The fields stretching out to the east, green and gold in the fading light. The ridge where Elowen had taken him on his first week and where they'd sat holding hands while the valley turned to amber below them.

This place had changed him. These people had changed him. He had arrived as a scared, broken boy who flinched at raised hands and kept the world at arm's length. He was leaving as something else — not unbroken, never that, the cracks would always be there — but stronger where the breaks had healed. A boy with a knife bearing an old man's name. A boy with a green stone on a cord around his neck. A boy who had stood in a village square and been seen.

Torin appeared beside him. The farmer stood there for a moment, looking at the same view, his scarred hands at his sides.

"You are always welcome here," Torin said to Cade. "The room is yours. The door is open."

Five sentences. The most words Torin had ever spoken to him at one time. And every one of them worth more than gold.

"Thank you, Torin," Cade said. "For everything. From the first day."

Torin nodded. He put his hand on Cade's shoulder — brief, firm, the hand of a man who showed love through action instead of words — and then went back inside.

Tomorrow morning, Cade would walk into the forest with Sammy and Elowen and Elysian. He would follow the dog south, toward the boulders, toward the shimmer, toward whatever was waiting on the other side. The backpack would crush his shoulders. The treasure would dig into his spine. But he would carry it, because Eydan and Ashen were waiting, and Cade Thompson was done being the boy who couldn't carry anything.

He went to his room. He set the backpack against the wall, feeling the weight of it settle against the timber. He lay on the bed. Sammy jumped up beside him and curled against his chest, the dog's heartbeat steady and warm against his ribs.

The last night. The last sounds of the village drifting through the hide flap. The last time he would fall asleep in this room, in this world, in this life that had rebuilt him from the ground up.

Cade closed his eyes and held his dog and listened to Verdant Haven breathe.

Chapter Twenty-Three - *Fifteen Minutes*

They left at dawn.

Cade, Sammy, Elowen, and Elysian walked out through the south gate as the first light touched the tops of the trees and the village horn sounded once — a single, low note that hung in the air like a held breath. Behind them, on the wall, a dozen villagers stood watching. They didn't call out. They didn't wave. They just stood and watched the four of them disappear into the forest, and the silence they kept was more powerful than any farewell.

The backpack was crushing. Cade had shifted the treasure three times that morning, trying to distribute the weight, and it didn't matter. The gold coins pressed against his spine like a row of fists, and the straps cut into his shoulders with every step. He'd tied extra padding under the straps — strips of leather Torin had cut for him — and it helped, but not enough. By the time they reached the creek crossing, his shoulders were burning.

He didn't slow down. He didn't shift the pack. He didn't ask for a rest. Eydan was on the other side of those boulders, and Ashen was on the other side, and every coin digging into his back was a month of rent or a pair of shoes or a drawing pad or a night when his mother didn't have to choose between groceries and electricity.

He carried it.

Sammy led the way. The dog had been pulling south since first light, straining ahead on the path, his nose up, his body vibrating with the same focused urgency Cade had seen the day this had all started — the day Sammy had pushed through the gap in the chain-link fence and sprinted into the woods behind Maple Creek Drive. Whatever connection existed between the dog and the portal, it was alive now, pulling Sammy forward like a rope only he could feel.

Elysian walked beside Cade. The old tracker moved through the forest with his usual silent ease, his walking stick finding the ground between roots and stones without a sound. He hadn't spoken since they'd left the village. His face was composed, steady, giving nothing away. But his hand had found Cade's shoulder twice during the walk — brief, wordless touches that said everything his mouth refused to.

Elowen walked on Cade's other side. She carried her bow, her quiver, and her mother's blade on her hip — the same way she'd carried them the night they'd gone to the canyon. She hadn't said much either. She'd said everything that needed saying on the ridge. What was left now was just the walking, and the breathing, and the terrible shrinking distance between where they were and where they were going.

The forest was quiet. The predawn sounds had faded into the steady hum of morning — insects, birds, the rustle of small things in the undergrowth. The light filtered through the canopy in long golden shafts, catching the mist that drifted between the trees. It was beautiful. It was always beautiful. And Cade was walking away from it.

They crossed the creek. They climbed the ridge where the old oaks grew. They passed through the section of deep forest where the ferns grew waist-high and the air smelled of damp earth and old wood. The terrain was familiar now — Cade had walked it on his first day in Emerald Vale, stumbling and terrified, chasing a dog into a world he didn't understand. He knew every turn, every fallen log, every cluster of the luminous fungus that glowed faintly against the bark even in daylight.

He was walking the same path in reverse. Everything the same, and everything different.

Sammy stopped.

The dog was thirty feet ahead, standing rigid in a small clearing where the trees thinned and the light came down in a wide column through a gap in the canopy. His ears were forward. His tail was still. His entire body was pointed at something Cade couldn't see yet.

Then Cade saw them. The boulders.

Two massive stones, gray and ancient, covered in moss at their bases, pressed close together with a narrow gap between them. A single oak root grew over the top of the left boulder like a gnarled arm reaching across to the other. They looked exactly the same as the day Cade had first squeezed between them — two sentinels standing in a forest clearing, guarding a doorway that shouldn't exist.

Sammy whined. A low, urgent sound, the kind the dog made when he needed something and couldn't explain it in any language Cade understood. The dog took three steps toward the boulders, then looked back at Cade.

Come on. That's what the look said. *It's time. It's here. Come on.*

The air between the boulders changed. Cade felt it before he saw it — a warmth, subtle at first, then stronger, pressing against his face like a breath. The shimmer appeared in the gap — a ripple in the air, like heat rising from summer pavement, bending the light, making the forest behind the boulders waver and distort. The same shimmer he'd seen nearly a year ago, standing in the woods behind his house with his heart hammering and his dog on the other side.

Fifteen minutes. That's what they'd figured, based on Cade's memory of the first crossing — the shimmer had appeared, held, and faded in roughly that window. Fifteen minutes to say goodbye and step through before the door closed.

The clock was running.

Elysian stepped forward. The old man looked at the boulders, at the shimmer, at the impossible doorway between two worlds. His expression didn't change. He had lived his entire life in a world of wonders — dinosaurs, ancient forests, a civilization built in partnership with creatures that shouldn't exist. A portal to another world was just one more wonder in a life full of them.

He turned to Cade.

There were no words. They had said everything in the dwelling by the fire, when Cade had cried and Elysian had waited and the silence between them had held more truth than a thousand speeches. So Elysian didn't speak. He stepped forward and pulled Cade into an embrace — the first time the old man had ever held him, his arms strong and steady, the walking stick clattering to the ground because both hands were needed for this.

Cade held him back. He pressed his face against Elysian's shoulder and breathed in the smell of leather and forest and smoke, and he felt the old man's hand come up to the back of his head the way a father's hand does when he's holding his son for the last time.

Elysian released him. He stepped back. He picked up his walking stick. His eyes were bright, but nothing fell. The old tracker held it all inside, the way he held everything, with the discipline of a man who had spent a lifetime controlling what the world got to see.

"Remember what I taught you," Elysian said. His voice was rough.

"All of it," Cade said.

"All of it," Elysian confirmed. He nodded once. Then he stepped back and gave the space to Elowen.

She was standing beside the boulders, one hand on the moss-covered stone, her amber eyes locked on Cade. She wasn't crying. Her jaw was set and her back was straight and she was holding herself together with the same fierce, stubborn strength she'd shown from the first day — the girl who had aimed an arrow at his chest and then fed him bread and changed his life.

Cade walked to her. He stopped in front of her. The shimmer rippled between the boulders beside them, warm and bright, patient and impatient at the same time.

"Don't say goodbye," Elowen said. Her voice was steady but thin, like a wire pulled taut. "I hate that word. Say something else."

Cade reached up and touched the green stone hanging around his neck — her mother's stone, warm against his skin, the weight of it so familiar now that he'd forget it was there until moments like this, when it meant everything.

"I'll see you again," Cade said.

"You do not know that," Elowen said.

"No," Cade said. "But Sammy's still here. And he found the way once."

Elowen looked at the dog. Sammy was standing at the gap between the boulders, his tail wagging slowly, his mismatched eyes moving between Cade and the shimmer with the patient urgency of a dog who knew it was time to go and was waiting for his person to figure it out.

"You had better come back," Elowen said to the dog. "Both of you."

She stepped forward and kissed Cade. Not the soft, brief kiss from the ridge — this one was harder, fiercer, a kiss that held a year of mornings and evenings and fights and laughter and the quiet moments on a rock overlooking a valley that stretched forever. She kissed him like she was pressing something into him that would last longer than memory, longer than distance, longer than whatever separated two worlds.

Then she stepped back. Her eyes were wet. She didn't wipe them.

"Go," Elowen said. "Before I change my mind and tie you to a tree."

Cade almost laughed. Almost. He looked at her one more time — the braid, the bow, the amber eyes, the girl who had believed him when nobody else would — and he held that image in his mind like a photograph on a phone that would never die.

He turned to the boulders. The shimmer was still there, rippling, warm, waiting. He could feel it pulling at him the way it pulled at Sammy — a gentle, insistent tug, like a hand on his sleeve.

He adjusted the backpack. The straps cut into his shoulders. The gold shifted against his spine. He took a breath.

He looked at Sammy. The dog looked back at him.

"Let's go home, boy," Cade said.

He took Sammy's collar in one hand and stepped into the gap between the boulders. The rock was cold against his chest and the backpack scraped the stone behind him and the shimmer wrapped around them both like warm water. The light changed. The sound changed. The smell of ancient forest and deep earth and flowers with no names faded, replaced by something different — cooler, drier, familiar in a way that hit him like a fist in the chest.

Leaves. Dirt. Damp bark. The smell of October in the woods behind a suburban neighborhood.

Cade pushed through the gap and stumbled into a clearing.

The trees were different. Smaller, thinner, ordinary. Oaks and maples and a few pines, their leaves turning gold and red. The sky above was gray — an October gray, the kind that promised rain and smelled like the end of something. The ground beneath his feet was covered in dry leaves, not ferns. The air was cool and thin and carried the distant sound of a lawnmower.

A lawnmower. Someone was mowing their lawn on a Saturday morning in a neighborhood that existed in the same world as algebra homework and Walgreens and chain-link fences.

Cade stood in the clearing and breathed. The backpack was on his shoulders. The gold was real. Sammy was beside him, tail wagging, looking up at him with an expression that said,

See? I told you. I always knew the way.

He turned and looked at the boulders. The two massive stones were there — the same ones, gray and ancient, moss on their bases. But the shimmer was gone. The air between them was just air. Cold stone and nothing else.

On the other side, Elowen and Elysian were standing in a clearing in another world, watching the shimmer fade.

Cade couldn't see them. Couldn't hear them. Couldn't reach them.

But the green stone was warm against his chest. And the knife with Elysian's name was in his backpack. And somewhere in his mind, he could still hear Elowen's voice.

You had better come back. Both of you.

Cade put his hand on Sammy's head. The dog leaned into him.

"Okay," Cade said. His voice was thick and his eyes were burning and the weight on his shoulders was the heaviest thing he'd ever carried and the most important. "Okay. Let's go."

They walked out of the clearing. Through the trees. Through the thin strip of woods that separated two worlds. Past the creek where Cade had stumbled a year ago — or a few days ago, depending on which world was counting. Through the gap in the chain-link fence at the back of the yard on Maple Creek Drive.

Cade stood in his own backyard. The grass was overgrown. The bench on the porch had a leaf stuck to it. The back door was closed. The house was quiet.

Home.

He was home.

Sammy's tail wagged so hard his whole body swung. The dog bolted for the back door and pawed at it, barking — the sharp, joyful bark of an animal who had been on the longest walk of his life and was ready to be inside.

Cade adjusted the backpack one more time. He took a breath. He walked across the yard, up the porch steps, and put his hand on the door.

He opened it.

Chapter Twenty-Four – *Home*

The kitchen smelled like coffee.

That was the first thing Cade registered when he opened the back door — not the sight of the house or the sound of the television murmuring in the living room, but the smell. Coffee. The cheap kind Eydan bought in the big red can from the bottom shelf because it was two dollars less than the brand she liked. The smell was so ordinary, so completely and utterly normal, that it hit Cade like a wall and he had to grab the door frame to stay on his feet.

Sammy had no such hesitation. The dog bolted through the door, claws skidding on the linoleum, and launched himself into the house with a bark that shook the windows.

A crash from the living room. A voice — Eydan's voice.

"Sammy? Sammy!"

Then footsteps. Fast, urgent, stumbling. Eydan appeared in the kitchen doorway.

She looked terrible. Her face was drawn and pale, with dark circles under her eyes so deep they looked like bruises. Her hair was pulled back in a messy knot. She was wearing the same clothes she'd worn the day Cade had left — the sweatpants, the old T-shirt — and they hung on her like she'd lost weight she couldn't afford to lose. She looked like a woman who hadn't slept in days.

She looked like she'd been dying.

Her eyes found Cade. They went wide. Her mouth opened, but nothing came out. Her hand went to the door frame, gripping it, and her knees buckled.

"Mom," Cade said.

Eydan made a sound that wasn't a word. It was something older than language, something that came from a place deeper than her throat — the sound of a mother seeing her child after believing she might never see him again. She crossed the kitchen in three steps and her arms were around him and she was holding him so tight he couldn't breathe and he didn't care.

"Cade," Eydan said. She was crying. "Cade. Cade. Oh God, Cade."

She said his name over and over, like saying it enough times would make it real, would prove he was here, would undo whatever nightmare she'd been living since the day he'd disappeared. Her hands moved across his back, his shoulders, his face — touching, checking, making sure he was whole.

Cade held his mother. He was taller than her now — a year of farm work and training and growth had added inches and muscle that Eydan couldn't have expected. Her head barely reached his chin. He wrapped his arms around her and held her the way she was holding him, and for the first time in his life, Cade Thompson felt like the one doing the protecting instead of the one being protected.

"I'm here, Mom," Cade said. "I'm home. I'm okay."

Footsteps on the stairs. Small, fast, bare feet on hardwood.

"Cade?"

Ashen stood at the bottom of the staircase. Nine years old, wearing pajamas with stars on them, her dark hair tangled from sleep, her face caught in the space between disbelief and hope. She looked at Cade. She looked at Eydan crying. She looked at Sammy, who was spinning in circles on the kitchen floor, barking with the uncontained joy of a dog who was home.

Then she ran.

She hit Cade at full speed, wrapping her arms around his waist, burying her face in his shirt, and Cade dropped to his knees and pulled her in and held her against his chest. His mother on one side, his sister on the other, Sammy jumping and barking between all of them, and the kitchen filled with the sounds of a family being put back together.

Cade held them and closed his eyes and felt something he hadn't felt in fourteen years. Not safety — he'd found that in Verdant Haven, with Torin and Elysian and Elowen. This was different. This was the feeling of being exactly where he was supposed to be. The feeling of home. Not a place. A people.

These people. His people.

They sat at the kitchen table. Eydan wouldn't let go of his hand. "Ashen sat on his other side, pressed against his arm, Sammy at her feet with his head on her knee." The coffee had gone cold and nobody cared.

Eydan told him what he'd missed.

Five days. He'd been gone five days. Saturday to Thursday — the Saturday he'd chased Sammy through the fence, gone. Eydan had come outside twenty minutes later to call him for lunch and found the back gate open and the gap in the chain-link fence and nothing else. She'd searched the yard, the street, the neighborhood. She'd called his phone. It rang twice and then went dead — dropped off the network completely, as if the phone had been destroyed or had simply ceased to exist.

She'd called the police at six that evening. By Sunday morning, there were officers in the woods behind the house, search dogs, volunteers from the neighborhood walking the streets with flashlights. Missing person flyers went up at the gas station, the library, the Walgreens where Eydan worked. Cade's school was notified. Carla had called seventeen times.

They'd found nothing. No tracks in the woods. No sign of the dog. No evidence of anything — no struggle, no clothing, no trace. It was as if Cade and Sammy had walked into the trees and evaporated.

"The police thought you ran away," Eydan said. Her voice was flat, wrung out, holding together through sheer force of will. "They asked me if you were upset. If there were problems at home. If you had any reason to leave."

She looked at Cade, and in her eyes he saw the weight of those questions — the knowledge that the answer was yes, there had been problems at home, terrible problems, the kind that left scars on a boy's back and taught his sister to sleep with her door locked. The police hadn't known about Don. But Eydan had, and the guilt of it was written across her face.

"I didn't run away, Mom," Cade said. He squeezed her hand. "I promise. What happened — I can't explain all of it right now. But I didn't run away."

Eydan nodded. She didn't press. She was a woman who had learned the hard way that some truths took time, and right now, having her son at the table was enough.

Then she told him about Don.

"There's something else," Eydan said. Her grip on his hand tightened. "Your father. Don."

Cade waited. Something in her voice — a shift, a weight — told him what was coming before the words did.

"He's dead, Cade," Eydan said. "Monday night. A car accident on Route 9. The police called Tuesday morning. He was — they said he was driving fast. It was late. They think he fell asleep."

The kitchen was quiet. The refrigerator hummed. Sammy's tail tapped against the leg of Ashen's chair.

Cade sat with the words. He didn't speak. He didn't move. He waited for the feeling to arrive — the feeling that was supposed to come when you learned your father was dead.

It came. But it wasn't one feeling. It was all of them at once, layered on top of each other like the strata of rock in the canyon where Kaelthas had built his compound. Relief — pure, shameful, undeniable relief that the man who had beaten him and terrified his sister and broken his mother was gone from the world forever. Guilt — because feeling relieved about your father's death was something no amount of justification could make feel clean. Anger — the cold, hard anger of a boy who would never get to look that man in the eye and say what needed to be said. And underneath all of it, buried so deep he almost didn't recognize it, sadness. Not for the man Don had been. For the man Don could have been. For the father who might have existed in some other version of the story, the one who came home and picked up his kids instead of breaking them.

That father had never existed. But the ghost of him — the possibility — was dead now too. And that loss, the loss of something that was never real, ached in a way Cade hadn't expected.

"Are you okay?" Eydan asked softly.

"I don't know," Cade said. It was the most honest thing he could say. "I don't know how to feel about it."

"Neither do I," Eydan said. And in those four words, Cade heard the truth of his mother's grief — complicated, contradictory, impossible to sort into clean categories. She had loved Don once, before the hitting started. She had married him, chosen him, built a family with him. And he had destroyed all of it, and now he was gone, and the wreckage he'd left behind didn't get any cleaner just because the man who'd caused it was dead.

Ashen was quiet through all of it. She sat beside Cade with her hand on Sammy's back, her face still, her eyes on the table. She was nine years old and she had just learned that the man who had taught her to lock her bedroom door was never coming back. Whatever she felt about that, she kept it where nine-year-olds keep the things they can't process yet — somewhere deep and protected, where it would stay until she was ready to look at it.

Cade put his arm around her. She leaned into him.

That evening, after the phone calls — to the police, to tell them Cade was home; to the school; to Carla, who cried so hard she couldn't speak — after Ashen had finally fallen asleep on the couch with Sammy curled at her feet, Cade sat at the kitchen table with his mother.

The house was quiet. The kind of quiet that follows a storm.

"Mom," Cade said. "I need to show you something."

He reached for the backpack. He'd set it beside the table when he'd come in, and it had sat there all day like a piece of luggage from a trip nobody could explain. He lifted it onto the table — Eydan heard the weight of it, the heavy thud, and her eyebrows went up.

Cade unzipped it. He reached inside and pulled out the first thing his hand found — a gold coin, thick and heavy, gleaming under the kitchen light.

He set it on the table.

Eydan stared at it. Her lips parted. She reached out and picked it up, turning it over in her fingers, feeling the weight, the density, the unmistakable reality of solid gold.

"Cade," Eydan said. "What is —"

He upended the backpack. Gold coins spilled across the kitchen table like water from a broken dam — dozens of them, thick and bright, clattering against each other and rolling to the edges. Polished stones tumbled out after them — green, red, blue — catching the overhead light and throwing it back in sparks. Bracelets of hammered gold. Pendants set with stones that burned with internal fire. Rings etched with symbols from a world Eydan had never seen and couldn't imagine.

The treasure of Verdant Haven covered the kitchen table. The same table where Ashen drew dogs on grocery receipts. The same table where Eydan ate standing up because sitting down felt like a luxury. The same table where the Thompson family had shared a meal of scrambled eggs and turkey slices on a Saturday morning that felt like a lifetime ago.

Eydan stared. Her hand was over her mouth. Her eyes moved across the gold, the jewels, the impossible fortune that her fourteen-year-old son had just poured out of a school backpack onto her kitchen table.

"Where —" Eydan started. "How —"

"I can't explain it all tonight," Cade said. "But it's real. All of it. I earned it, Mom. People gave it to me because I helped them, and they wanted me to bring it home to you."

He looked at his mother. The woman who worked days at Walgreens and nights at a restaurant. The woman whose hands were cracked and whose back ached and who hadn't bought herself new shoes in two years. The woman who had driven her son to the emergency room at two in the morning and told them he'd fallen off a fence because she was too afraid of Don to tell the truth.

"We're going to be okay, Mom," Cade said. "We're going to be okay."

Eydan picked up a gold coin. Then another. Then a green stone that caught the light and held it like a tiny sun. The tears came back — not the desperate tears of a mother finding her lost son, but something quieter. Something that had to do with years of counting pennies and stretching paychecks and lying awake at three in the morning doing math that never added up.

She held the green stone in her palm and looked at her son. This boy who had walked out the back door five days ago and come back taller, broader, with muscles that hadn't been there and eyes that were older and a backpack full of gold. She didn't understand. She might never understand. But she understood the look on his face — the steady, certain look of a boy who had been somewhere that had changed him, and who had come home carrying the proof.

"Okay," Eydan said. Her voice broke on the word, and she didn't try to fix it. "Okay, baby. We're going to be okay."

In the living room, Ashen slept. Sammy's tail thumped once against the couch cushion. The refrigerator hummed. The streetlight outside the kitchen window cast a pale glow across the gold on the table, and for the first time in the history of the house on Maple Creek Drive, the future didn't feel like something to survive.

It felt like something to look forward to.

Chapter Twenty-Five - *A New Start*

The gold was real.

Eydan took one of the coins to a jeweler in Ridgewood the day after Cade came home. She walked in wearing her Walgreens vest, holding a coin the size of a silver dollar in her palm, and asked the man behind the counter if he could tell her what it was.

The jeweler put a loupe to his eye. He turned the coin over. He weighed it on a small scale. He tested it with acid from a glass bottle. Then he set the coin on the counter, took the loupe out of his eye, and looked at Eydan like she'd just walked in carrying a piece of the sun.

"Where did you get this?" the jeweler asked.

"It's a family heirloom," Eydan said. Cade had coached her on the story. Inheritance from a distant relative. Old coins, old jewelry, kept in a collection for years. Nobody knew what they were worth.

The jeweler picked up the coin again. "This is solid gold," the jeweler said. "The purity is extraordinary — higher than most modern minting. The stamp isn't from any mint I recognize. It could be ancient. It could be worth significantly more than melt value to a collector."

"How much?" Eydan asked.

The jeweler gave her a number. Eydan's hand went to the counter to steady herself.

That was one coin. Cade had brought home close to a hundred.

They didn't rush. Eydan was too smart for that, and Cade had learned enough about patience in Emerald Vale to know that moving too fast attracted the wrong kind of attention. They sold the coins slowly, a few at a time, at different shops in different towns. The jewels went to a gemologist in the city who spent twenty minutes examining a single green stone and then offered a figure that made Eydan sit down in the man's office and not speak for a full minute.

Within two weeks, Eydan quit the restaurant. Within a month, she quit Walgreens. She cried both times — not from sadness but from the sheer, overwhelming relief of a woman who had been carrying a weight for so long that putting it down felt like flying.

They didn't move right away. Eydan wanted to be careful, wanted to make sure the money was real and lasting and managed properly. She found a financial advisor — a woman recommended by the gemologist, someone who dealt with inherited wealth and knew how to make it last. The advisor looked at the spreadsheet Eydan had made on her phone, tallying the sales so far, and told her the truth in plain language.

"If you're careful," the advisor said, "your family will never worry about money again."

Eydan came home that afternoon and sat on the couch and stared at the wall for twenty minutes. Cade sat beside her and said nothing. He understood. When you've spent your whole life surviving, the idea that you don't have to anymore takes time to settle in. It's like stepping out of a storm and not trusting the sun.

The changes came gradually. New shoes for Ashen — not from the clearance bin, not from the outlet store on Route 4, but from a regular shoe store where a nine-year-old girl could pick the pair she actually wanted instead of the pair they could afford. Ashen chose purple sneakers with white laces and wore them every day for two weeks straight, even to bed, until Eydan pried them off her feet at night.

A new bed for Eydan, replacing the mattress that sagged in the middle and made her back hurt every morning. Groceries without the calculator. A coat for Cade that actually fit. Small things. Ordinary things. Things that had been luxuries and were now just life.

But the biggest change was time. Eydan was home. Not for an hour between shifts, not for a rushed breakfast before the alarm sent her out the door. Home. She cooked dinner at the stove and sat down to eat it. She helped Ashen with homework at the kitchen table. She fell asleep on the couch watching a movie and nobody had to wake her up for a shift.

Cade watched his mother discover what rest looked like, and it was one of the most beautiful things he'd ever seen. Not the beauty of a valley in Emerald Vale or a sunrise over the mountains. The beauty of a tired woman finally sitting down.

Ashen was changing too. Not overnight — the quiet, careful girl who locked her bedroom door and drew dogs on grocery receipts didn't transform into someone else just because the money problems were gone. The damage Don had done lived deeper than a bank account could reach. But the edges were softening. She laughed more. She talked more. One evening, Cade heard her singing in her room — a song from a cartoon, half the words wrong, her voice small and off-key and the most hopeful sound the house on Maple Creek Drive had ever held.

She was drawing again, but not on receipts. Eydan had bought her a proper sketchpad and a set of colored pencils, and Ashen spent hours at the kitchen table filling pages with animals and trees and houses with big windows and open doors. She drew Sammy constantly — Sammy sleeping, Sammy running, Sammy with his tongue out. And once, Cade found a drawing she'd left on the counter that made him stop and stare.

It was a picture of a boy and a dog standing between two big rocks. The boy had a backpack. The dog was looking up at him. Behind the rocks, the trees were green — not regular green, but the vivid, impossible green of a place that didn't exist in any world Ashen had ever seen.

Cade picked up the drawing. He looked at it for a long time.

He hadn't told Ashen about Emerald Vale. He hadn't told anyone. But children see things. They hear things. They feel the shape of a story even when the words aren't spoken. Ashen knew her brother had gone somewhere. She knew it had changed him. And she had drawn it the only way she could — a boy and a dog and a doorway between two worlds.

He put the drawing back on the counter. He didn't say anything about it. Some things were better left in the space between knowing and not knowing, where they could be true without needing to be explained.

Sammy adapted to being home with the same ease he'd adapted to Emerald Vale. The dog fell back into his old routines — sleeping on Cade's bed, begging at the table, harassing squirrels in the backyard — as if the past year had been a long walk and he was simply glad to be back on the couch. The neighborhood children didn't follow him around the way the village children had, but the mailman still gave him treats and the woman next door still called him "sweet boy" over the fence, and Sammy accepted it all with the serene contentment of a dog who had herded baby dinosaurs and knocked a tyrant to the ground and was perfectly happy to resume his career of chasing butterflies.

But sometimes, in the evenings, Sammy would stand at the back fence and stare at the tree line. His ears would come forward. His body would go still. And he would look at the woods behind Maple Creek Drive with those mismatched eyes, and Cade would watch him from the porch and feel the green stone warm against his chest and wonder if the dog could feel it too — the pull, the shimmer, the doorway that might or might not be waiting between two boulders in the deep part of the forest.

Cade never went back to check. Not yet. He wasn't ready. And the people on this side of the boulders needed him more than the people on the other side. For now.

Don's funeral was on a Tuesday. Small. Quiet. A service at a funeral home on the east side of town, attended by a handful of people Cade didn't recognize — coworkers, maybe, or drinking buddies, men who had known the version of Don that smiled in public and told jokes and shook hands. The version that went home and became something else.

Eydan went. She dressed in black and stood at the back of the room and didn't cry. Cade stood beside her, wearing the new coat, his hands in his pockets, his jaw tight. Ashen stayed home with a neighbor.

Cade looked at the casket and felt the collision of everything he'd carried for fourteen years. The man in that box had taught him to flinch. Had taught his sister to lock her door. Had taught his mother to lie to emergency room doctors. The man in that box had broken everything he touched and left the wreckage for other people to clean up.

And the man in that box had also, without meaning to, given Cade the reflexes that saved his life in Emerald Vale. The instincts that let him read Kaelthas. The hardness that kept him standing when the razormaws came through the walls. Don had tried to destroy his son, and instead he had built something inside him that couldn't be destroyed.

Cade didn't forgive him. He wasn't sure he ever would. Forgiveness was a door he might walk through someday, or might not, and either choice was okay. What he did, standing in that funeral home looking at the casket, was something smaller and harder and more important than forgiveness.

He let go.

Not of the pain. Not of the memories. Not of the scars on his back or the flinch in his shoulders or the wall he'd built between himself and every man who raised a hand too fast. He let go of the hold. The grip Don had on him — the voice in his head that said he wasn't enough, wasn't strong enough, wasn't worth the space he took up. That voice had followed him through a portal to another world and Elysian had spent a year teaching him to silence it. Standing in the funeral home, looking at the box that held the source of that voice, Cade let it go. Not all at once. Not completely. But enough to take a breath that went all the way down to the bottom of his lungs for the first time in fourteen years.

Eydan looked at him. She saw something in his face — a loosening, a release, the barely perceptible shift of a boy setting down a weight he'd been carrying since before he could remember.

She took his hand. They walked out of the funeral home together, into the October sunlight, and they didn't look back.

Chapter Twenty-Six - The World He Left Behind

Cade went back to school on a Monday.

Eydan drove him. She'd bought a car the week before — nothing fancy, a used sedan with low miles and a back seat that didn't smell like someone else's fast food. It was the first car the Thompson family had owned that didn't make a sound like a dying animal when you turned the key. Sammy rode in the back with his head out the window, ears flapping, living his best life.

Ridgewood High looked exactly the same. The flat brown building, the parking lot, the flag out front. Students moved through the entrance in the familiar morning shuffle — backpacks, headphones, half-awake faces, the low hum of conversations about homework and weekend plans and who said what to whom. It was so ordinary that it made Cade's chest hurt.

Five days ago for them. A year ago for him.

He'd prepared a story. Eydan had helped him build it — he'd gotten lost in the woods, disoriented, wandered for days before finding his way to a road. The police had accepted it, mostly because there was no better explanation and because Cade was home and healthy and they had bigger cases to work. The school would accept it too. Missing student returns safely. File closed.

The story was a lie, and the lie sat inside Cade like a stone he couldn't swallow.

He walked through the front doors and the hallway swallowed him. Lockers, fluorescent lights, the squeak of sneakers on tile. A poster on the wall advertised the fall dance. Another one reminded students that library books were due Friday. The world of Ridgewood High was exactly as he'd left it — small, enclosed, concerned with things that had once felt important and now felt like they belonged to someone else's life.

A boy from his history class passed him in the hallway and did a double take. "Dude, you're back," the boy said. "Where'd you go?"

"Got lost in the woods," Cade said. The rehearsed answer.

"For real?" the boy asked. "That's wild. You didn't have your phone?"

"Battery died," Cade said.

"That sucks," the boy said. He shrugged and kept walking, already looking at his own phone.

Five days. For the people in this hallway, Cade had been gone five days. He'd missed some homework, a quiz in algebra, and whatever drama had unfolded over the weekend. That was the size of his absence in their world. Five days. A blip.

In Cade's world, he had spent a year learning to move through a forest without making a sound. He had trained with a stone blade until his arms burned. He had watched a girl kill a razormaw with three arrows and not flinch. He had stood in a village square and been applauded by people who had tried to exile him. He had carried a backpack full of gold through a portal between two worlds.

And now he was standing in a hallway at Ridgewood High, and the kid from history class wanted to know if his phone had died.

The distance was enormous. Not the physical distance — the distance between who he had been and who he was now. The boy who had walked these halls with his head down, avoiding eye contact, keeping the world at arm's length — that boy was gone. In his place was someone who stood straighter, moved differently, looked people in the eye. Someone who had killed a predator with a knife and knocked a grown man unconscious with a staff and held a girl's hand on a ridge overlooking a valley that shouldn't exist.

Nobody at Ridgewood High could see any of that. They saw a kid who'd been gone for less than a week and looked like he'd grown an inch.

Carla was waiting at his locker.

She was leaning against the wall with her arms crossed and her dark hair falling across one eye, and the moment she saw Cade her face did three things at once — collapsed with relief, tightened with anger, and then broke open into something that was part smile and part sob.

"You absolute idiot," Carla said. She was crying. She crossed the distance between them in two steps and hit him in the chest with both fists and then wrapped her arms around him and held on like the hallway was a lifeboat. "Five days. Five days, Cade. I thought you were dead. I called you seventeen times. I walked those woods with the search team. I found your shoe print by the creek and I —"

She couldn't finish. She pressed her face against his shoulder and shook.

Cade held her. He put his arms around Carla Martinez and held her in the hallway of Ridgewood High while students walked past and pretended not to look, and he felt the weight of what his absence had done to the people who cared about him.

"I'm sorry," Cade said. "I'm here. I'm okay."

Carla pulled back. She wiped her eyes with the back of her hand and looked at him — really looked, the way she always did, the way that had made him uncomfortable before because Carla saw things other people missed.

"You're different," Carla said.

"I got lost in the woods for five days," Cade said. The lie again.

"No," Carla said. Her eyes were sharp, searching his face. "That's not what I mean. You're — bigger. And I don't just mean taller. You're standing different. You're looking at me different. Something happened to you out there that you're not telling me."

Cade looked at Carla. This girl who had texted him about snacks and saved him a seat at lunch and worried about him for five days while he was gone for a year. She deserved the truth. She deserved all of it — the portal, the dinosaurs, the village, the battle, the girl on the ridge who had taken his hand and changed him.

But the truth was impossible. The truth was a story nobody in this world would believe.

"Something did happen," Cade said. "I can't explain it all. Not yet. Maybe not ever. But I promise you I'm okay. Better than okay."

Carla studied him. She was deciding whether to push. She was the kind of person who pushed — direct, honest, unwilling to let people hide behind comfortable lies. It was one of the things Cade valued most about her.

But she didn't push. She saw something in his face that told her this wasn't a wall she needed to climb right now. She nodded once.

"Okay," Carla said. "But when you're ready to tell me, I'm here. I've always been here, Cade."

"I know," Cade said. "That's one of the things I figured out while I was gone."

She almost smiled. Then she punched him in the arm, hard enough to leave a bruise.

"Don't ever disappear again," Carla said.

"Deal," Cade said.

The days that followed were strange. Cade went to class. He took notes. He turned in the assignments he'd missed. He sat in algebra and worked equations that felt like a foreign language after months of tracking animals through ancient forests, and he sat in history and listened to a lecture about the American Revolution and thought about a different revolution — the one he'd fought in a village square with a staff and a knife.

He looked at his classmates and felt the distance. These kids were worried about grades and relationships and college applications and who was going to the fall dance. Their problems were real — Cade didn't dismiss them, didn't look down on them. But he couldn't share them anymore. He had fought trained predators. He had helped topple a tyrant. He had held a dying razormaw's weight on his chest and felt its breath on his face. The distance between that and a pop quiz in algebra was unbridgeable.

But he didn't resent it. That was the thing Emerald Vale had given him that surprised him most — not the strength or the fighting skills or the gold in the backpack. It had given him gratitude. He sat in a warm classroom with electric lights and running water and a teacher who had never tried to kill anyone, and he was grateful. He ate lunch in a cafeteria where the food came from a kitchen and not from a hunt, and he was grateful. He walked home on a sidewalk where nothing was trying to eat him, and he was grateful.

The small things mattered more now. Ashen laughing at the dinner table. Eydan reading a book on the couch because she had time to read. Sammy sleeping on the bed with his paws in the air, dreaming about whatever dogs dreamed about. These things were precious in a way they hadn't been before, because Cade had lived in a world where none of them existed, and he knew what it felt like to miss them.

Eydan found a counselor. A woman named Dr. Reyes, whose office was in a building near the library, with a waiting room that had soft chairs and a fish tank and magazines nobody ever read. Eydan had wanted to get her kids into therapy for years — had known they needed it, had known the damage Don had done couldn't be fixed by time alone. But therapy cost money, and money had been the one thing they never had.

Now they had it. And Eydan was not going to waste a single day.

Cade went on a Thursday afternoon. He sat in a chair across from Dr. Reyes — a small woman with kind eyes and a patient voice and a box of tissues on the table between them — and he didn't know where to start.

"Your mother tells me things were difficult at home," Dr. Reyes said. "Before your father left."

"Yeah," Cade said.

"Would you like to talk about that?" Dr. Reyes asked.

Cade looked at the fish tank. A blue fish drifted past the glass, slow and calm, existing in a world that was six inches wide and perfectly safe.

"My father hit me," Cade said. "He hit my mother. He scared my sister so bad she stopped talking. He did it for years, and nobody stopped him, and then he left, and now he's dead."

The words came out flat and direct, the way Elysian would have said them. No decoration. No softening. Just the truth, laid on the table like a map.

Dr. Reyes didn't flinch. She didn't gasp or look sad or reach for the tissues. She just nodded.

"That's a lot," Dr. Reyes said. "That's a lot for anyone to carry. Especially someone your age."

"I've had help," Cade said. And he thought of Elysian putting a hand on his shoulder. Of Elowen sitting beside a fire and not pushing. Of Torin saying "We have more jugs" and turning away so Cade could breathe.

"From your family?" Dr. Reyes asked.

"From people who cared about me," Cade said. "People who showed me that not every man who raises his hand is going to use it to hit you. People who taught me that being afraid doesn't have to make you small."

He couldn't tell her the full story. He couldn't talk about Emerald Vale or Verdant Haven or the knife with an old man's name etched on the spine. But he could talk about what those people had given him — the lessons, the strength, the understanding that he was worth more than Don had ever let him believe.

He could start.

"I'm not fixed," Cade said. "I still flinch sometimes. I still dream about the bad nights. I still have a wall up that I don't always know how to take down. But I'm better than I was. And I want to keep getting better."

Dr. Reyes smiled. It was a small smile, professional but genuine, the smile of a woman who had heard a hundred versions of this story and still found something to hold onto in each one.

"That's a very good place to start, Cade," Dr. Reyes said.

He went back the following Thursday. And the Thursday after that. The healing wasn't fast and it wasn't dramatic. It was slow, steady work — the kind Elysian would have understood. One session at a time. One truth at a time. One brick at a time from the wall that Don had built inside him.

Ashen started seeing Dr. Reyes too. Eydan drove her on Tuesday afternoons, and afterward they went for ice cream — a new tradition, small and sweet and exactly the kind of normal that the Thompson family had never had.

The house on Maple Creek Drive was becoming something it had never been. Not just a shelter. Not just four walls where a family hid from the world. It was becoming a home. The kind of home where a mother could cook dinner without flinching when a pot clanged. Where a nine-year-old girl could leave her bedroom door open at night. Where a boy could sit on the back porch with his dog and feel the last of the October sun on his face and not be afraid of what was coming next.

They were healing. All three of them. Slowly, imperfectly, together.

And that, Cade had learned, was how it worked. Not all at once. Not in some dramatic moment of transformation. But one day at a time, one small act of courage at a time, one open door at a time, until the house that had been full of fear was full of something else instead.

Something that felt, finally, like hope.

Chapter Twenty-Seven – *Healing*

Thanksgiving came on a Thursday, the way it always did, and for the first time in the history of the Thompson family, it felt like a holiday instead of an endurance test.

Eydan cooked. Not the rushed, exhausted cooking of a woman squeezing a meal between shifts, but real cooking — the kind that started at nine in the morning and filled the house with smells so good that Sammy parked himself under the kitchen table and didn't move for six hours. Turkey, mashed potatoes, green beans, cornbread from a recipe Eydan's mother had written on an index card thirty years ago. And a pie. A real pie, from scratch, with a crust that Eydan rolled out on the counter while Ashen sat on a stool and watched with the wide-eyed focus of a girl who had never seen her mother have a full day off on a holiday.

"Can I help?" Ashen asked.

"You can put the apples in the bowl," Eydan said.

Ashen put the apples in the bowl. She did it slowly, carefully, arranging each slice in a pattern only she understood. Then she looked up at Eydan and smiled, and the smile was so open and unguarded that Cade, watching from the doorway, had to look away for a moment because the brightness of it was too much.

She was coming back. His sister was coming back. Not all the way — Dr. Reyes had told them it would take time, that the kind of fear Don had built into a little girl didn't dissolve in weeks or months. But the edges were softening. The locked door was open now. The silence was filling with words — small words, careful words, but words. And the smile. That smile was worth every coin in the backpack.

Cade set the table. Three plates, three glasses, three sets of silverware. He put Sammy's bowl on the floor beside his chair, because the dog was getting a plate too and everybody knew it. He arranged the napkins and stepped back and looked at the table and felt something shift inside his chest — a settling, like a stone finding its place at the bottom of a river.

This was what a family looked like. Not the version Don had built — the version where meals were minefields and silence was survival and the table was a place where you kept your head down and prayed the night would end without an explosion. This was the other version. The real version. The one Cade had seen at Torin's table in Verdant Haven, where food was shared and voices were steady and nobody flinched when a hand reached across the table.

Torin had given him that. The quiet farmer who showed love through action instead of words had shown Cade what a dinner table was supposed to feel like. And now

Cade was standing in his own kitchen, looking at his own table, and the feeling was the same.

They ate. They ate until they couldn't eat anymore, and then Ashen had a second piece of pie and Eydan laughed and Sammy got turkey scraps and the kitchen was warm and loud with the sounds of a family that was learning how to be a family.

After dinner, while Eydan washed dishes and Ashen drew at the table — a turkey this time, with feathers in every color the pencil set contained — Cade went to his room.

He sat on the bed and opened the drawer of his nightstand. Inside, next to his dead phone and the house key on the Ridgewood High lanyard, were the things that mattered most.

Elysian's knife. The dark wood handle, the stone blade shaped with extraordinary care, the three marks on the spine that meant the old man's name in the old script. Cade picked it up and turned it in his hands. The weight of it was familiar — the weight of forty years of knowledge, of patience, of a man who had chosen to be a father because blood wasn't the only thing that made one.

He thought about Elysian. The old tracker would be in his dwelling by the northern wall right now, or walking the deep forest, or sitting by a fire telling stories to nobody in particular. Did he think about Cade? Did he look at the empty chair across the fire and feel the absence? Did he stand at the southern wall and stare at the tree line the way Sammy stared at it from the backyard fence?

Cade didn't know. He couldn't know. The distance between them was bigger than miles — it was the distance between two worlds, unmeasurable, uncrossable except by a dog and a shimmer and fifteen minutes of impossible grace.

He set the knife down and picked up the green stone. Elowen's mother's stone, smooth and warm, hanging on its braided leather cord. He held it in his palm and closed his fingers around it and felt the warmth of it against his skin, and for a moment he was back on the ridge, sitting on the flat rock, looking out over the valley with Elowen beside him and the wind moving through the grass and the whole world spread out below them in green and gold.

He missed her. The missing was a physical thing — a weight in his chest, a space in the room where she should have been standing. He missed her voice. He missed her laugh. He missed the way she looked at him like he was the only thing worth looking at, and the way she fought like she was born with a bow in her hand, and the way she said his name with the slight emphasis on the second syllable that nobody in this world would ever replicate.

He missed all of them. Elowen. Elysian. Torin. The children who called Sammy soft-one. The ridge. The valley.

The smell of the forest after rain and the sound of stoneshells rumbling in their pens at night and the way the stars looked through the canopy — thick and bright and endless, a sky so full of light it made you feel both enormous and invisible at the same time.

He put the stone back in the drawer. He didn't wear it around his neck anymore — too many questions he couldn't answer. But he held it every night before he slept, and every night the warmth of it carried him to a ridge overlooking a valley in a world between worlds, and every night Elowen was there, amber eyes and braided hair, waiting on the flat rock with her legs drawn up and the sunset turning everything to gold.

A knock on his door. Light, careful — Ashen's knock.

"Yeah?" Cade said.

The door opened. Ashen stood there in her pajamas with the stars on them, holding a piece of paper.

"I made you something," Ashen said.

She held out the paper. Cade took it.

It was a drawing. Not the quick sketches on grocery receipts — this was done with care, in colored pencil, on proper paper. It showed a boy standing on a hill. He was looking out over a valley — green hills, a river, mountains in the distance. A dog stood beside him. And behind the boy, drawn small but clear, was a group of people. A girl with a braid. An old man with a walking stick. A big man with scarred hands. They were watching the boy from a distance, and even in colored pencil, even drawn by a nine-year-old, you could see it on their faces.

They were proud of him.

Cade looked at the drawing. He looked at it for a long time. His throat was tight and his eyes were burning and the drawing in his hands was shaking slightly because his hands were shaking.

"Ashen," Cade said. His voice was rough. "How did you —"

"I dream about it sometimes," Ashen said. She said it quietly, matter-of-factly, the way children say impossible things. "The green place. The big animals. The girl who likes you. Sammy is always there."

Cade stared at his sister. Nine years old. Drawing things she couldn't have seen, couldn't have known, couldn't have imagined without something feeding her the images in her sleep. The portal. Sammy. Whatever connection existed between the dog and the space between two boulders — maybe it didn't stop at the dog. Maybe it touched the people the dog loved. Maybe it reached through the walls between worlds and planted seeds in the dreams of a nine-year-old girl who drew pictures at the kitchen table because it was the only language that made sense to her.

Or maybe Ashen was just a child with a vivid imagination who had sensed that her brother had been somewhere extraordinary and had built it in her mind the way children build everything — with color and wonder and absolute belief.

Either way, the drawing was the most beautiful thing anyone had ever given him.

"Thank you," Cade said. "This is perfect, Ash."

Ashen smiled. The open smile. The one that had been gone for years and was coming back, one day at a time, one drawing at a time.

"The dog in the picture is Sammy," Ashen said. "He's the one who finds the way."

"Yeah," Cade said. "He always does."

Ashen turned and padded back down the hall to her room. Her door stayed open behind her. Cade listened to her climb into bed, heard the rustle of blankets, heard the soft sound of her breathing settle into the rhythm of sleep.

He looked at the drawing one more time. The boy on the hill. The dog beside him. The people watching from behind — Elowen, Elysian, Torin, drawn by a child who had never met them but somehow knew their faces.

He pinned the drawing to the wall above his bed, next to the window, where the streetlight caught it at night and the morning sun would find it first.

Sammy jumped onto the bed and turned three circles and collapsed beside him with a sigh that communicated absolute satisfaction with the state of the universe. Cade put his hand on the dog's side and felt the heartbeat — steady, warm, constant. The heartbeat that had led him through a portal and brought him home again. The heartbeat that had never once, in three years, failed him.

"You're a good boy, Sammy," Cade whispered. "The best boy in any world."

Sammy's tail thumped once. Agreement.

Cade closed his eyes. Through the wall, he could hear Eydan in the kitchen, putting away the last of the dishes, humming something under her breath. Through the window, the streetlight cast its pale glow across the drawing on the wall — the green valley, the distant mountains, the people who had changed him.

He was healing. They were all healing. Not in a straight line — Dr. Reyes had told him healing didn't work that way, that it circled back on itself, that there would be bad days mixed in with the good ones and that was normal. But the direction was forward. The trend was up. And the house on Maple Creek Drive, which had been a place of fear for so long that the walls themselves seemed to hold the memory of it, was filling with something new.

Laughter. Open doors. A nine-year-old singing off-key in her bedroom. A mother humming in the kitchen. A dog snoring on a bed. And a boy who had traveled to another world and come back carrying gold and scars and the knowledge that he was worth more than the man who had tried to break him.

The healing wasn't done. It might never be completely done. But it was happening, and that was enough.

Cade slept. And in his dreams, the valley was green, and the sky was endless, and Elowen was sitting on the ridge waiting for him, and Sammy was running through the ferns with his tongue out and his tail high, and everything was exactly as it should be.

Chapter Twenty-Eight - *Not Yet, Boy*

December came in cold and clear, the kind of evening where the sky turned purple at the edges and the first stars appeared before the streetlights kicked on.

Cade sat on the back porch steps with his jacket zipped to his chin and his hands in his pockets. The yard was small and ordinary — chain-link fence, brown grass, the bench with the peeling paint. Beyond the fence, the woods stood dark and still against the fading sky, the bare branches of oaks and maples reaching upward like hands.

Inside the house, things were warm.

Eydan was in the kitchen, cooking something with garlic and onions that smelled so good Sammy had spent ten minutes standing at the back door trying to decide whether to stay inside near the food or go outside with Cade. He'd chosen Cade. He always chose Cade.

The dog lay at Cade's feet on the porch, his chin on his paws, his mismatched eyes half-closed. The cold didn't bother him. Nothing much bothered Sammy anymore. He had herded baby dinosaurs and tackled a tyrant and traveled between two worlds, and the December chill on a suburban back porch was not even worth lifting his head for.

Through the kitchen window, Cade could see Ashen at the table. She was doing homework — math, from the look of it, her pencil moving across the page with the careful focus of a girl who was learning that school could be a place where she belonged instead of a place where she hid. Her purple sneakers were under the table, still laced, because she'd worn them to school and hadn't taken them off yet.

She was humming. Cade could hear it through the glass — faint, tuneless, the absent humming of a child who had forgotten to be afraid.

Eydan moved behind her, setting a glass of juice on the table without interrupting the homework. She touched the top of Ashen's head as she passed — a light touch, automatic, the kind of casual affection that had been impossible in Don's house because every gesture had been monitored and every moment of softness had been a potential trigger.

Not anymore. Don was gone. The fear was fading. And the house on Maple Creek Drive, which had held so much darkness for so long, was full of light.

Cade watched them through the window and felt the fullness of it — not happiness, exactly, because happiness was too simple a word for what he felt. It was something deeper. Something that had to do with knowing where he was and why he was there and what it had cost to get here. He had walked through a portal to another world. He had been trained by a man who saw him when nobody else did.

He had fought for a village that wasn't his own. He had carried a backpack full of gold through a gap between two boulders. And he had come home.

Not because Emerald Vale wasn't real. It was real. Every moment of it was real — the valley, the forest, the ridge, the battle, the girl. He carried the proof of it against his skin every night when he held the green stone, and he carried it in his hands every time he picked up the knife with the old man's name.

He had come home because this was where he was needed. Because Eydan was his mother and Ashen was his sister and they deserved a life that wasn't defined by what Don had done to them. Because the boy who had walked into the woods behind Maple Creek Drive had been running from something, and the boy who had walked out of them had been running toward something.

Toward this. This kitchen. This light. This family.

Cade reached into his pocket and touched the green stone. He'd started carrying it again — not around his neck, but in his jacket pocket, where his fingers could find it when he needed to remember. The leather cord was warm. The stone was smooth. And when he closed his hand around it, he could feel her.

Not literally. Not the way he'd felt her hand in his on the ridge or her lips against his in the clearing. But a warmth.

A presence. The sense that somewhere, in a world he couldn't reach, Elowen was sitting on a flat rock overlooking a valley, thinking about a boy who had come from nowhere and changed everything.

He thought about Elysian. The old man would be by the fire right now, working a blade with antler bone, his dark eyes seeing everything the way they always did. Cade wondered if Elysian thought about him. He hoped so. He hoped the old tracker sat in his chair and looked at the empty space across the fire and felt the absence the way a man feels a missing limb — not with pain, but with the constant, quiet awareness that something that was there is gone.

Courage is not staying where it is safe. Courage is going where you are needed.

Elysian's words. Cade heard them in the old man's voice — low, rough, certain. He would hear them for the rest of his life. They were etched into him the same way the three marks were etched into the spine of the knife. Permanent. Unbreakable. A lesson written in stone by a man who had never needed a classroom to teach.

The sky darkened. The stars came out — not the thick, endless sky of Emerald Vale, but enough. A few bright points above the tree line, steady and constant, the same stars that shone over both worlds.

Sammy lifted his head.

It was sudden. One moment the dog was half-asleep on the porch, chin on paws, ears flat. The next he was up — ears forward, body rigid, every muscle in his forty-five-pound frame locked and pointed at the woods beyond the fence.

He whined. A low, soft sound. The sound Cade had heard a hundred times — in the backyard before the first crossing, at the edge of Verdant Haven in the weeks before they'd come home. The sound of a dog feeling something he couldn't explain, pulled by a thread only he could feel.

Cade looked at the tree line. The bare branches were still. The woods were dark. Nothing moved.

But Sammy's tail was wagging. Slow, steady, certain. The dog stared at the woods with those mismatched eyes, and in the fading light Cade could swear he saw something in the dog's expression that went beyond instinct, beyond animal awareness, beyond anything a forty-five-pound mutt from a suburban shelter should have been capable of.

Recognition. Sammy recognized something out there. Something calling to him from between two boulders in the deep part of the forest, from across the space between worlds, from a clearing where a shimmer waited to ripple and warm and open.

Cade's hand tightened around the green stone in his pocket. His heart beat once, hard, against his ribs.

He could go. Right now. Stand up, walk across the yard, push through the gap in the fence, follow Sammy into the woods. Find the boulders. See if the shimmer was there. Step through and be standing in the ancient forest in thirty seconds, surrounded by ferns and mist and the smell of a world that had rebuilt him from the ground up.

Elowen would be there. Elysian would be there. The ridge, the valley, the village. Everything he'd left behind, waiting.

But behind him, through the kitchen window, Eydan was setting the table. Three plates. Three glasses. Ashen was putting her homework away and reaching for her juice. The light was warm and the garlic smell was drifting through the cracked door and the house on Maple Creek Drive was, for the first time in its history, a place worth staying in.

Cade smiled.

He reached down and put his hand on Sammy's head. The dog's fur was warm under his fingers. The tail kept wagging, slow and steady, but Sammy leaned into Cade's palm the way he always did — the lean that said,

I'm yours. Wherever you go, I go. You decide.

"Not yet, boy," Cade said softly. "But someday."

Sammy looked up at him. The dog's tail thumped once against the porch. Then he turned his head, looked at the woods one more time, and lay back down at Cade's feet with a sigh that held no disappointment. Just patience. The patient certainty of a dog who knew the way and would find it again when the time was right.

The back door opened. Eydan's voice.

"Dinner's ready," Eydan called. "Bring Sammy in before he freezes."

"Coming, Mom," Cade said.

He stood. He took one last look at the tree line — dark, still, ordinary. But not empty. Never empty. Not to him. Not to the dog at his feet.

The green stone was warm in his pocket. The knife was in his nightstand drawer. The drawing was pinned to the wall above his bed. And somewhere, in a world between worlds, a girl with amber eyes was sitting on a ridge, waiting.

You had better come back. Both of you.

Cade Thompson opened the back door and walked into the warmth and the light and the smell of garlic and the sound of his sister humming and his mother setting plates on the table. Sammy trotted in behind him, tail wagging, heading straight for his bowl.

The door closed behind them.

The woods were quiet.

The stars came out.

And somewhere in the deep part of the forest, between two boulders covered in moss, the air shimmered. Just once. Just for a moment. A ripple of warmth in the December cold, a flicker of light where there should have been none.

Then it was still.

For now.

THE END

Acknowledgments

This book would not exist without the people who believed in it before it was anything more than an idea and a stubborn old man who refused to quit.

To my family, for a lifetime of stories worth telling.

To the men and women I served with in the United States Navy from 1959 to 1979 — you taught me what courage looks like when nobody's watching. Some of you are still here. Some of you aren't. I carry all of you.

To every kid who ever felt invisible, who kept their head down and their mouth shut and survived things no child should have to survive — this book is for you. You are not what happened to you. You are what you become after.

And to Sammy. Every dog I've ever known. The ones who loved us better than we deserved and found the way home when we couldn't.

About the Author

Jackie L. Smith is a retired United States Navy veteran who served from 1959 to 1979. After his military career, he spent eight years in hospital administration for the State of Oklahoma and twenty years as a civilian supporting the United States Air Force. He began writing novels in his eighties, proving that it's never too late to start telling the stories that matter.

He is the author of Hank Blankenship and the Longest Fall, Echoes of 1969, Wilbur Northcutt and the Boonesborough Fall, Charlie Fitzgerald's Folly, The Customs Conspiracy, The Last Whisper of Innocence, Colby Utterback: Finding His Place, Brynn Thornwick: Guardian of the Crimson Crown, Atlas Drummond: Fragments of Deceit, and The Arrest of Wilder Rhodes.

He lives in Staffordsville, Kentucky, with a deep appreciation for stamp collecting, computer technology, and the belief that every good story needs a dog in it.

The Fractured Path to Emerald Vale is his tenth novel.

Also by Jackie L. Smith

<u>Hank Blankenship and the Longest Fall: 154 Years from Home</u>

<u>Echoes of 1969: A Veteran's Memoir, a Murder, and the Fight to Be Heard</u>

<u>Wilbur Northcutt and the Boonesborough Fall: One Year Behind the Walls</u>

<u>Charlie Fitzgerald's Folly: A Boy, a Field, and the Country His Father Buried</u>

<u>The Customs Conspiracy: A Corporate Fraud Thriller</u>

<u>The Last Whisper of Innocence: A Family Crime Thriller</u>

<u>Colby Utterback: Finding His Place</u>

<u>Brynn Thornwick: Guardian of the Crimson Crown</u>

<u>Atlas Drummond: Fragments of Deceit</u>

<u>The Arrest of Wilder Rhodes: A Thriller of War, Corruption, and Vengeance</u>

Connect with the Author

Enjoyed The Fractured Path to Emerald Vale?

Please consider leaving a review on Amazon, Goodreads, or your favorite book platform. Reviews help other readers discover books they might love and support authors — especially an author who started writing at 84 — in continuing to tell stories that matter.

Recommend this book to readers who enjoy:

Fantasy adventures with real emotional depth

Stories about overcoming abuse and finding strength

Unique worlds with dinosaurs, ancient civilizations, and portal crossings

The unbreakable bond between a boy and his dog

Coming-of-age journeys about courage, healing, and finding where you belong

Stay Connected

Twitter/X: @CheckerBoa81267

Facebook: jacksmith1591

Thank you for reading The Fractured Path to Emerald Vale. Your support means everything to this author and to Cade's story.

At 84, I've finally found my voice. With your help, I hope to keep telling stories that keep you turning pages —

and maybe, someday, to find out what happens when Sammy
pulls toward the woods again.

— Jackie L. Smith

Staffordsville, Kentucky

2026

A Note from the Author

I wrote this book at eighty-four years old.

People ask me why I started writing novels so late in life, and the honest answer is that I didn't start late. I started when I was ready. Twenty years in the Navy, eight years in hospital administration, twenty years supporting the Air Force — those weren't detours. They were the education. Every story I tell comes from something I lived, something I witnessed, or something I couldn't stop thinking about until I put it on the page.

The Fractured Path to Emerald Vale is different from my other books. My thrillers come from my military background. This one comes from something else — the belief that the hardest journeys are the ones that take us the farthest from where we started and the closest to who we're supposed to be.

Cade's story is about a boy who was broken by the person who was supposed to protect him. It's about finding the people who put you back together. It's about a dog who always knows the way home. And it's about the truth that courage isn't staying where it's safe — it's going where you're needed.

If this story meant something to you, I'd be grateful if you'd leave a review. Reviews help readers find books, and finding readers is all an author can ask for.

Leave a review here: amazon.com/dp/B0GRD5K76K

(Or just search "The Fractured Path to Emerald Vale" on Amazon and click "Write a customer review.")

Thank you for reading. Thank you for caring about Cade and Sammy and Elowen and Elysian. They're as real to me as anyone I've ever known.

And if you're wondering whether the door between the boulders ever opens again — well. Sammy's still here. And he always finds the way.

— Jackie L. Smith

Staffordsville, Kentucky

2026